DEPARTURES

J G WALLACE

JG Wallace
Justin, TX
jgwallace249@gmail.com
JG@HardTurnSeries.com

Hardcover/Dust Jacket ISBN: 979-8-9885846-3-6
Hardcover ISBN: 979-8-9885846-2-9
Paperback ISBN: 979-8-9885846-1-2
Ebook ISBN: 979-8-9885846-0-5

Cover and book design by Brian Phillips Design
Edited by Carlo DeCarlo

First Edition

Printed in the United States

*This book was written because of someone who
changed my life in many, many good ways. I started this book
before you came into my life—but I finished it because
you changed my life, Beverly, and I love you very much.*

PROLOGUE

Major Dan Hatfield was finally alone with his thoughts... and a bottle of Dewars. Pilots tend to look at memories the way people flip through YouTube. His head was filled with short videos of his life, and he replayed them from time to time, but tonight he was mostly looking back on the last twenty-four hours. The images took on the feel of watching a war movie about someone else. Maybe it was the intensity of what had happened during the last two days, or maybe it was the scotch. What he knew for certain was that he had survived the series of events of the prior day, and that it would forever change him. A folding chair behind the planning shack within the Prince Sultan Air Base in the desert southeast of Riyadh, Saudi Arabia, was the location for Hatfield's internal debriefing. It was secluded and quiet and with the oh-so-hard-to-get bottle of scotch.

It was perfect.

Yesterday had started like dozens of other missions: late wakeup, coffee in the briefing room, memorizing some key details while getting suited up to fly. Hatfield could barely recall the routine preflight checks, engine start, and taxi out. So routine, it would be like trying to recall one uneventful drive to the office from another. The climb to altitude and rendezvous with the tanker, also routine. The authorization to begin their bomb run and the insertion point, that was where the day began to sharpen in focus. Hatfield was number four in line, with a pair of 2,000-pound bombs to deliver. The original target had been a refinery, but the package commander had called a weather abort for that target as the conditions would not have allowed for a precise delivery. Hatfield was far less troubled by the concept of collateral damage than many others prosecuting this war.

The weather was far better in the area of a possible Republican Guard command and control facility. The "nice evening" the Iraqis were having was about to change. When a high-speed aircraft is flying right at you, there is no obvious sound until they pass. If they are dropping high-explosive ordnance on you, well, the surprise is just that much more profound. The first three F-16s put their ordnance right on target, and the detonations were spectacular. Number four in line was Major Hatfield, and he was focused.

When Dan Hatfield was fourteen, he watched his alcoholic father murder his mother in the kitchen of their modest home. Dannie then picked up a twelve-inch butcher knife from the counter by the sink and drove it into the chest of his father. Hatfield's life would change a thousand different ways that day, but one of the changes was to instill in him a sense of justice that would drastically lower his threshold for violence via revenge. Such a proclivity, for most people, would rarely find an outlet. An adult Major Hatfield in the seat of an instrument of violence as honed as the F-16 felt right at home. The fact was he liked killing the enemy.

When someone gets a lucky shot on target, it is often indistinguishable from talent and skill. The surface-to-air missile (SAM) slammed into Hatfield's aircraft just as he was releasing his ordnance. It's quite possible the shooter wouldn't live long enough to celebrate his perfect timing, but that was of no consolation to Hatfield. All of his sensations immediately came into play. The jolt of a missile explosion; the shuddering of the aircraft as its clean aerodynamic lines turned jagged. The sound of cockpit warning systems alerting to failures, flashing lights, and the ever-increasing number of steady lights illuminating. As the cockpit filled with smoke, he could sense his aircraft slowing down. The loss of speed was his greatest concern, as his trajectory was from safe airspace and taking him farther over enemy-held territory. Hatfield couldn't turn what was left of his disintegrating aircraft. What a prize a captured pilot would be.

The feel of his aircraft had changed, and Hatfield was suddenly gripped by the sensation that he was going down. In that cool, calm pilot radio voice, he broadcast that he was going to eject.

1

"*Fort Worth Center, Blue Sky 2448 is looking for lower.*"

"*Blue Sky 2448, Fort Worth Center. I'll be able to start you down in five miles.*"

"*Roger.*"

Captain Hatfield had been a pilot long enough to transmit a little frustration with that single word. There is a language within the language pilots use on the radio, and Dan Hatfield was fluent.

"*Blue Sky 2448, Fort Worth Center. You are clear of traffic. Descend and maintain flight level 240.*"

"*Descend and maintain flight level 240. Blue Sky 2448, thanks.*"

"I guess he got your message. Traffic my ass." First Officer Mike Chelsea was not new to the game either. The onboard TCAS system allows the pilots to see other traffic around them, and there was no one below them. Of far greater concern was the weather that plagues the central Texas area much of the year. There are times when thunderstorms pop up in seemingly random fashion in the area, wreaking havoc with air traffic control. There are also days when they form in lines and block off parts of the airspace, creating traffic jams in the sky. Today was one of those days, and unfortunately for the inbound traffic, the storms were close to the airport.

"*Fort Worth, Blue Sky 2448 is going to need to deviate to the left around that cell at our twelve o'clock and fifteen miles.*"

"*Blue Sky 2448, Fort Worth. Left deviations approved. Proceed direct*

YUCCA when able. Contact Fort Worth approach now on 119.85 and tell them when you are direct YUCCA."

"Approach on 119.85 and will advise. Blue Sky 2448."

"That's a bad sign." Captain Hatfield immediately recognized YUCCA as a fix on the approach into runway 18-R. For center to be giving them that fix to proceed to usually meant the weather was closing in on the airport.

FO Chelsea widened his radar to a distance that reached out to the approach corridor and grunted. "The line is now about five miles north of the field. This is going to be sporty getting in today."

"Approach, Blue Sky 2448 is flight level 248 for 240, heading 080 for weather. Have direct YUCCA when able and ATIS information Bravo."

"Blue Sky 2448, Regional Approach. Change of plans. Expect runway 13-R, heading 180 when able and descend and maintain ten thousand."

Hatfield acknowledged the transmission and painted it with a tad more frustration than before. That wasn't lost on the seasoned controller.

"Yeah, sorry about the late switch, 2448, but that weather is starting to crowd the 18-R arrivals. Reduce speed now to 210 knots and then continue descent to ten thousand."

A late runway switch means reprogramming the box, the navigation controller that contains the database of airports and the arrival and approach procedures for each. It was Chelsea's leg to fly, so that meant Hatfield was taking care of all the busywork. Chelsea was concentrating on finding the smooth air in between the tall cumulus buildups that contained air no one likes to find. Bad weather arrivals make for busy and often stressful cockpits. As is common in the profession, the two handled it all in a cool, easy manner that would have fooled anyone who hadn't spent much time in the cockpit.

"What does the ATIS say the surface winds are?" Chelsea asked.

There was now a stack of small printouts from the cockpit printer sitting on the center console. It took Hatfield a few seconds to find the right one and decipher it for Chelsea. "The ATIS is twenty minutes old; winds were 190 degrees at eighteen knots gusting twenty-five knots. Kid stuff!"

The joke had them both smiling, and while a fifty-degree crosswind gusting to twenty-five knots was within the limits of the Boeing, it was hardly child's play. This day was going to be sporty right up to turning off the runway.

The lightning put on quite a show as the two of them guided the aircraft toward the approach. It was seemingly all around the airport, but lightning always looks more spectacular while flying around it at night. Chelsea threaded the needle during the descent, turned the Boeing left and right around all of the cells and kept it in the surprisingly smooth air that exists outside of the vertical clouds. One hundred forty-five passengers watched the light show out of their windows, many waiting for the heavy turbulence that they expected any second, yet never appeared.

"I'm going to roll it on, out of pure spite for this weather!"

"Beers tonight in Seattle are on me if you do," Hatfield said.

"Hope you cashed your paycheck. You're on!" A beer bet is a serious matter, thought Chelsea, who put his game face on. They both knew with gusty winds, making a very smooth landing by "rolling it onto" the runway would require a little luck in the last five seconds. A gust at the wrong time, and they might float, or the aircraft could drop the last five feet and thump onto the concrete. Hatfield was already thinking about the long flight to their Seattle overnight. If they could just get in and then get out, the weather the rest of the night to Washington State would be easy. All Chelsea had on his mind right now was the feel of the wheels touching the ground.

Chelsea let loose a self-satisfied smile. "Like a BOSS!"

"Okay, okay, you got me. Beers are on the captain tonight."

Chelsea handled the crosswind with learned skill and smoothly ended the flight on the long concrete strip. Hatfield took control of the aircraft, and as they turned off the runway, Chelsea was flipping switches with one hand and pressing the transmit button with the other. On a bad weather day, the ramp and gates get crazy.

"Alpha Ramp, Blue Sky 2448 is on the ground for gate A-29."

"2448, the ramp just opened back up, and A-29 is open. Call approaching spot fifteen."

"And the hits just keep on coming!" Chelsea was happy to be telling Hatfield they had an open gate.

Hatfield taxied the Boeing past numerous aircraft sitting on holding pad areas as they waited for their gate to open up. It was hit or miss tonight for gates, with many more misses than hits. Flight 2448 was one of the lucky ones.

Standing in the cockpit door, Hatfield thanked the passengers for "flying with us" as they ambled off the airplane. More than a few wore a look on their face as if they had cheated death. In reality, the flight would be the safest thing they would do all day. They would not give a second thought to driving at night in the rain, a task containing far more danger. Having assembled their own bags and saying their goodbyes to the flight attendants, Hatfield and Chelsea made their way up the jet bridge in search of their next gate.

They never found it.

2

Blue Sky Airlines had bases, also called domiciles, in several cities spread across the U.S. Ed Ronkowski was the Chief Pilot of the DFW base, and today his biggest concern was the weather threatening to completely wreck the flight schedule. Ronkowski had been checking his watch and the flights several times an hour since the radar started to bloom in color at about two P.M. Ed had plans for this evening, so if things got bad enough at the airport, he could be delayed—or worse, even asked to cover a trip by crew scheduling. It didn't happen often, but he was still a serving line pilot, available to fly and conveniently located at the airport. Crew schedulers had called him three times that afternoon to discuss a schedule conflict, and each time he saw the caller ID, he sucked wind as he picked up the phone. It was now four-thirty, and he was eyeing the door.

The weather was leaving the field alone for the time being, just causing arrival and departure delays. Actual cancellations were few, and it was looking like he had dodged a bullet. There are few things that a man will get his hopes up for and look forward to. At the top of that list for most men is the company of a woman. This particular woman and the memories of their previous time together made it difficult for Ed to concentrate. The afternoon lent itself well to planning the entire evening in detail. Leave the airport, home for a shower, pick up a bottle of wine, and head over to her place. With no entanglements, he was planning on an eight o'clock arrival. He hoped to be making more distracting memories by nine.

Ed was a chief pilot for a few reasons, but the largest of them was his auto dealership. Ed's father had built the Chevrolet dealership in Grapevine, Texas, from the ground up at a time when far fewer people lived in that town. As the surrounding area grew, the dealership grew, and the area next to his location went from large, vacant fields to two rows of auto dealerships. One on each side of the expanding Texas Highway 114. The money Ed's father made was considerable, and Ed's future was secure. At an early age, Ed was infected with the Pilot Virus, and he could not remember a time when he wanted to be anything else. Most pilots would say the same. Ed's father had no issue with Ed becoming a pilot and had no trouble paying for it. As Ed's father grew older, he knew it would be difficult for Ed to fly and run the dealership, so his father brought on the right people to run the operation with Ed as CEO and owner. Ed's actual involvement was little, and he always drove a Corvette less than a year old. His salary, as stipulated in the documents drawn up to accompany the father's will, saw that Ed was rewarded handsomely by the dealership.

Ed's mind floated into daydreaming about the woman he had most recently been seeing and what she liked to do to him in that sports car. A ringing phone brought him back to the current time. The caller ID came up as Crew Sched. *Oh please, God, no*, he thought as he reached for the phone.

"Hey, Ed, it's Brandon in Crew Scheduling."

"Hey, Brandon, what's going on?"

"I just wanted to give you a head's up. We are working with Dispatch on a few cancellations. Looks like we may have to cancel five overnights."

"Have you finalized them?"

"They are not written in stone, but it is pretty solid that it is going to be New Orleans, Austin, Orange County, and the last Chicago. We may cancel the last La Guardia, and there's an outside chance Orlando as well, but we are trying to limit it to the first four."

"Okay, well, I'll be leaving the office in a half hour or so. If you need me, call the cell."

"Aah, the life of a chief pilot. I'll be here till one A.M. playing Whac-A-Mole."

"Good luck with that, Brandon. No offense, but I hope we don't talk again today."

"Right, chief, good night."

At ten minutes to five, Ed was beginning to let himself believe he was going to duck out of the office on time and make it a great evening. *In the car by five-ten*, he thought, *in and out of the liquor store by five-thirty-five, then about fifteen minutes to get home, so walking in the door about ten to six. Shave, shower, and dress will be about half hour or so. Plenty of time to be at her house by eight. By eight-thirty I'll have a bottle of Merlot opened, and I'll be taking in the sight of that lingerie she said she bought just for me.* Ed's new lover had changed his life significantly. On the days when he knew he was going to see her, he had trouble concentrating on anything else all day.

The timepiece on the wall was an old, black analog clock that had probably been stared at by twenty other Chief Pilots since it was hung there. At one minute to five, he could take it no longer and stood to leave. Briefcase in hand, Ed climbed the stairs to the terminal and with anticipation driving his feet, he was whistling as he walked. Three minutes later, he was standing at the employee bus stop, silently willing the bus to hurry up and arrive. He was certainly too far from his desk to hear his office phone ring.

It was Brandon calling to give Ed an update. As soon as Brandon had hung up with Ed, a dispatcher called back with an idea. The late afternoon Seattle had been delayed due to maintenance in DFW. That flight, and the late Seattle, both had light passenger loads. The late Seattle flight didn't leave Seattle the next day on its return leg until late afternoon, so

if they canceled that flight instead, it would have little impact on operations. Brandon agreed. Seattle was out, and Orange County was back
in. It is good to be a meticulous person as a crew scheduler, and that was
how Brandon became a supervisor. It bothered his personality that he
was not able to check all the boxes by notifying Ed, but he tried. In the
end, he decided it wasn't worth looking up Ed's cell number.

3

While Hatfield chatted with the gate agent, someone he had known for years at Blue Sky, Chelsea checked the computer for their Seattle information.

"Hey, they canceled Seattle. Sweet. We pick up the rest of our trip tomorrow afternoon here in DFW."

They were on the first day of a three-day trip. Cancelling the Seattle overnight meant they were going home right away. The long flight back tomorrow was also canceled, so they would have a long overnight at home. It doesn't happen that way very often, so when it does, it is a wonderful surprise. Hatfield jumped onto the other gate computer, logged on to acknowledge that he saw the trip change, and was right on his first officer's heels headed toward the exit.

"Hey, Mike, I'll see you tomorrow. I'm going to duck into the Chief Pilot's office and drop off a parking reimbursement."

"Say 'hi' to Ed for me. You know I don't like to say it in person. See ya!"

The CPO was a place that pilots generally avoided. Most felt that the less time they spent in that office, the better. It was largely thought of the same way the Principal's Office is in grade school. It was where pilots were told to go when they needed to be "spanked" for some issue that didn't go well. It wasn't that way for Dan. He met Ed Ronkowski when they were both students at Purdue University, many years prior. Ed was a rich man's son, a fraternity member, and studying Management. The two of them had a party to go to every weekend, and sometimes during the week. They stayed in touch after they graduated. But while Dan went off to the Air Force, then settled down, Ed never really left the fraternity. He continued to act like he was still in college, with plenty of money from the dealership, and never found that one woman. He liked chasing tail, and as a pilot who also had money, he found his share. He took his time building flight hours, while Dan was building flight hours flying missions in combat. Dan and Ed were happily surprised when they were both offered acceptance letters from Blue Sky Airlines, and they almost ended up in the same class of new hire pilots.

The CPO was only a gate away from their arrival gate. Glancing at his watch, he knew it would be unoccupied at seven thirty P.M. Hatfield blew out a little huff and muttered under his breath about how nice it would be to have the Chief Pilot's life and schedule. Sure, the job could be a pain, especially when disciplinary requirements popped up involving the pilots of the base. But knowing you'd be home every night, *that* might make it worth it. Might.

Dan found his way to one of the elevators that can be found inside almost any airline terminal—the ones marked "Authorized Personnel Only." Inserting the special key, he boarded and pressed the lower-level button. DFW sits a story off the ground, with the lower level containing the inner workings that go on mostly out of view of the public. Baggage is handled and sorted, cargo is distributed to the various flights, and crew lounges and offices are found on the lower level.

Dan strode into the Blue Sky pilot crew lounge, greeting the familiar faces as he weaved his way to the back toward the Chief Pilot's office. It is the goal of many pilots to go as long as possible without ever having the Chief Pilot know their name. Most avoided the office if it was at all possible. Dan had always taken the opposite tack, and had tried to maintain a first-name, good relationship with every Chief Pilot with which he worked. Although he had yet to "need" a friend in the Chief Pilot's office, he felt that it was better to be prepared—and he was lucky that this Chief Pilot was already a good friend. In many a situation in the past, Dan had managed to get by on his sense of humor and good looks. At six foot one, a lean, muscular 165-pound frame, dark hair, and dark eyes set on a strong face, if he was wearing a smile, it was impossible not to smile back.

He had been popular in high school and college. His looks got him dates in high school, and his sense of humor ensured he was always skirting trouble. It was his looks that also got him introduced to his future wife in college, but it was his sense of humor that she was most attracted to. Dan had managed to hang onto that body despite four years of college food and fifteen years as a professional pilot eating airport food and rich restaurant meals within walking distance of the hotels he spent half of every month in. As an airline pilot, however, his good looks had gotten him more than his fair share of situations requiring him to distance himself from another crew member in order to keep his marriage vows intact. He had managed to do that without a single indiscretion, something he was proud of and something he saw other crew members violate often. While his sense of humor came in handy with getting along with first officers, it would do him no good during a "carpet dance" in the Chief Pilot's office if ever he was summoned there to explain a mistake.

Stuffing a few pieces of paper and a parking receipt through the drop slot in the door, Hatfield turned and headed back to the elevator. As he strolled through the terminal with bags in tow, he hesitated as he passed the brightly lit machine filled with bouquets of flowers. Things at home with Sharon had been strained lately, and their last words to each other as he left for the trip were harsh.

Dan had met Sharon while they were in college, and her immediate expectations of affluence were much lower back then. She believed that eventually Dan would be making serious money and that their lives would be full of glamour and travel. What had become clear was that her reality did not match her dreams, and it was beginning to show in her handling of Dan. Her disappointment, while unspoken, was obvious. Dan had always seen her materialism as something that was annoying at times but would not threaten the marriage. He had always loved her deeply. In fact, Sharon was the only woman he'd ever loved. But recently, loving her began to feel more of a burden than a blessing. He'd lately been entertaining thoughts of divorce, but always came to the same conclusion: it was cheaper to keep her. *Once again, I'll try to bridge the gap*, he thought as he dug a credit card from his wallet.

"And I thought airport food was expensive," he said aloud as his card was charged for the dozen roses. Thinking that if it smoothed things over, and maybe even got him laid tonight, it would be worth the $85.95. Stowing his wallet, grabbing the handle of his typical rollaway overnight bag, and holding the bouquet of roses as if it were an Olympic torch, he turned toward the exit. His eyes caught the glance of a passenger—a woman—who smiled as she looked at his face, then the bouquet, then back to his face. He'd seen the look many times before. It said, "it must be awesome to be married to an airline pilot, the money, the travel, all that time off..." Civilians didn't have a clue about the reality of the airline business but were convinced it was desirable.

AIDS, to the airline pilot, stands for Aviation Induced Divorce Syndrome, and it plagues the rank and file of pilots. One of Dan's good friends at Blue Sky had just finished a very ugly, costly divorce. Sam and Cameron Parker—Sam and Cam as everyone called them—seemed as if they would be married forever. Dan never found out exactly what led to the divorce, but he was read into the details of the divorce itself. Cam made the mistake of lining up a divorce attorney, then listening to her friends much more than her attorney. She based her financial math on what they owned when the divorce was filed. In reality, the first thing the divorce attorney hands their client is a form to fill out listing all marital assets. The attorney then assesses just how much of those assets they can take in billable hours and gets right to work. By the time Sam and Cam were finalized, most of the money was gone, safely in both legal firms' bank accounts. Alimony doesn't exist in Texas. Cam was on her own with half of the 401k, living in an apartment. Sam was in the same situation, with a job, but saddled with all the marital debts by a judge that hated men.

As he climbed on the bus with the "Employee Parking" sign, Hatfield was wondering if he was contracting that disease, or if he'd be able to at least fight it off tonight with the combination of Colombian flowers and American Express. His watch said 7:45 P.M. With any luck, he'd be home by 8:30. The decision to make the marriage work left Dan with an odd sense of relief. Coupled with that was the hope that the flowers and the surprise overnight at home would be good for them.

4

Dan was starting to relax as he drove his crew cab pickup down the six-lane highway that led to his neighborhood. The job of being a pilot requires an artificially high level of concentration while in the cockpit, a state that pilots get used to and don't even notice as it's happening. Once out of the cockpit, there is a certain amount of time required to slow down the body and mind, to place it back in a more normal state. Borrowing a diving term, that time has been labeled Decompression Time.

An even longer amount of time is required to get in a state where sleep is possible. That can be an occupational hazard sometimes because many of the overnights on multi-day trips are short. Some barely allow for eight hours of sleep. Then there are the red-eyes and all-night flights. Hatfield was just decompressing as he drove, listening to the music on the radio and enjoying the luck of going home.

This is an opportunity for me to patch up things with Sharon, he thought. *I'm really going to try to make it a good night with us.*

Sharon's background, her life before Dan, included opportunities few people get in life. Few people come from the kind of money Sharon's family had. But Dan had taken her from all that and had tried hard to make her happy. They met as students at Purdue, Sharon working on a management degree and Dan in the University Flight Program. He was also in the Air Force Reserve Officer Training Program, AFROTC for short. They had been invited to the same fraternity party where they literally ran into each other, Dan pouring a full cup of beer down the front of her shirt in the process. He offered to take her to a nice restaurant as an apology, and Sharon accepted. There was an ROTC drill the afternoon of the date, and Dan being late showed at the restaurant in uniform. Sharon was immediately smitten with Dan. Neither of them really knowing love in their lives prior to their meeting, they fell quickly and fell hard for each other. Since that time and until recently, despite the recent strain in their relationship, Dan knew with not a shred of doubt that they truly loved each other and were the best of friends.

As reality replaced the fairy-tale expectations of Sharon's hopes, things got tense. No amount of travel, money, vacations—nothing, really—seemed to make her truly happy. The move to a big house in Texas seemed like a plan that would work, but the novelty of a new home and surroundings wore off quickly. Sharon seemed impossible to satisfy, and Dan found it increasingly difficult to even try. When Sharon slid into losing basic respect for Dan, he found it hard to love her in return. It is true that women value love first, men value respect first, and a lack of either makes it hard to show the other. Dan had high hopes that the love and respect would return, that their love would conquer all. *I know guys that have been married thirty years to the same woman. They all say the same thing—they had their share of bad times, but their love always got them through. That's it. I'm going to make this work no matter what. I'll call the union tomorrow and line up marriage counseling. We truly love each other, and I am going to see this through.* He glanced down at the flowers. *This. This is going to be the moment I turn it all around. Maybe we could plan a second honeymoon.*

It rained off and on during the drive, and in true decompression mode, Dan drove the speed limit in the right lane without any urgency to get home. He wanted to get home, but driving fast on wet roads only raises tension. He knew that if he was going to make any headway with

Sharon tonight, walking in the door wound up like a spring was not going to help.

Dan was in a pretty good mood when he finally turned into their neighborhood. It was one of those standard Texas neighborhoods with huge houses, wide-open streets, and little landscaping. Texas gets very brown in the summer when the heat is turned up. He had chosen this house because it had the garage separated from the house, with room enough for a shop.

I'll park in the alley and not bother with the garage so I can surprise Sharon. No sense in bringing the bags in. I'm heading back to the airport tomorrow.

To ensure the surprise, he turned off the headlights as he made the bend into the alley so as not to alert his wife. Running lights only, he maneuvered his truck up close to the fence that was his backyard and shut off the engine.

Almost forgot those ninety-dollar flowers. Wow! He turned to the passenger seat and picked up the bouquet. Dan purposely closed the truck door quietly. He did the same with the fence gate, quietly opening and closing it. When he looked back at the house, he stopped in his tracks.

His house was almost completely dark, with only a small light that serves as a night-light giving the kitchen a warm glow. *I don't remember Sharon saying she was going out.*

Taking two more steps forward, he looked through the small window of the door to the garage. He could make out the lines of her BMW sedan in the dark, confirmed an instant later when a flash of lightning briefly lit up the scene. Turning back to the house, with eyes adjusted to the dark, he saw the movement of a person walking toward the kitchen. The grace and flow of the movement was familiar.

Sharon, you are home.

Preparing to take another step toward the house, another flash of lightning lit up the kitchen. He froze solid at what he saw. There was Sharon standing on the other side of the sliding glass door, pouring a glass of wine, wearing matching lacy bra, panties, and stockings, finished in very high heels. The flash was so quick and the sight so unexpected, it didn't really register until the next flash of lightning confirmed that he wasn't seeing things. He glanced down at the flowers in his hand and a smile spread across his face.

I'm not the only one trying to patch things up. Then confusion. *How did she find out I was coming home?* He still hadn't moved from that corner of the yard.

The next flash of light felt as though the bolt traveled right through him. There was a man, walking up behind her. *Sharon!*

Dan went into rapid formulation of a plan to best deal with the intruder and keep Sharon safe. So far, it was something like run in there and kick his ass. The lightning put a stop to that plan. As the man reached arm's length from her, Sharon turned around and embraced him, kissing him deeply. The glow of the night-light and the flash of millions of volts of static electricity burned the image into Dan's brain. He never felt the flowers slip from his hand.

With each flash of lightning, the scene changed slightly. Sharon backed up to the island in the big kitchen.

Flash.

The man lifting Sharon onto the island.

Flash.

Sharon leaning back and raising widely spread feet high into the air.

Flash.

The man's head disappearing between her thighs.

Flash.

Sharon's head all the way back, touching the granite counter.

Flash Flash Flash.

The man lifted Sharon into his arms and carried her through the adjacent living room and into the attached master bedroom. The big bay windows of the master that Sharon had raved about when they bought the house provided a spectacular view of the unfolding scene.

Flash.

Sharon posed seductively on the bed while the man removed his clothing.

Dan felt as if he were on an elevator, and with every flash he was descending lower and lower toward a dark place where he knew he would be different. Each flash illuminated a scene that stripped from him a part of himself and replaced it with a darker person. By the time the man and Sharon were making love, he knew that the Dan who bought the flowers, the Dan who wanted to surprise his wife, was gone, changed by the man in his house. The Dan who was standing there in the rain, next to a pile of roses laying on the ground, was a man who had nothing but seething spite for the two lovers.

Dan's demeanor was surprisingly level-headed as he thought, *I'm going to kill them both.*

So caught up in his thoughts, he hadn't noticed the two had apparently finished what they were doing. The man had walked up to the window of the master bedroom and was looking out at the night sky.

Flash.

Just when Dan thought he couldn't go any lower, the face of the man who was with his wife became clearly illuminated. *Well now, that just made the job easier.* Even at a distance in the rain, the face of Ed Ronkowski was familiar. Dan felt a level of pain and betrayal like nothing he'd felt since he watched his father kill his mother. What was missing while Dan stood in the rain was the instant justice that happened when Dan killed his father. Dan was feeling the pain of the betrayal of both Sharon and a man he considered his friend. It was burning through his heart with nothing in the way of justice to put out the flames. He stood a few moments longer before he came to a decision.

Time to go formulate a plan.

Dan left his old life and his old self in that backyard like the pile of beautiful roses at his feet. An already permanently changed Dan Hatfield turned and walked toward the exit of his old life. The gate to the fence was opened and closed again with the same stealth as before, as was the door of the truck. Not this time to be polite or to surprise, but so as not to alert his future victims.

5

Leaving the neighborhood was easy, as there was just one way out of the gated community. It was the car behind him honking at the intersection that forced him to choose left or right at the entrance. On autopilot, he turned right as if going to the airport. Dan had two desires that were immediate: a room for the night and alcohol. The highway service road he had just turned onto presented solutions to both. The Pink Cabaret bar and the aging motel next to it. *Perfect.* He pulled into the motel parking lot and glanced over at the strip club sign. *I'll be right back.*

The room was adequate, and Dan had everything with him already for a hotel stay. That was what he'd intended to do in a state over a thousand miles away. It didn't take long to change into the clothes he'd packed for going out on his trip. However, this was not what he'd pictured when he had packed them. It was a short walk across the two parking lots to the front door of the Pink Cabaret.

The music leaked out the front door so that it could be heard with twenty feet of parking lot left to cross. By the time Dan opened the door, he could clearly make out the Eighties rock song playing inside, complete with just a little bit too much base. There was a fairly attractive young woman at the door, who collected the cover charge, flanked by a large man whose job it was to look intimidating. Dan was far more interested in Dewars doubles on the rocks than he was with whoever would be spinning around a brass pole inside.

"Why do strip clubs always have the same smell?" he muttered as he turned the corner and looked around the place. It was the standard strip club layout, and his feet began moving again when his eyes found the bar. Dan made sure to pick a stool with empty seats on both sides. He wasn't interested in conversation. In any other bar, that would have been a good idea. The dancers saw that as an invitation and didn't leave him alone long.

. . .

Cindy Simpson had just left the dressing room area, the inner sanctum of the club for the dancers. Her shift had started an hour and a half ago, and so far, it had been a slow night. Scanning the club, she saw that most of the men were already accompanied by dancers, with the exception of the unusually handsome man sitting solo at the bar. For many dancers, this was just a job, and while they put on a good show of enjoying themselves, for the most part they didn't. Cindy—or "Sindee," as she referred to herself at work—had always been sexually promiscuous and actually did enjoy the job. The money was good, but what really did it for her were those rare occasions when she accompanied men who turned her on. The closer she got to Dan, the bigger her smile grew and the lower her morals settled in her brain.

"Hi, I'm Sindee. Mind if I join you?"

Dan, deep in thought, was mildly startled. "Have a seat. I'm Dan. Nice to meet you."

They sized each other up, and even a casual observer would have seen that they both liked the view. Sindee was five foot seven, one-fifteen, blonde, well-endowed, and all of twenty-five. She watched for a man to look her up and down, then took that as her cue to do the same. She made sure he saw her doing it and smiled as she did. It usually worked like a charm. She could see that Dan would need a little more loosening up, the tension in him obvious. Now that she got a good look at him up close, she realized how hot he was. She wanted to touch him immediately, and it was clearly something he needed.

"You look like you have a lot on your mind," she said as she slid off the stool and gracefully snuggled up behind him. Her hands went to his shoulders and began a skillful massage.

"That feels nice," Dan said, and Sindee heard the sincerity in his voice. She didn't know if he was talking about the massage, or the way she was purposefully rubbing her breasts on his back. *Probably both*, she thought.

When the bartender approached Dan, he turned his head to Sindee and asked, "Would you like a drink?"

Sindee looked to the bartender, who probably used to be a dancer but had aged out and graduated to drinks. "Vodka and cranberry please," she said. "Thank you, Dan!" Then she leaned in and whispered in his ear. "If you like this massage, you'll love one of my private dances."

He could smell her now, and the entire experience had nearly made him forget why he was there. Nearly. "Sure, let's go." He made eye contact with the bartender. "Can I get a refill sent to our new location?"

The smile and nod from her gave him confidence the Dewars would find him.

Led by the hand to the back of the club, the pair passed three other dancers, two of whom openly gave Sindee looks as if she'd scored a prize. Sindee sensed a bit of hesitation in Dan, as if he felt that the private dance was either a good idea or it was not.

It seemed as if the third dancer they passed removed his doubts. "Looks like you both are going to have a real good time." Dan's posture visibly relaxed at the remark as Sindee led him toward the private area.

What they couldn't see was the large European sedan parking outside the club. It backed into a space not far from the door, the way a cop or someone expecting to make a quick getaway would do. That was standard practice for the driver, who doubled as the bodyguard for the single occupant of the back seat: a middle-aged, sharply dressed man. He was fit, confident, and had clearly been to this club before. His name was Angelo Genofi, a mob boss who had worked in the past as a collector and, when needed, a hitter.

He was there to pick up the weekly protection money and to see his favorite dancer, Sindee.

6

It was out of pure habit that Sindee looked at the lit doorway. She was looking forward to the dance she was about to perform for—or rather on—Dan. *Definitely someone whose phone number I want to get. He'd be a great repeat customer*, she thought. But when the door opened, the light from the outer lobby spilled in like a flood of water. The potential of a new customer trains the dancers to glance at the doorway to see who is entering. Sindee recognized him immediately.

FUCK. I forgot today is Friday. That's Nico. Angelo will be right behind him.

She was panicking inside, but no one would have seen the change in her demeanor. Sindee knew that they would go to the back office through an unmarked door so inconspicuous you had to know it was there to see it. They would spend ten to fifteen minutes in there with the owner, then Nico would look the place over while Angelo would head to the bar to get a drink. That was supposed to be her sign to join him. When Nico was sure the place was safe for Angelo, he'd go back to the car to give Angelo alone time with Sindee. It was their routine, every Friday, like clockwork. He rarely stayed for more than three private dances, but by then, Dan, the man giving her tingles, would be in the hands of someone else. She needed a plan.

Angelo and Nico arrived at a semi-private, even more dimly lit spot in the back of the club with multiple individual seating areas. The angles allowed the dancers to give private dances that, at times, broke the rules, out of sight of everyone else in the club. It was an unspoken agreement between labor and management: break the rules as you see fit, show the customers a good time, they will request more dances and will be back again. The house gets $5 of every $20 private dance, and a motivated dancer could make more than $100 an hour. Of course, there were higher levels of dances that paid even better and pretty much required breaking all the rules. Sindee began violating the rules immediately. With experienced skill, she also began the interrogation.

"So, Dan, what do you do?"

"I'm an airline pilot." Dan saw that look creep across her face that was nearly identical to the woman in the airport. Sindee's look had heat in it, though, bordering on lust.

"Really? That's awesome, I *love* pilots!" Sindee stepped up her calculations. No way was she letting Dan go. Not even for Angelo. Time to make a move. "Dan, I want to ask you a favor, and I will make it worth your while. There's a friend of the owner here, and I know he is going to be asking for me in a little bit. He won't stay long, and he's actually a great guy. He travels a lot and would probably like to meet you. If it's okay with you, can we all sit together, and after he leaves, I will be yours the rest of the night. I'll give you two private dances for free. What do you say?"

It didn't take Dan long to agree. She was attractive, sensuous, smelled great, and her "dance" had gotten the full attention of his entire body. Small talk for a little while with a stranger was a small price to pay. It wasn't the $40 he'd save. That was chump change. It was the offer. It said a lot about Sindee. All of it good.

"Sure, why not?"

"Thanks, Dan! I promise you will not be disappointed."

The word "promise" took twice as long to say as it should have. He was confident she was right. The third Dewars arrived at the table just as the door to the back office opened. Angelo strolled out and right into the arms of Sindee. He was clearly delighted to see her, and she at least gave the appearance of being happy to see him.

Let's see if I can pull this off, she thought. "Angelo, come with me. There's someone I'd like you to meet." She parted the curtain. "This is my friend, Dan. He's an airline pilot."

. . .

Angelo's interest was piqued. He'd always admired pilots. In a way, their demeanor and job were like his. There was a coolness and confidence in them that came from having a job that was life and death, where they were expected to keep their calm during difficult and even dangerous situations. He always thought he would have made a good pilot, but few people from his neighborhood ever became professionals in that sense of the word. Far more became the kind of professional he was.

"Dan, nice to meet you. Pilot, impressive. When I was a kid, I'd see the war movies in the theater; the first one hooked me. I wanted to be a pilot, but let's just say not many pilots grew up on the streets where I lived. I didn't do too bad though."

They sat down in the small private area. Dan picked up his drink and took a sip. Sindee had not left Angelo's side since he first walked up and was now practically sitting in his lap. She was making it clear who she wanted to think she saw as the alpha male. Sindee sold it well, but there was a tension in the mix. Angelo's ego had to feel that Sindee was there for him only—it was the reason he always left Nico in the car. But he liked pilots and wanted to make the acquaintance. He also liked the distraction from his life that was Sindee and looked forward to his time with her. Sindee was his favorite toy, and Dan was a new toy. Sindee obviously didn't want to lose either of them. She'd made her deal with Dan, but at that moment, she needed for Angelo to clearly understand that he was the one that was important to her.

The next song started and without a word or hesitation, Sindee started her affections on Angelo. He gave her a wide smile and clearly was enjoying himself but looked over at Dan to continue the small talk. It was a guy thing, as if to say he was enjoying this beautiful woman and her sexuality, but he was in control enough to still engage in conversation the man who was being left alone.

"Sindee is the perfect end to a busy week. I love it when you do that baby. Do it again."

Another rule broken by Sindee—Angelo clearly was in charge.

"So, what do you do for dancer money?" Dan was smiling as he said it.

"I'm a business financial consultant." It was the kind of thing someone said when they either wanted you to ask or didn't want you to know what they really did.

"Business looks like it's been good to you."

"HA! Yeah, business has been booming in the—" Angelo didn't finish the sentence. It was difficult to talk with Sindee's thirty-four double-dees applied firmly to his face. Sindee didn't know what Angelo did for certain, but there was enough talk that she had a pretty good idea. Talking about it with Dan seemed like a pretty bad idea.

A smiling waitress placed another double Dewars on the table in front of Dan. He had only been half-kidding when he told her earlier to bring him another any time his glass got down to half an inch. Apparently, the waitress had good eyesight and followed instruction well.

Perhaps too well. By his fifth Dewars, Dan had received his two freebie dances and Angelo was still there. Sindee was in overdrive, trying to outdo herself with each dance. All the club rules had been broken and broken badly by the time Dan picked up his seventh Dewars from the table. Before that drink was gone, Sindee had gone right past club rules and was now breaking the laws of most states in the union. Halfway through the eighth Dewars, she was breaking the laws of all of them.

Dan was giving up a lot of information as the night went on, and Angelo was soaking it up. Dan would have no memory at all of his eighth drink, the ninth drink, most of what they talked about, or his credit card bill of just under $500. He certainly wouldn't remember Angelo telling Sindee to take him back to his motel room to "tuck him in."

Or the way she giggled when he said it.

7

Waking up after a night like Dan had was more of a process than an event. The first step involved taking a quick physical inventory and an orientation of his exact location. The light hurt his eyes, his throat was dry, and water was first on his mind. Behind his eyes, his head was aching, but that was all to be expected. He must have gone through at least some of his hotel routine because there was a bottle of water on his nightstand. He got as far as recognizing and remembering checking into this hotel, then walking into the club. He felt the distinct sensation of a naked ass rubbing up against his naked ass, and for a few shocked seconds had no idea who it could be.

Turning to look, he recognized the face of Sindee, still with her eyes closed and still clearly desiring sleep. The next step of the morning-after process began: the search for information. Dan couldn't remember coming back to the room, or anything after that, so he started chronologically from when he walked through the door of the Pink Cabaret. *Dewars, Angelo, dances, oh the dances, talking, and then...*

And then nothing. He slowly raised his head up and looked around the room.

My clothes in a heap next to the bed. Don't remember that. Her clothes on the chair. Nope. Condom wrapper on the floor. WOW. Nothing. Crap, I still have to fly late today, what time is it?

Dan saw his cell on the nightstand: 9:43 A.M. Being late or missing a flight is a huge sin for an airline pilot. He relaxed again as he realized he had plenty of time to ask the naked woman next to him how his night went. He assumed she wanted to sleep, and that with her job, she probably rarely woke before noon. The one-hour hotel shower, as he called it, seemed like the best course of action. Dan slid out of bed as carefully as he could and took his cell, the water bottle, and the ibuprofen from his overnight bag to the bathroom.

It was a pretty tame indulgence, the one-hour hotel shower, but it was something Dan would only do on the road. His upbringing had been modest. Well, the part before his life and his childhood fell apart. His father was a delivery driver after a stint in the navy. Life on a ship taught his father the opposite of the one-hour hotel shower: the Navy shower. Water was at a premium on the ship, so standard procedure was to get wet, water off, lather up, rinse quickly, and done. Dan had never timed them, but he was sure he had at least a few two-hour showers. He would just hang a towel over the shower curtain rod to wipe the condensation from the front of his phone from time to time.

This particular morning, the phone was left out on the counter in the hopes that running water over his head would wash away the ache. He'd been standing under the showerhead for at least ten minutes, eyes closed, and it seemed to be working. The sound of the shower and the water over his ears masked any sounds Sindee made as she carefully entered the shower and sank to her knees. She went right to work, and he never even opened his eyes. His hand on her head, his fingers in her hair, she was as graceful and skillful at this as she was with her private dances. The shower did *not* last an hour. Even with the application of soap to both their bodies by what felt like the hands of an artist, it was over in twenty minutes.

"That was already more successful than last night, but that is what a bottle of Dewars will do to a man. Even a man like you. Time to take me to bed now and return the favor," she whispered in his ear as she turned off the water.

She was as demure as a woman could possibly be. He had no idea what had happened the night before, but he was enthralled by the thought of what was about to happen. Returning that favor was one of Dan's favorite horizontal activities. He had studied it, and like all pilots, had an innate desire to master any skill he wanted to acquire. Dan took a little longer to exit the bathroom than Sindee had. He walked out to see her laying on the bed in what could be described as the ready position.

A knock on the door came before he was two steps closer to the bed. It was the knock of someone motivated and who knew exactly which door he was knocking on. Half knock, half pound. Oddly, Sindee didn't seem phased. Dan wrapped a towel around his waist.

I hope I paid my bar tab, he thought. Looking through the peep hole in the door, the face uncovered another layer of the night before. Angelo, holding three cups of coffee. Coffee sounded good, but it was still a distant second to making Sindee writhe in bed.

"Hi, Angelo," he said as he opened the door.

Before Dan had finished saying his name, Angelo was already pushing past him into the room. Sindee never moved other than an outstretched hand.

"I figured you for a caramel macchiato. Looks like you tucked him in. Actually, looks like you were about to tuck him in again!"

Angelo laughed, as did Sindee. Dan was still trying to take it all in.

"And for you, my man, a coffee, tall, and black as your hair. How much of last night do you remember?"

Dan took the coffee, actually grateful for it, and pondered Angelo's question.

"Clearly you don't remember it all, so you won't remember me telling you I'd stop by the room so we could talk more. I wanted to finish our conversation, but it's looking like we might have to have some of it over again."

"Maybe most of it. Refresh my memory: what were we talking about?"

"Oh, we talked about a lot, flyboy. Okay, I'll start from early in the evening, and we'll just go again. Maybe from about your fifth drink, you know, when Sindee started sticking her hand in our pants."

Angelo began laying out a conversation that, at first, Dan remembered most of, but then it faded off into nothing. Dan had been telling him about the events prior to checking into that hotel room. Angelo had been asking him about his background, his training, and the life of a pilot. Dan had filled him in on his upbringing, his Air Force experience, flying in combat in the Middle East, and what being an airline pilot is really like. Seemingly tame conversation so far. Angelo seemed to hesitate, as if something wasn't right, something he needed to correct.

"Hey, sweetie, I'm hungry, and after last night, I'm sure Dan needs food. Could you be a doll and get us all some breakfast? You can take my car. You'll love driving it. It's the black 550SL parked right outside. It's backed into the space, can't miss it."

"Sure, baby, anything you say."

Angelo peeled a hundred off a thick fold of bills. "I want you to keep what's left as a gift for a fun night last night."

Sindee was dressed in an instant, but then she didn't put much on. She gave Dan a smile and a wink, then gave Angelo a kiss and a squeeze. It was her ass Dan was looking at as the door closed. Angelo was back to his relaxed self and clearly ready to talk about something Sindee shouldn't hear.

"Do you remember discussing your wife, her guy, and their futures?"

"No, but I can guess what I said."

"Do you remember filling me in on the way you airline pilots and flight attendants travel?"

"I talked about that?" Dan knew now he may have shared information he wasn't supposed to. It was hard for him to believe that he did. He had a security clearance as an Air Force pilot and clearly understood the sanctity of classified information. More puzzling was the connection Angelo seemed to be making. As airline crew, they cleared security in the airport in ways that were different than the public.

Angelo made eye contact with Dan and paused. It was a thoughtful pause and a deliberate stare. It was the demeanor of a person who understood they were about to cross a line, about to open a door that then could not be closed.

"Last night you said you wanted your wife and that man dead. Over the years, I've heard many people say many things like that, and I can tell when they mean it, and when they are just talking shit. You said it several times, and you meant it every time. How do you feel about that now?"

"Nothing has changed."

"Then say it again."

"Dead, Angelo. I want them dead and out of my life."

Angelo's eyes never left Dan's, and he remained in that tentative demeanor.

"After you said that a few times last night, I told you I could help you with that. I told you that I had an idea how we could help each other. You told me to come here this morning, and we'd talk about it. One last thing. You told me last night that you watched your father kill your mother when you were fourteen, and that you killed him. Got sent to a home until you were old enough to move out. Is that all true?"

Holy shit, I told him about that? I don't talk about that with anyone. "Yeah, Angelo, that's all true. They called it self-defense, but that was a stretch, and I had nowhere else to go."

Another pause, only this time Angelo looked off to the right, making a mental decision. Then he made that eye contact again with Dan.

"Okay, now listen to my story and my proposal."

8

Ejecting from an F-16 could be compared to cliff diving. It begins with a single, deliberate act, and the rest of it is vivid and automatic, completely out of control of the actor. The actual experience of cliff diving pales in comparison to the ejection sequence. With the same speed as a car's airbag, the sequence begins with a few measures designed to protect the limbs of the pilot while simultaneously shedding the canopy above his head. Then a split second after the canopy is safely behind the cockpit, the rockets on the base of the pilot's seat erupt and give the pilot a 16G to 19G kick in the ass. That kick rapidly removes the pilot from the aircraft, seat and all, and the system is designed to reorient the seat and occupant vertically away from the earth, even if the ejection happened with the aircraft upside down. So hard is this kick, it is not unusual for a pilot that has ejected to lose an inch in his vertical height for a long period of time, or even permanently! After a time, the sequence continues, separating the pilot from the seat, releasing the parachute canopy, and a survival kit that remains tethered to the pilot.

Major Hatfield's "cliff diving" experience began with the realization and evaluation of the fact that he was no longer in an airplane. It was a $2.5 billion dollar dumpster fire, half a mile above a planet that it was streaking toward at three hundred miles an hour. Head back, knees in, and both hands between his thighs on the ejection handle, Major Hatfield pulled hard and was immediately rewarded with the sequence he'd read about, imagined, experienced simulations of in practice ejection trainers, but never actually felt until that moment.

In anticipation, Hatfield had reflexively filled his lungs with air and held his breath. The seat kicked him in the ass so hard, he blew every ounce of that air out of his lungs before the seat had cleared the rails it was attached to in the aircraft. That moment would be one he would relive and dissect thousands of times over the next few years, but in the moment all Hatfield felt was physical punishment and the uncomfortable feeling of being completely out of control.

The seat and occupant were howling through the black night sky above southern Iraq, but the sound of the wind was decreasing as the resistance to the air began to slow the assembly. Perfectly in sequence, a drag chute deployed, and the seat separated from the pilot. The dynamic changed from a kick in the ass to the weightlessness of falling through the sky for a moment, and then as the parachute deployed Hatfield felt the hard pull on the harness that attached him to the parachute canopy deploying over his head. It is a tribute to the human brain that in Hatfield's memory, all of that sequence happened in slow motion and his brain recorded amazing detail. In a mere five seconds after pulling the handle, Hatfield was separated from the seat and floating down toward the earth under a fully deployed parachute canopy, with his survival kit hanging below him by a strap connected to his harness.

The deafening sounds of the ejection sequence were replaced by almost complete silence. Hatfield, still wearing his helmet, could see his aircraft arcing toward the ground in front of him, but he didn't hear anything until a few seconds after it impacted the desert floor and exploded. Then abruptly it was almost complete silence again. He reached up and pulled at his left parachute strap. Hatfield could see from the smoke of the aircraft fire that if he turned away from the impact site, the winds would carry him farther away from it. The only lights off in that direction were faint and far away. Hatfield wanted to create as much distance as he could from his crashed aircraft, any structures, and roads. Pickup would be by helicopter if it was by friendlies. Hostiles would be alerted by locals and would arrive in vehicles.

Looking beneath his feet, he could make out the outline of the survival kit. It contained a myriad of items, but most important to Hatfield were the radio and the infrared beacon. *Time is now the enemy*, thought Major Hatfield. There's only so much darkness left. It will take time to get out of my harness and open the survival kit. Then in darkness, find the radio, establish contact with someone—anyone—on the emergency frequency. The right person will then have to authenticate that Hatfield is who he says he is and isn't under duress. It takes time for a rescue helicopter to get manned, spun up, and an escort coordinated. Then, of course, the flight time to location, finding the Major on the ground, and picking him up. Hatfield was making two calculations in his head: is there enough darkness left for a pickup to happen at night, and how much longer before his boots hit the ground. Just a few seconds before his feet touched the sand, his plan was complete.

Sand, Hatfield thought, grateful that the sand softened the impact with earth. If it was daylight, he'd have been able to flare the chute a bit and make a running landing. In the darkness, there wasn't but a few seconds between becoming aware the impact was imminent and the impact itself. Not all of the desert is sand, but if he broke an ankle on a hard surface, he'd never hear the end of it from his fellow pilots: "How the fuck did you manage to eject over the desert and miss the sand?" they'd rib him.

In short order, Hatfield was all business. Punching out of the parachute harness, pulling the strap closer to retrieve the survival kit. Finding the radio and extra flashlight. He did all this while keeping as quiet as possible, listening for any noise at all that wasn't the light breeze tracing over the desert. While feeling in the dark for the life-saving items, he turned his head ninety degrees at a time for a few seconds. Hatfield was using his eyes to see if there was anything nearby and using his ears as listening beacons. Satisfied that he was alone, at least for now, he turned his focus to the radio. Until he heard the sound of an approaching rescue helicopter, he was trapped in the paradox of time moving very slowly, but every second precious enough not to be wasted.

I hope that GPS locator beacon is doing its job.

What Hatfield hoped, but couldn't know at the time, was that the beacon *was* doing its job, and that there were teams of people already springing into action. No one was wasting time.

9

Angelo's eyes narrowed as he stared at Dan, giving the correct impression that Angelo was about to speak of something deeply important.

"Now Dan, I don't believe in God. The path this meeting is about to take will make you believe that. With that said, I also don't believe in coincidences. I believe there are forces in this world we simply don't understand completely, but that doesn't make them not real. Gravity, we understand. It's real and observable. It's a force that causes a pull, an attraction if you will. I believe there are other forces that attract and repel, forces I have seen at work in my life and the lives of others, but that we don't really understand. Like the force that brought you and me together."

"I'm not sure I follow you, Angelo..."

"My father was a mean motherfucker. All the time I'm growin' up, I'd watch him slap my mother for any little thing, sometimes for nothin'. I'm not sure what made him that way. Maybe his father beat him up. I don't know."

The pain behind Dan's eyes was easing up. *Thank God for ibuprofen.* But now images of his own childhood were popping up. What Angelo said next felt like an electric shock.

"One day, when I also was fourteen, my mother made it clear to my father that she'd had enough and wasn't gonna be slapped that day. She stood in front of him with a butcher knife that looked like it was older than the house. I watched him slowly look down at the knife, then slowly back up to my mother's face. Then calm as if he was reaching for his wallet, he pulled a revolver from his back pocket and shot her right in the chest. I was at her side almost before she hit the floor. She whispered my name, and then I saw the life just leave her. My father couldn't see me take the knife from my mother's hand. I stood and turned, taking his gun hand in my left hand, and sunk that knife in his fuckin' chest with all my might, all the way to the fuckin' handle. We both sank to our knees, and I watched the life leave his eyes as well. He never said a word."

Angelo and Dan sat there, staring at the floor, silent for a moment. Dan was trying to process everything that Angelo was clearly revisiting in his head at that moment. Dan was imagining the scene; Angelo was playing it back like a recording in his head. When Dan looked up, he had an odd, new feeling: perhaps Angelo was right, and something had drawn them together. If it was a coincidence, it was amazing. If you didn't believe in coincidences, well then it was proof.

"So, you see, Dan, something brought us to this room, but what we do from here, that is our choice. Unlike you, I did have somewhere to go. My uncle, my father's brother, was a made man in the Mafia. The first cop to arrive on the scene was someone on the payroll. He called my uncle, and the cop gave the phone to me. I told him what happened, and he said, "No, Angelo. Your mother stabbed your father, and he shot her. You tell anyone who asks, that's what happened. Now give the phone to the cop." When the detective showed up, the cop backed up the story to him, and I did too. My Uncle Vito took me in as his son and put me to work in the business. That's what we called it back then, the 'business.' Now, what do you airline pilots say when it is about to get bumpy? Uh... fasten your seatbelts!"

Dan had said that very phrase many, many times, but Angelo's impression of a pilot making a cabin announcement to the passengers was comical.

44

"As circumstances would have it, it didn't take long for Uncle Vito to figure out what my strong suit was. I was backing Vito up one day at a, shall we say, transaction. I see one of the other guys reaching for a gun, and then a second guy doing the same. Looks like they are going to try to rip us off. So, I reach for mine while I take a step forward. Vito has all eyes on him, so they don't see me at first. When they both start pulling guns, I pull mine. First one gets it in the chest, second one gets one in the chest, one in the gut. Two guns and two guys hit the floor. The third is standing in front of Vito, and he's now begging for his life, telling Vito how sorry he is, and was following orders. I'm trying to see Vito's face. Am I a hero, or did I just fuck up? Vito never lost that expression of being in control. He looked into my eyes and nodded once, and then looked at the guy in front of him. He didn't need to say it. He got his in the face. Once we were in the car, Vito said, 'I think we found your calling, Angelo.'"

Dan thought he was beginning to understand why they were having this conversation. Angelo had a service to offer Dan. "So, you can help me with my problem?"

"Dan, I think we can help each other."

"How so?"

"That thing with Vito happened thirty years ago. Since then, I have moved up from enforcer to hitter to running my own territory. One part of my organization provides a service to organizations all over the country. Sort of a pest removal business. Now, you and I have already engaged in what some might call 'conspiracy to commit murder,' so I'm going to stop all of the small talk. Organizations call me when they got someone they want dead. They set up the mark for me, my guy comes into town, pulls the trigger, and then leaves. That organization takes care of the cleanup and money changes hands."

"So, you have guys that can help me?" Dan was understanding that

Angelo's operation could do the job, but he wasn't understanding where Dan's part of the favor was going.

"Fucking computers, cameras, biometric shit is the fucking problem! Nowadays, there are law enforcement agencies tying in computers with cameras, biometric scanning, passenger lists, credit card transactions, cell phone records, you name it—all kinds of shit flying through the air. It is closing in on my business. I'm having to go more cash and cryptocurrency transactions when I can, and I have to be careful with everything. Can't even simply buy an airline ticket without creating a false identity and fake identification. You present a unique solution to my problems."

"Okay, as we pilots say, land the plane, Angelo. I am lost on where you are going."

"You fly all over the country, right?" Dan nodded. "You are an airline pilot, there's no ticket for you wherever you fly, right?" Again, Dan nodded. "You don't show up on passenger lists, and I doubt these agencies are including internal airline crew databases in their searches. As far as any investigation goes, you travel as a ghost. You told me last night that the transportation to and from the hotel and the room itself are in the airline's name, right?" Dan nodded yet again.

"You said you have some control over your schedule, so you would be able to, what did you say? 'Trade' trips? You would be able to request overnights in specific cities?" Dan didn't even nod this time, and Angelo continued as if he was pitching a sale he was excited about.

"A local organization member comes to your hotel, has with him pistol and a magazine full of ammo. I'm thinking a threaded barrel, suppressor for the pistol, and subsonic hollow points. They take you to the mark, you kill the mark, and if you spend only cash on your overnight, you show up on no databases. They take you back to the hotel, they clean up the mess, and you ghost out of town the next day. Thanks to Covid, everyone is wearing masks now, so no biometrics to worry about. Even if they had them, you still aren't on any databases. It's perfect!"

"That is intriguing, Angelo, but I'm trying to figure out why. Why don't I just pay you, and we call it even?"

"I have a full-service operation, my pilot friend, and there are multiple services we provide. When Chicago calls and requests my service for, say, a snitch that is a made guy, they get quoted one price. If the guy is not made, is lower level but still a criminal no one will miss, they get quoted a different price. Price goes up when risk goes up. Price goes up when there are special instructions or situations. What you are asking for is two very high-risk hits. When your wife dies in a single car accident, or 'falls' off a bridge, it would be best if your bank accounts didn't show a withdrawal of a hundred grand in cash a week before. What about when her lover dies the next week, and the cops connect the two? However, if you were to come to work for me, I could get some contracts filled, and you could bank some earnings with me. When your account reaches two hundred thousand, I arrange for a few unfortunate accidents. If you want to continue after that, it's up to you. My hits usually pay about twenty-five grand each. Give or take."

Angelo spoke as if he was talking about selling used cars. But Dan recognized the truth of what he was saying about his own situation. He didn't just have a mound of cash laying around, and he couldn't just hit an ATM. It wasn't as if he had much experience with hitmen, let alone the head of a "full-service" hit operation, but Angelo was only selling him on coming on board. Dan had the feeling that he'd been led down a hallway with one door at the end. But it was a door he wanted to step through.

"Okay, Angelo, I'm in. We need to work out a few small details, but the big ones you've already thought through. To get started, I will need $5,000 in twenties to put in my bag so I can cover anything I need to on overnights, especially emergencies. I want bribe money. And we need a way to communicate."

"One of my legit businesses is a travel agency. No, I didn't use it to buy travel for my soldiers, but I did use it for intel and to keep tabs on what the agencies are doing. Give me a good email address, and I will have them send you emails with dates and destinations where we need you to go. They will come as alerts for travel 'Deals.' When you get one, work your magic with your schedule, then send an email back with your 'requested' travel date, flights, and the name of the hotel you will be 'requesting.' We will handle the rest."

"Okay, so how do I contact you?"

Angelo reached in his pocket. "Here's a phone. I'm the only contact on it. When it rings, answer it or call back."

At that instant, they both heard the electronic lock on the door energizing, and Sindee strolled through with bags and drinks in her hands. *Perfect timing*, both men thought.

"Did you miss me?"

10

Sindee walked in, transforming the room completely in the blink of an eye. All business ended abruptly, and the small talk of friends resumed. Sindee played the host, passing out warm fast-food breakfast sandwiches, and only slightly warmer coffee to herself and the two men in her immediate life. Angelo's affinity for pilots was on display in the conversation as he asked Dan a few "war story" questions, then listened intently while Dan told them. Dan could tell a good flying story, and he had plenty of material from both military and civilian life. Sindee listened as well, flashing that demure smile at him whenever she could. She'd barely touched her food. She worked hard to maintain her "stage" body, and fast food was an enemy to that.

"Babe, could you be a doll and work on my shoulder? It's all tensed up again, and you are so good with your hands..."

Sindee stood and began gliding over to Angelo. *God, is she smooth*, thought Dan as he watched her take up a position behind Angelo's chair. Her hands started working on Angelo's right shoulder before her feet stopped moving. The expression that flowed over Angelo's face, the slowly closing eyes, told the tale that Sindee's hands were working magic.

"Don't wear yourself out on me, baby. That's good, but I want you to save some for our new friend. He has a flight tonight, and I want you to rub some of his tension out before he goes."

"Sure thing, Angelo, but I already rubbed some of that tension out of him before you got here."

They all laughed at the joke. Still laughing, Dan and Sindee made eye contact, and Dan gave her a slow nod of approval.

"I have to fly one leg today to Miami, late flight. Then one flight back tomorrow, I'll be landing about 1900. Then I have three days off."

Dan understood the mistake he made when he noticed Angelo's eyes looking up to the right.

"Sorry, Angelo. I'll be landing about seven P.M."

"Okay, sure thing, hotshot. Think up an excuse to have lunch day after tomorrow. That gives me a couple of days to put some things together, make a few calls. We should be able to get business going in a few weeks, I think. Till then, do nothing that breaks routine with your wife, friends, or work. Biz as usual, you got it?"

"Yeah, I got it. Lunch is..."

"On me. How's about, uh, 1300 at an Italian place in Grapevine. Ever heard of Vincent's? I know the owner; it's a great little joint." Angelo chuckled, mentally patting himself on the back for getting one P.M. right. He was already sliding toward the door.

Dan thought for a second. "Yeah, little Italian place, downtown Grapevine. Stumbled upon it about six months ago."

"Okay, good, see you then. Babe, bye, shoulder feels great, thanks!"

Sensing Angelo was about to make his exit, Sindee sauntered over to his side, sliding up against his back and putting her arms around him. Her next words would be breathed almost directly into his ear. "Anytime, sweetness. Will you be in the club tonight?"

"No, baby, I have business to take care of for the next few days. You'll definitely see me on the regular day next week, maybe sooner, if I can. You know I can't stay away from you long, angel."

"I'm gonna miss you and little Angelo..." The healthy squeeze to Angelo's crotch left no doubt what she was talking about.

She placed a kiss on the side of his neck that would melt any man with a heartbeat. Angelo, keeping up his man-in-control persona, reacted just enough to acknowledge the gesture. Sindee knew exactly the effect she had on him, and Dan, for that matter. Dan was watching it all unfold in a way very much like someone who knows their turn is next.

"Baby doll, remember what I told you. And Dan, appearances."

Sindee nodded, pivoted out of the way, and Angelo made his way to the door.

Angelo looked over his shoulder as he walked through the doorway. What he saw was Sindee blowing him a kiss. Dan was thinking that "...remember what I told you..." was Angelo telling Sindee to take care of Dan. What Dan didn't know, and Sindee did, was that Angelo was talking about a conversation he had with Sindee the night before, after Dan had passed out. Angelo had explained to her that he thought he would be going into business with Dan, and that he needed someone to get close to Dan. Someone who could report back to him, and keep tabs on Dan. That job, Angelo explained, paid well and there would be benefits. When Sindee told him she was in and that it sounded great, she almost blurted out that she would do the job for free. Almost.

The moment the door latch clicked, Sindee looked over her shoulder at Dan for a long second. She had the look of a predator, and Dan had the look of prey that really wanted to be eaten. Slowly, Sindee turned, and without a sound, her practiced hands removed what little she was wearing as she slowly closed the distance to a seated Dan, who, mesmerized, looked at the naked woman, now kneeling in front of him. In a few seconds, he learned that her hands were practiced on the clothing of both sexes.

"Stand up, lover," she whispered.

Dan slowly rose, Sindee stayed right where she was, never losing eye contact. It would be a while before they made it to the bed.

. . .

It is standard practice for pilots to take their "go time," the time a flight leaves, or the "van time," the time the van leaves the hotel, and calculate backward to determine when they need to get ready for work. Some cushion is usually built into the timing, but there weren't enough hours in the day for what Sindee wanted to do with, and to, Dan. He had managed to disengage and get in the shave/shower routine at the calculated time. However, Sindee joined him in the shower, and they were still in it thirty-five minutes later.

"Okay, sweetheart, I have got to get ready and out the door. Believe it or not, showing up late for work and causing a delay is a huge sin in the airlines."

"Just call in sick, flyboy, and I'll treat you to more than a few huge sins."

"Oh, I believe you! Plan them all in your head while I'm away, and I'll let you have your way with me when I'm back in town."

Sindee's face broke out in a huge, confident smile. "My way would kill you. What I have planned only requires a bed, some Gatorade, and a lot of towels."

"I'm looking forward to it already, but I *gotta* go." He rinsed a final time and left Sindee in the shower with the water running. Having already packed his stuff, Dan knew he was only about ten minutes from the door. By the time Sindee was walking out of the bathroom holding a towel, Dan was already in uniform, zipping up his rollaway bag.

"Oh my God, you are so fucking sexy in that uniform! I know you have to go, but, next time I see you, it is that uniform I want to be stripping off of you. Deal?"

"Deal, baby. I'm glad you like it."

"Like it? It's got my knees weak. In fact..." Sindee started to sink to her knees and in a burst of willpower, Dan stopped her. He brought his lips to hers, and gave her a sincere, passionate kiss that was returned in kind. The kiss was slow and lingering, as if neither wanted it to end, with Sindee allowing her hands to roam all over Dan's body. Both of her hands ended on the back of his neck as they separated, looking into each other's eyes. Sindee's face showed true passion. It was a moment of unspoken words, clearly understood.

"Do you want a girlfriend?" Sindee whispered, and her voice didn't have her familiar confidence. Angelo had asked her to get close to Dan; being Dan's lover served the purpose well. At the same time, Dan checked a lot of Sindee's boxes: a handsome pilot, smart, well-off, great body, very good in bed, and apparently about to be available. Sindee had a lot of men in her past, but very few she had gotten close to. And even fewer checked half of those boxes. Dan was different. Special.

"If you are applying for the job, I want to let you know, the interview went really well for you. I'm prepared to offer you the position."

Sindee laughed. "I'm prepared to offer you all the positions." The pair broke into laughter. Dan also smiled and loved the shameless hand that now massaged his crotch, and the smoldering kiss she put on his lips.

"I'm going to drop my contact to your phone." It was something she had clearly done many, many times.

"Papa Tony's Pizza?" It took just a second before Dan smiled, realizing why she put her number in his phone contact list that way.

"I want you to know, Dan, that when I'm with a guy, he is the only guy. If you're okay with me working at the club, it will just be work. What happens in the club stays in the club. I'm just doing a job. Otherwise, I'm yours."

Dan understood the complexity. Many men couldn't handle seeing someone who five days a week had her hands all over random men. He had enjoyed one twenty-hour period with her so far, and that was all. But he wanted to keep all of his options open. "I appreciate that. Thank you, beautiful. You're hired!"

Dan reached behind his back and found the handle to his rollaway without breaking eye contact. Brief goodbyes were all that was exchanged as he strode to the door. When Dan looked over his shoulder, it wasn't a blown kiss he saw. It was a beautiful woman with the tilted head and fading smile. Dan didn't know if it was a pose or if it was genuine, but the look seemed like a true separation. It was a look he hadn't seen from a woman in a very long time.

The drive to the airport was a blur. Dan felt as if his entire life had changed. Aside from a few big decisions and a few new players, in actual fact, not much of it had really changed. Yet. Always seeing his life through pilot analogies, he was thinking that he had only just taken off and had been given the first vector to the destination. His first waypoint had been Sindee, the second Angelo. The first *big* waypoint to cross was lunch the day after tomorrow. One thing that definitely had changed was that he was stepping onto an employee bus for the first time in a long time actually not wanting to be there. He was already missing something.

Then he realized that the highlight of the last day, the thing that stuck out most in his mind, was the kiss. That was followed closely by the look on her face at the parting moment they shared. Before he knew it, Dan was approaching the security checkpoint and knew that for the next twenty-four hours, he needed to be wearing his captain hat.

He had to keep his mind in the game.

11

The leg from Dallas to Miami is a route that takes the flight out over the Gulf of Mexico. On a moonless night, at thirty-seven thousand feet over the Gulf, every star is visible. Also shining clearly is the meandering carpet of stars known as The Milky Way. *Passengers think their view is great. They should see this*, thought Captain Hatfield. The numerous oil platforms below, sprinkled on the surface of the water, looked like stars below them as well.

The First Officer next to him was not Mike Chelsea. They were supposed to finish this trip together, but instead Dan had a newly hired FO sitting in the seat to his right. Tony Patrick was a reserve pilot. "Sitting Reserve" is the airline practice of having a certain number of pilots who have days when they are available to the company, on an on-call basis. Chelsea had called in sick, a fact that First Officer Patrick relayed to his captain when the two met at the gate.

"I'm sure I'll hear some intriguing story when I see him next week," Dan had replied. Dan sized Tony up at that meeting. *Two first names. Great. I just hope he can fly and doesn't talk too much.*

So far, his hope had proven to come true. Tony Patrick had never met his captain before today, so what he didn't know was that Dan was being uncharacteristically quiet. Dan tried to run a friendly cockpit, and he enjoyed good conversation. But, there was a limit to what was considered an appropriate amount. If both pilots had something they thought was important or timely, they might talk all the way to the destination. If both pilots didn't have an obvious shared interest, a bit of mundane chit-chat of the "so where do you live" nature would suffice. If something was on a pilot's mind, he might want to just sit there for the whole leg and stare out the window. In that case, if the other pilot kept talking, sometimes an obvious signal, like shutting off the pilot intercom system, could pass the message that talk time was over. Some got the hint, but not all.

Dan was grateful for the time to think, and an FO that let him. He kept replaying in his head the conversation alone with Angelo. Without all the details worked out, the mental exercises playing out in Dan's head were leading to more questions than answers. He wanted to organize his thoughts, and make sure he asked all the right questions when he met Angelo the day after tomorrow. Normally, he'd turn to his phone, or an iPad to compile some lists and notes. This was not normal. The logic of not typing his thoughts into an iPad was obvious. Dan didn't want to create an Exhibit A.

Dan was not a hitman—not yet anyway. But he correctly guessed that like any other important operation involving humans, a fair amount of planning, intelligence-gathering, and knowledge of the players was necessary. *How could they possibly expect me to do any of that on an overnight?* Dan and Angelo were going to have to piece this new method together from the ground up, and this enterprise had to go smoothly every single time.

There's also a tremendous amount of mental preparation that would be necessary, and Dan knew that as well. Not just the "brain stocking"— filling the mind with the details for each individual job. The mental prep of taking on a whole new role and doing things that many people simply could not do. It didn't occupy more than a minute of time for him to conclude that he would, in fact, be able to kill people up close and personal. After all, he'd done it many times before. *Who knows how many I've killed with an F-16 and strike coordinates. But, will I be able to live with, talk to, eat with, and possibly fuck—for at least a few months—a person that I'm going to have removed from my life in a permanent way?*

And then he selected the recording in his brain marked *Sharon Fucking Around on Me*, and he played it back. Standing there in his own backyard, holding a bouquet of flowers for the leading actress in the porn movie unfolding in front of him. In the dark, Patrick could not clearly see Dan's face. If he had, he would have noticed the look of anger mixed with resolve on it.

Dan spent the next hour trying to game out every angle of his personal life, as opposed to his airline life. Dan started playing all the *A Day in the Life of Dan Hatfield* recordings in his head, but imagining it was the future. It was a useful exercise, as it would be best if they continued on as a somewhat happily married and semi well-adjusted couple right up until the "death do you part" clause happened. It wasn't until he had missed three radio calls in a row from air traffic control that he realized he needed to put the personal life away for a little while and concentrate on being a pilot. Besides, the west coast of Florida was getting close, and there was pilot stuff that needed to be done.

"Blue Sky 2249, Miami Center. You can expect lower in ten miles. You are now cleared direct to SSCOT intersection. Expect vectors to the ILS runway nine approach into Miami."

"Miami, Blue Sky 2249. Understand lower in ten miles, and now direct SSCOT. Thanks."

It was a pretty good shortcut, and Dan was grateful for it. He was still five miles in the air and flying through it at three quarters of the speed of sound, but he was having a hard time not thinking about the hotel van. *Okay, time to focus. It'll be a lot easier to organize my thoughts in the lobby bar with a scotch in my hand.*

"Blue Sky 2249, Miami Center. Cross the SSCOT intersection at ten thousand feet and 250 knots."

"Uh okay, cross SSCOT at ten and two-fifty, Blue Sky 2249."

One more center controller, two Miami Approach controllers, MIA tower, ground control, ramp control, a walk to the curb, too long a wait for the hotel van (it was always too long, but South Florida is among the worst), a front desk sign-in sheet, an elevator, and a long walk down the hall to the last room on the right were all that stood between Dan and that moment all airline pilots look forward to: peeling off that uniform. "There are days this moment feels as good as sex," Dan proclaimed to his empty hotel room. Out of habit, he picked up his phone to check in with Sharon, then stopped himself. "Fuck that." Dan tossed his phone on the bed and began his hotel routine.

. . .

He hasn't checked in yet, which is odd. He usually does when he gets to his room. Sharon had just gotten out of the shower when she heard her phone ringing. She didn't get to it fast enough. When she looked at her phone, it displayed five missed calls. She smiled at the contact. "Aw... I think somebody misses me." Sharon was about to call Ed back when the phone rang again. She could hear the anticipation in his voice when she answered.

She replied, "If you know he is in Miami, come here any time. I'd like to stay in tonight, and you can stay if you like. See you soon!" There was anticipation in her voice as well.

. . .

Sharon was laying in her bed processing all of the changes in her life, contemplating her future. Ed, snoring next to her, held the keys to a future she desired. *I gave up so much for Dan, and here I am in a middle-income bracket while my childhood friends, and most of my family, ski in Switzerland, rent yachts, and shop on Rodeo Drive.* Ed represented the opportunity to leave Dan and live the life she'd dreamed about. She still had some love for Dan, but she knew she'd never be satisfied with his level of income, and she simply loved herself more.

She was reacquainted with Ed at the Christmas party she and Dan hosted at their house months ago. The first time they met was back in college when she and Dan had dated. Ed struck up a conversation with her, and his story appealed to her immediately. She later called him on the pretense of wanting to buy a car, and Ed was more than willing to handle her personally. The dress she wore to the test drive left Ed wondering who was test driving whom. He didn't wonder long. Sharon came on to him immediately, and having been alone for a while, Ed gave in with little resistance. *I will just have to play housewife a little longer, until I can put a plan in motion. When I leave this marriage, I'm leaving with half of everything.*

12

The bar in the lobby of the hotel was typical, adequate, and very conveniently located. It was amusing to Dan how all of the hotel bars wanted to portray themselves as unique. In reality, most of them had the same layout, same feel, and same goal of somehow justifying their high drink prices. But it was hard to beat the travel time of fifteen seconds from elevator to barstool. And they knew that that was appealing enough.

Dan thought he found some middle ground. It would be ridiculous to make a list on his iPad of all the questions and ideas he wanted to explore with Angelo. About the same time he was putting on comfortable clothes in the hotel room, he came up with a solution that allowed him to organize a list while not creating "Prosecution Exhibit A." Dan walked into the lobby bar, noticing there were only a few people in it. Standing at the bar was a forty-something waitress, who had clearly spent too much of her life in the Florida sun. Dan saw her eyes go all the way down to his feet and back up to eye contact as she bounced over to him. "Sit anywhere you like, honey!"

"What could you recommend that is out of the way and has a plug reasonably close?"

"Follow me, sugar. I know just the place." Before she spun around to lead the way, Dan spied the big name tag with *AMY LYNN* plastered across it. Amy led Dan to the back of the bar floor to a corner booth. She did a fairly graceful Vanna White, waving the menu in her left hand toward the booth.

"All the tables on this wall have plugs, but I think this one will give you the most privacy, and I will come visit you often."

Dan smiled as he recognized her flirting with him. He flirted back. "Come as many times as you like."

"I always do, sugar!" Amy tilted her head down, making sultry eye contact.

Dan went for the kill. "I bet you do, and I would be no different for you, Amy Lynn."

Her mouth dropped open in a little smile, touched that he had noticed her name. "Well, my handsome new friend, what can I do you for?"

"I'd like a scotch rocks. And each time you visit, bring me another. I will tell you when I've had enough."

"Sure thing." She offered her hand the way a Southern girl would have since before *Gone with the Wind*. "You know my name, so may I have yours?"

"It's Dan, and I'm pleased to meet you." He took her hand in the way any Southern gentleman would have.

"I'm pleased to meet you, Dan." She held his hand, looking into his eyes purposefully until it was just a bit too long. She let her fingers slide over his palm as she drew it back slowly. "I'll be right back with your drink." Amy spun away and headed for the end of the bar.

Cordial, demure, nice figure, and an A-minus ass. I really shouldn't. I got work to do and will probably need to save my strength for Sindee anyway. Focus. Dan couldn't see Amy looking over her shoulder at his booth. He was busily getting the iPad out, portable keyboard set up, and plugging his device into the table's power port. Over the years, there had been numerous times when he'd been tempted in situations where he could easily have cheated on Sharon. If he had wanted to, it could have happened dozens of times, but he'd never let it come to pass. Now it all felt different. Dan knew that all he would have to invest would be a little more conversation, and most likely Amy would be up in a room he didn't pay for while doing a lot of things as often as she liked.

He shook his head. *Nah, it's going to be complicated enough with Sindee and keeping up appearances.* Dan focused his attention on the Notes app on his iPad, starting a new note. He titled the list *Home Depot.* His idea was to make a list of things you could find at Home Depot, with each line on the list having a word that reminds him of a question or idea. Closing his eyes for a moment, Dan started pulling the ideas out of his thought cloud and making entries.

Intelligent door locks *Who gathers the intel on the marks; sets them up; gets it to me?*

Stain remover *How does the situation get cleaned up after I go?*

Light timer *Angelo is going to have to understand flight crew scheduling for this to work.*

Weed killer *How does Angelo plan on handling Sharon?*

"I brought you another scotch, handsome Dan!" Buried in his iPad, he hadn't seen her coming. "This one is on me," she whispered.

"Well, thank you! Care to join me?"

"Sure thing!" Amy slinked onto the bench and right up to Dan. "Whatcha workin' on, lover?"

"My Home Depot list."

"'Weed killer'? Got some weeds that need to die, Dan." Amy was putting more air into the way she said his name every time she said it.

"Nope, just two. Two big weeds that need to die." Dan lost the smile on his face.

"Well, when you get back home, you do just that!" Amy's encouragement was accompanied with a wink and smile.

"Oh, not me. I have people that will kill them for me." He chuckled. "Those pesky weeds don't know it, but they're dead already."

Amy Lynn gave Dan a playful slap on the chest and chuckled right back.

. . .

With his list finished, one hour killed, and three more scotches knocked back, Dan paid the bar tab and left Amy what anyone would consider a very good tip. He had made sure to circle his room number on the merchant copy of the credit card receipt. It didn't feel like he was back in the room even ten minutes when he heard a gentle knock on the door. *That was easy. Hell, why not?* Dan opened the door, and Amy closed the distance, wrapped her arms around him, and they fell into a deeply sexual kiss. He could feel her trembling as they continued to kiss, hands roaming over each other's bodies.

Wow. And I almost passed on this.

13

The leg back to Dallas was Dan's leg to fly. In a two-pilot cockpit, the captain sits on the left, and the first officer sits on the right. The shared duties of flying the plane are broken down as two roles: the Pilot Flying and the Pilot Monitoring. There are different methods favored by pilots to determine who is who for any given flight, but most of the time pilots just alternate the legs. Patrick had flown the aircraft to Miami, so Dan would fly back. There's quite a bit to keep both pilots busy during take-off, climb, approach, and landing, but at cruise, there's just babysitting. One pilot keeps an eye on the airplane and what it's doing, while the other monitors the radio for incoming transmissions from ATC, and a few other duties. Of course, they backed each other up. Mistakes, omissions, and carelessness lead down bad roads in aviation, and they can go there quickly.

The overnight was fairly long, sixteen hours, which gave Dan time to be able to go to the bar and work on his list, and still not have to awaken too early. He had in fact awoken early, as it was impossible to sleep with what Amy was doing to him when he woke up. Dan was trying to recall if Sharon had ever woken him that way. *It's all over now*, he thought, almost surprised at how he now felt nothing at all for Sharon. Well, almost nothing. No love, no loyalty, no allegiance, no responsibility, not even pity. It was as if that night when he witnessed her betrayal, a bolt of lightning burned the fuse connecting her to him. That connection was now melted, severed forever by her choices and something he'd never unsee.

He despised her now. He did feel that. And a desire for revenge.

It was time much better spent, Dan decided, playing back his morning starting with opening his eyes. Amy's face may have told the story of a woman who spent a lot of time in the Florida sun, but she had clearly spent a lot of time in the bedroom as well. Her horizontal skill set was very good, but the most exciting thing about her sexuality was the casual raunchiness she possessed, to the point of being dirty. Playing back the video in his head was like watching a porn movie with himself as the male lead.

Dan turned on his iPad. *Okay, gonna look over the Home Depot list one more time.* He closed one app, opened another, and was looking over his work from last night. A dozen or so items in a vertical column of words, each with a meaning to jog his memory about something he felt he and Angelo needed to discuss.

The impression Angelo gave Dan was one of a man with a life bearing some similarities to his own. Dan realized that Angelo also had two lives: Business Life and Casual Life. He clearly seemed to be interested in enjoying himself as much as possible in his Casual Life. That may be because he was intense, detailed, and focused on his Business Life. And the nature of his business! Dan suspected that Angelo had numerous other ventures requiring his full attention. As Dan was imagining the meeting tomorrow in his head, he imagined Angelo being on point and not bullshitting. Dan didn't believe Angelo would take kindly to him doing any bullshitting either.

There must be something about that restaurant Vincent's. Angelo wouldn't pick that place at random. He must have a reason. Dan went to the bottom of his list to add that question. He thought about what to put on the list to remind himself, and he settled on, "Look at selection of stoves." *Yeah, I'll remember that.*

So deep in thought was Dan, he hadn't noticed that they had been back over land for quite a while, leaving the Gulf of Mexico and its oil platforms behind them. Patrick was replying to a radio call handing their flight off from Houston Center to a Fort Worth Center controller. That surprised Dan, as that meant they were getting close to home. He put the iPad away and began focusing on the list of tasks that takes a 140,000-pound aircraft flying six hundred miles an hour all the way down to a full stop on a relatively small piece of land of their choosing.

Thirty minutes later, Dan and Patrick accomplished that very feat. "Cheated death one more time." Dan said as they parked the aircraft at Gate A-24. Seemed unlike the captain to Patrick, who had heard very little from Dan all the way to Miami and back. But Dan was happy to be done, and so was Patrick. Everyone likes a non-eventful "go home" leg with an early arrival at the gate. Smooth air allowed them to fly near maximum Mach, and a few shortcuts had given them that coveted early "in."

After completing the final checklist items, both pilots packed up their kit bags, and made sure they took everything, especially phones. Patrick turned in his seat and extended his hand. "It was good flying with you, Dan. I'm sure it will happen again."

"Yes, good flying with you too, and I'm sure it will. Sorry I wasn't good company. I have some business details I'm mulling over."

"Oh, no, it's fine. Good luck with your business. You can tell me about it next time," Patrick said.

Dan gave a genuine chuckle. *No, I can't.* "Okay, enjoy your days off. You go ahead first."

"Thanks. Take it easy!" Patrick stood, taking his bag with him. The narrow cockpit door faced a long line of passengers trying to leave the aircraft. Patrick offered a "thank you" and "have a good day" more times than he cared to count while he waited for a break in the line that was long enough to grab his overnight bag and get off the airplane. He found one about the same time Dan left his seat. Patrick was already on the jetbridge saying goodbye to the flight attendants in the forward galley as Dan took his place in the cockpit door. Every remaining passenger would be thanked by Dan until none were left. Since the day he flew his first flight as a captain, that had been Dan's policy, as well as always being the last off the aircraft. Once he'd verified it had been put in proper condition and his crew all had their feet on the ground, he would leave that aircraft for the next flight.

There was the sound of a ringing phone on the jetbridge. It didn't sound to Dan like the jetbridge's phone ringing, and it wasn't his cell ringtone. It took him a few seconds of standing there alone to realize it was his phone—or more accurately, the phone Angelo had given him. It could be only one person. Well, two. Dan fished through the big pocket on his overnight bag and found it. No caller ID.

Dan answered. "Hello?"

Angelo sounded like he was in a good mood. "Hey, buddy. How about one P.M. tomorrow, where we said?"

"I'll be there, Angelo."

"Who is that? No Angelo here."

Dan knew it was him, and he also detected the slight annoyance in the tone. *He's right. No need to use names. Just another opportunity to get yourself in trouble.* "Yeah, sorry. I don't know what I was saying. I do now. One P.M. See you then."

Click

Dan passed the next two pilots on the jetbridge, going down to "their" jet. He passed on a tip about their flight. "It's a good aircraft. Was smooth all the way from Miami."

"Great, thanks!"

Gate A-24 was a short walk to the employee bus. *I'll be in the truck in ten minutes,* he calculated. He wouldn't get to the truck before that phone was ringing again. It wasn't Angelo.

14

The E-3 Sentry aircraft is a modified Boeing 707, with a look unlike any previous aircraft. Attached to the top of the fuselage is a huge radar antenna in the shape of a rotating disk—thirty feet in diameter, six feet wide—giving the operators the ability to "see" 250 miles in any direction. It can also look down, detect low altitude aircraft, and even surface vehicles. Also known by the acronym AWACS (Airborne Warning And Control System), the interior of the aircraft looks much like a ground-based air traffic control center. Just longer and narrower.

The men working in AWACS Pegasus 7 were watching over the combat area and knew in real time what happened to Hatfield's F-16. The controller working Hatfield's flight called out to the flight leader, requesting status of his four aircraft the moment he heard Hatfield announcing his ejection.

"Switchblade 1, Pegasus 7, flight status?"

"Pegasus 7, Switchblade 1. Switchblade 4 is down. Pilot has punched out."

"Roger, Switchblade 1. Switchblade flight, RTB, we will begin SAR."

Radio frequencies with multiple combat aircraft performing mission can get quite busy, so commonly used phrases like "return to base" and "search and rescue" became acronyms. Air Force search and rescue was based at Prince Sultan Air Base – the 15th Special Air Operations squadron flew the MH-53J Pave Low helicopter. If it was a daytime operation, some kind of air cover for the helicopter was routine, such as a pair of

A-10 Warthogs. At night, the helicopter pilots flew without lights, while wearing night vision goggles. A-10s could orbit above but would not be as effective for cover at night. Fortunately, night vision gear in the Iraqi army was fairly rare.

Pegasus 7 had a direct line of electronic communication with the Special Air Operations control center. Situation, status, position, identification of the downed aircraft, and other information was all transmitted nearly instantly to them by the AWACS aircraft. Transmitted back was a handshake signal, letting the Pegasus 7 operators know the information was received and what the call sign of the alert helicopter was at that moment. "New Castle 9" would be the responding SAR helicopter, with the goal to safely retrieve the downed pilot from the desert floor.

Major Hatfield knew all of this was going on without him, and he knew it was only a matter of time before he would hear the distinct rotor noise of the heavy Pave Low. His GPS beacon appeared to be working properly. He had only spent a second or two looking it over, seeing that it was completely intact, and the status light on it was glowing green. The only sound he had heard so far was a few secondary explosions from the site of his crashed aircraft. Each time, the detonations sounded distant, a good thing considering the Iraqis almost certainly knew he had ejected and was in the desert somewhere. The desert is a big place, but an F-16 being lit up by a SAM, then impacting the ground, is pretty spectacular. The SAM operators knew they had scored a hit.

It only took Major Hatfield a few minutes to bury his parachute, harness, G suit, and other unnecessary equipment in the desert sand. It had taken him longer to remove the suit than bury it. Not only is it protocol, but it gives the mind some tasks to complete while waiting for the rescue helicopter. Minutes will feel like hours, and hours like days. This is worsened if there is nothing to do but wait. Hatfield was doing all of the tasks on the downed airman protocol, all designed to maximize the chance he would end up stepping off a helicopter at a friendly airbase, and not bundled in the back of a truck behind enemy lines. Pilots make for great television news stories, and Hatfield was determined not to be a feature on Iraqi news.

The fire from the downed aircraft site had nearly burned out. Hatfield had been looking in that direction from time to time, noting that the glow in the distance was fading and was now almost imperceptible. He was busying himself trying to take stock of his situation. If he was still there at daybreak, he would have only moments in the early morning twilight to decide what he had available for cover and concealment, and then make his move. For now, he was seeing with his feet and hands, only discovering more sand and the occasional small stones. When he had made his way only about two hundred yards from where he buried his gear, he heard voices for the first time.

The muddled voices, not surprisingly, had Arabic tones. Hatfield couldn't make out what they were saying. It wouldn't have mattered, since his vocabulary words in any of the languages spoken in the country were countable on a single hand. What he was able to perceive was the cadence of military orders being given and acknowledged. Someone was talking on a radio. By Hatfield's estimation, he had at least a few more hours before morning twilight. He made the decision to move a bit closer, surveil the situation, gather as much information as he could before moving as far as he could in a different direction.

Hatfield took another thirty minutes to close the distance to the Iraqi army soldiers. When he was about one hundred feet away, one of the soldiers switched on a flashlight, instantly showing Hatfield everything he needed to know. The soldiers were manning a large, mobile surface-to-air missile battery, and anti-aircraft gun. The Iraqis were moving them out of Baghdad and concealing them out in the desert while the U.S. Navy and Air Force aircraft were hunting them. The concealment was mostly for overhead threats; Hatfield on the ground, at a distance of one hundred feet, could clearly see the vehicle, the missiles, and the anti-aircraft gun positioned there to protect their position from close-in threats.

The soldier with the flashlight was clearly the man in charge, mustering his men. Hatfield couldn't understand the orders, but a pretty good guess was that he was mustering his forces to search for the downed pilot at first light. Hatfield was doing a math problem in his head: bullets he had on him, versus number of men he was looking at. Hatfield counted seven men. He had chosen to carry a Beretta 92, 9 mm pistol, giving him far more rounds than the old .38-caliber revolvers used to hold. The 92 had a fifteen-round magazine, and Hatfield had two additional magazines. Forty-five rounds versus seven men, an anti-aircraft gun, and a bunch of SAMs.

Hatfield removed the pistol from the holster, quietly racked the slide, loading the pistol so it was ready to go. He then flicked off the safety to familiarize his hands with the weapon, made the weapon safe again, and put the pistol back in its holster.

Then he started to game out the situation, and it went badly every way he took it to a conclusion. If he moved away from the missile site, there's no way he could get very far. That made any rescue helicopter vulnerable to the anti-aircraft gun and SAMs. The closer he was to them, the worse that risk became. The site was well-concealed, so there was an excellent chance it would remain undetected well after the sound of the approaching helicopter would be filling the desert air. *The only way this works out, without risk to an SAR helo, is to warn them on the radio, then move to a safe distance.* Watching an A-10 or Apache disassemble this site would be spectacular for him to see, as long as he wasn't a casualty as well.

That was Hatfield's last thought as he reached for his PRC-90 handheld radio to turn it on and break radio silence. No matter how many times he grabbed the empty pouch on his flight suit, no radio magically appeared. He wanted to scream "FUCK" to the heavens. Hatfield knew immediately, it didn't matter where or when he had lost that radio; until daylight, he would never find it. The Special Air Operations personnel moved with high motivation when there was a downed airman. With his rescue almost certainly coming at night, and no way to warn them, the brave airmen coming to dust him off the desert floor were in grave danger.

No matter how many times he gamed it out, Major Hatfield now came to a single conclusion. His mental math, coupled with some rapid, violent action, was going to be needed. He began moving closer to the Iraqi position, formulating a plan for how and when he would kill seven soldiers.

15

The call had no caller ID, but Hatfield knew it could only be one of two people. Or, it could have been someone wanting to sell him extended car warranty coverage. The breathy, sexy purr told him exactly who he had just said hello to.

"Hey, baby, did you miss me?" Sindee's voice was as smooth and graceful as a cat.

"Of course I missed you, sweetheart! When am I going to see you again?" The employee bus came to a stop. Recognizing it was his stop, Dan grabbed the handle to his rollaway bag and made his way out the door. He knew sooner or later this conversation was going to go toward one he wouldn't want to have on the bus, and it didn't take long at all to go there.

"Flyboy, you can *see* me aaaanytime you want."

"Well, I'd like to *see* you right now, but I have to keep up appearances, remember? Gotta go home and show my face. Not much to go home to right now, but I can't have Sharon thinking I'm going somewhere else."

"Yeah, about that. Do you plan on *seeing* her?" The purring cat voice disappeared instantly. Sindee was clearly marking her territory, and it was not at all lost on Dan. In fact, it put a little smile on his face. He was almost to his truck, but he paused his walking as he said something to Sindee that he knew may not go over well. "Well... we are talking about appearances. If it doesn't happen every once in a while, and it hasn't been happening that often lately, she's going to think I'm seeing someone else. Do I get an allowance?"

Sindee's voice went from sultry to uncharacteristically sincere. "Well... I am still working in the club, and you are okay with it. Okay, you can *see* her twice a month, three times if the month has thirty-one days, but I don't want to hear a thing. Not a detail, I don't even want to know when."

Relieved that Sindee understood, his feet started moving again. He switched hands and fished his truck key fob out of his pocket. "Deal, and I promise I won't enjoy it."

The smoke returned to Sindee's voice. "Dan, give me a break. No way you could not enjoy it. If I didn't enjoy what I do at the club, I wouldn't be so fucking good at it. Difference is, I'm going to just let them bring me to a boil. It's your spaghetti going in my pot."

"Jesus, Sindee, is there anything you can't make sound like sex?" He couldn't contain his laughter.

Dan could hear the smile on Sindee's face as she spoke. "Nope, just about anything. And remember where I work and what I do. We are going to be having pasta. Every. Fucking. Chance. We. Get. I come to a boil very easily."

"I know exactly how you come. Okay, baby, I gotta use both hands right now; I'm getting in the truck." It was obvious in his voice; Dan didn't want the conversation to end.

"Yeah, baby, next time I get you at arm's length, I'll be using both hands too." Sindee didn't just want the conversation to continue, she wanted Dan in person. That, too, was obvious in her voice.

"Me too, lover. Me too. Why don't we plan on meeting after my lunch tomorrow with Angelo?"

"Sounds good, flyboy. Till then, bye, baby."

"Bye, lover," Dan said, reluctantly ending the phone call.

The conversation had had an effect on Dan's demeanor, as well as the front of his pants. *Better get in the truck before someone sees me and thinks I'm excited about going home.* He chuckled out loud at that thought. His attitude remained upbeat for much of the drive home as he replayed some of the tapes from his Sindee folder in his head. Only when Dan passed through the gate of his community did the adult-rated video clips finally evaporate, and the reality of walking through his front door came crashing down.

Just then, very involuntarily, he pictured the cheating scene again, and his attitude quickly changed again. Dragging his bag behind him from the garage to the house, he could feel his heart sink lower with every step. Dan actually dreaded walking into a house that he owned but no longer felt like his home. *I wonder if that feeling will return when I'm the only person living here?*

One of the best parts of any airline pilot's life is that moment when they get to take off the uniform and get into something comfortable. Sharon was still out. *Working perhaps? Maybe fucking?"* Dan poured himself a healthy scotch before going to the bedroom. *Wherever Sharon is, I want to be on my third scotch before she gets home.*

16

Sharon breathed a sigh of relief at the sight of Dan on the couch in front of the living room TV, baseball game on, and half of a scotch rocks on the lamp table next to him. She was not looking forward to seeing Dan, especially after just *seeing* Ed. Her gait changed as her steps padded carefully toward the bedroom door. Dan heard the change in her walk, just as he had heard the keypad lock on the front door open and pretended to be passed out. The situation worked for them both. Sharon very carefully closed the bedroom door, and Dan caught the home run just as he opened his eyes.

By the time Dan climbed into bed, Sharon had showered, and was already under the covers. This time it was Sharon's turn to pretend to sleep. Didn't matter to Dan, he didn't have any plans.

. . .

Dan woke to an empty bed. Sharon's signature gym bag—a ridiculously expensive, high-fashion oversized tote that she used as a gym bag for the sole purpose of advertising her bling at the gym—was missing from the closet. That meant she was off to a spinning class or something equally cliché. She had been going to the gym more often lately. *Just another reason*, thought Dan.

He actually relished the next few hours. It was not his norm to awaken in his own space, no rush to get ready for a hotel van. There was time to leisurely make a pot of coffee, watch some news, and dress for a business lunch. In standard airline pilot fashion, Dan had calculated the countdown clock, and knew exactly when he would have to walk out the door of his home in order to be at the door of the restaurant ten minutes early. Five minutes before that, he was starting the engine of his Ford F-150.

Parking at the restaurant had actually been easy, and that surprised Dan as this was downtown Grapevine, a quaint little town within a big town. Situated just north of the Dallas-Fort Worth Airport, Dan had assumed parking would be an issue. The restaurant had its own, ample-sized parking lot on one side of the building. Following a few signs, he was guided to a narrowing corridor with a ninety-degree bend that made the doors to three adjoining businesses not visible from the street. Maybe the situation had heightened Dan's absorption of his surroundings, but this architecture seemed odd to him.

As Dan stepped through the door, he was greeted by an older man with Italian features. The introduction was a prepared one. "Good afternoon, Captain Hatfield. I am Vincent Ricci, owner of this establishment. Mr. Genofi is right this way. You will not be disturbed."

The restaurant was elegantly decorated with a fine balance of modern and traditional touches. The floor was maybe one-third filled with patrons, and Dan was quickly convinced that almost all had the aura of being a regular. Waiters, men only, in black aprons and white shirts, darted around the restaurant. Dan had regret. While he told Angelo he had "stumbled upon" the place, what he didn't admit is that he had passed on the place and never actually walked in. Looking around now, he wished he had. *If the food is as spot on as the appearance and staff, I'm going to be a regular here too.*

"Thank you, Mr. Ricci. Your restaurant is truly impressive. I only wish I had visited a few years ago," Dan said with obvious respect.

"Please, Captain Hatfield, call me Vincent. Everyone does. I am at your service; you are an important visitor. Mr. Genofi thinks highly of you. Naturally, then, I do as well."

The pair weaved their way through the restaurant floor to the back of the room. Before them were large double doors made of carved mahogany. As Vincent opened them, Dan found Angelo seated at a table for ten. Vincent stopped at the threshold, motioning Dan inside. "*Grazie mille*, uh, thank you very much, Captain Hatfield. I will get the doors so that you will not be interrupted."

Dan nodded and continued to the table. He could hear the heavy doors close behind him, and oddly, just as they closed, he heard his cell phone make a sound. He looked at it and noticed it wasn't getting a signal. He put the cell back in his pocket and sat in front of Angelo.

Angelo pointed at Dan's pocket. "Hey, flyboy, if you could, whip out that cell again and power it down. I'm sure you noticed; you got no signal in the room. It's more than that. We have a scrambler, and other tech crap my IT guy installed in the room. No cells, no bugs, no microphones, no recording devices in here."

As he powered down the phone, Dan replied, "Freedom of speech through technology."

"Or lack thereof," Angelo said between chuckles as he pointed to Dan's dead phone.

Angelo pressed a button on the table that Dan hadn't noticed until it was pressed. A barely distinguishable door in the wall behind them opened. Dan hadn't noticed that either. *I wonder what else I'm missing.* A waiter swiftly came through the door, two menus in hand.

Angelo waved his hand at the waiter. "Not gonna need those. Just take the order."

The waiter wordlessly nodded. Dan expected him to whip out a pad and pencil. The waiter's hands remained behind his back.

"I'll be having the veal ravioli; he will be having the fettuccini alfredo with grilled chicken. Bring us a loaf of bread, new olive oil, and ask Mr. Ricci to select a wine for the lunch ordered. Make sure it's Italian. I'm sure my friend would like a house salad, pasta fagioli soup for me. Two waters. Tell the chef to take his time, make it right. But then, I didn't have to say that."

"Of course not, Mr. Genofi. I will signal as usual."

The waiter left as swiftly as he arrived, and the two men were alone again. Angelo saw the puzzled look on Dan's face. He answered the unasked question. "I've been eating here twenty-five years, Captain. Vincent's people are top notch and fully vetted. They get the orders right every time, and they see and hear nothing."

Dan was beginning to understand completely what type of establishment he was sitting in. *Now I know the food is going to be good!*

17

The food was better than good, and Angelo was all business. Dan thought the conversation was edging on the surreal as Angelo closed all the loops regarding how the operation would work. He ran a tight ship, and Dan was impressed with the thorough, detailed plan. Of course, Dan had to provide some details as well, but it was clear that even in areas where Angelo needed actual details, he had gamed it out pretty well without them. By the time the coffee was served, Angelo made clear that he thought they had something that would work, so he proposed a practice run.

"I think we need to do a test flight of this operation. If I was to give you a city right now, can you show me how you would arrange to overnight there, and what it would look like?"

"Sure, Angelo, but I'd need the internet. "

Angelo reached down to his side and retrieved a laptop, placing it on the table in front of Dan.

"I thought you said…"

"My IT guy connected it special here. This particular laptop has internet access. I can trust *me*." Angelo smiled.

Dan opened the computer, and it was already running. In just a few seconds, he was opening a new browser window and accessing his airline's pilot trip trading site. Dan pulled up the list of open time for the rest of the month and showed the list to Angelo.

"These are all the open trips right now, the ones that don't have captains assigned to them. This is pretty typical. What city am I looking for?"

Angelo was staring at the computer, absorbing what was happening. "Indianapolis."

"Indy, okay. So, I just scan down the list and look for IND, the identifier for the Indy airport. I can see a handful open this month. Mostly four-day trips. There are about eight available. What I would do is put in a trade, to trade the trip I already have for something that's in open time, assuming I'm not already scheduled for a trip to Indy."

Dan pulled up his month just to make sure he wasn't already on an IND trip. He wasn't. "Do you want me to try to trade?"

"Yeah, first one available. How long you gonna be in Indianapolis on that trip, and where you gonna be?" Angelo asked, still staring at the laptop.

Dan pulled up that trip data and showed it to Angelo. He pointed to different parts of the trip data, explaining how it was displayed. "*This* shows the date we get in, *this* is the arrival time, and *this* is the departure time the next day. *This* shows that I will be on the ground in Indy for sixteen hours and twenty-five minutes, a fairly long overnight. We get in at seven P.M., so plenty of evening time. *This* entry pulls up the hotel and limo information, and *that* is where I'll be staying."

Angelo sat back, clearly gelling thoughts and making some decisions. The pause was long enough for Dan to finish his cup of coffee, also extraordinarily good.

"Okay. Okay. Go ahead and trade into that trip now."

"Yes, I can try to trade. Sometimes the computer won't let a trade go through for a bunch of reasons, and you never know until you try. Okay, one second. And there it is. It let me trade, so I am now on that trip. Whatever you are planning, Angelo, also keep in mind that flights cancel, are sometimes delayed hours, divert to other airports for weather, and I can be taken off flights and reassigned. Plans need to be flexible, and your people need to be able to keep an eye on real-time flight data." Dan made a few keystrokes and displayed the updated trip data for Angelo to see. "Okay, there it is. The trade went through, and up *here* you can now see my name listed as captain."

This time Angelo leaned completely forward, elbow on the table and hand on his chin. Some of what Dan had explained was new information, but not completely missed by his planning. The posture and face showed that he was very close to completing his thinking on his idea. And he approved.

"Okay. Alright. This will be how we run any job. You are going to get the emails from the travel agency offering special packages in special cities. You will then work your trade magic; get an overnight in that city as soon as you can, the longer the overnight time the better. You'll then log on to the travel agency website and request a ticket quote for your flight in and your flight out the next day, all under the login info I already gave you. You go on your overnight, make no plans, and when you get to your room, change into something casual; be ready for anything. There will be a knock on your door. Answer it and take whatever is given to you. A briefing on the assignment will be in there. Complete your assignment and follow all instructions. The next morning, there will be a knock on your door, and things will be collected. Possibly more instructions given. You follow all the rest of your routines; nothing out of the ordinary."

Dan asked, "This Indy a test run. Just an exercise, not a live operation?"

"Exactly, flyboy, exactly. You will get a quote email back from the agency every time you send a request. That quote is confirmation that it is a go. If there are any special things to pack, it will be in that email. Do it. Otherwise, just pack like you always do, thinking about the weather and knowing you'll be leaving the hotel."

For a fleeting second, Dan thought about whether or not he was at the point of no return. That moment evaporated, erased by the realization that backing out was no longer an option. Hadn't been for days. Besides, he had no desire to do so. The conversation was coming to a conclusion.

"Is there anything else, Angelo? I've got plans for the rest of the afternoon."

"Nope, I think we have the bases covered. I got lunch; you can head out."

Dan stood, thanked Angelo for lunch, shook his hand, and turned toward the door. Just as he reached for the door handle, Angelo spoke. "Hey, flyboy, do enjoy the rest of your day!"

Dan nodded, but there was something knowing in the way Angelo spoke, and the unmistakable smirk on Angelo's face. Dan stepped through the doorway and scanned the room as he made his way toward the door. As his eyes found the bar, he made eye contact. Sitting there, martini glass in hand and a widening, sultry smile, was Sindee.

18

Sliding off the barstool, Sindee melted into Dan's open arms. Dan felt as if she was hugging every part of his body. She almost was. Sindee followed it with a kiss, just touching his lips with hers ever so lightly. She possessed a rare, classy sexuality.

She half-whispered, "I missed you, my captain."

"I missed you as well. I've been all over the world, and I'm certain you are the sexiest, most sensual woman I have ever crossed paths with. I almost don't recognize you in that long dress."

"You think you missed me now, wait till you see what I have on under this dress."

Dan followed her form to the floor with his eyes and saw three-inch heels attached to black patterned stockings. She was right, his level of arousal spiked. "Do you have plans to show me what's under that dress?"

"Of course. I reserved a room at the airport Crowne. It's about a ten-minute drive." Sindee didn't just have a room reserved; she held up a room key card in her hand between her fingers, the way a magician would. When Dan's eyes returned to her face, that hot little smile of hers told him that she had much more than a room reserved for him.

. . .

Dan and Sindee were laying in the hotel bed, a napping Sindee being his little spoon. She earned a nap, having worn herself out trying her best to please her man. *She has quite the skillset*, thought Dan. This was time alone with his thoughts, something Dan rarely got outside of the cockpit. He reflected on all that had happened in the past few days, and in a substantial way, he felt like he was watching a movie about someone else.

As sexy as she was, as incredibly sensuous as she was, and in spite of only knowing her a short time, Dan knew that he was having feelings for her. He briefly hoped she was having them back. Then he went back in time to the night that had started all this, and a new feeling grew in him: regret. Dan was a mission hacker, a guy who got things done. He didn't give up easily or often, so he had caused his marriage to extend way past its expiration date.

All that time with a woman who clearly didn't love me, missing out on this the whole time. If only I had seen the writing on the wall and had the balls to divorce her, she never would have had the chance to hurt me like this. Sindee, lying next to him, reminded him of just how long he had had a hole in his heart, and just how big it was. Sharon was his first and only love, and Dan had as little experience with falling in love as he did falling out of it. At that moment, Sindee was everything Sharon wasn't, and it made Dan feel whole again.

Sindee stirring awake halted the movie Dan was playing in his head. *This is my life now.* And the realization made him happy. Sindee rolled over, kissed Dan on the neck, and buried her head in his chest. Then he felt her hands roam over his body, and all thinking stopped. Dan was a bit amazed how Sindee could so easily and so quickly put him in a state of being ready for her. Without a word spoken, for the next hour, the two of them were just two lovers apart from the world and together as one. Dan couldn't know that during their time together, Sindee's feelings had been growing with his.

. . .

Sindee let out a deep sigh and said, "As much as I hate to say this out loud, I have to get ready for my shift at the club tonight."

"Yeah, I have some things to do as well. I only get a few days off between trips. It's like living two lives: pilot and regular guy. Only regular guy has had some rather large changes in his life lately. I have to go, but I'm going to have you on my mind all day, baby."

"I wish I didn't have to turn a shift at the club tonight." Sindee's face lit up with the spark of an idea. "Can I take a night off during your next break, so we could do something together?"

Dan smiled at the thought. "I'd love that. Maybe a nice dinner, get a steak, maybe see a movie?"

"Sounds like a date, flyboy!"

The two of them dressed as they spoke, and with nothing else to do but walk out the door, that's what they did. They said their goodbyes all over again in the parking lot, and after one last, long kiss, got in their vehicles and separated.

Dan's drive home was on autopilot. Once he got on a familiar street, the path to his house was automatic. All his thoughts were on Sindee anyway. When he pulled into the garage, Sharon's car was not there. Relieved at not having to see her at that moment, he was allowed to continue to dwell on Sindee, even as he showered and put on comfortable clothes. *Think I will pack my bag and get a uniform ready, even though I'm off tomorrow.*

Dan went through his routine of readying a uniform shirt with his wings and epaulets, pens in the pocket, and passport. He laid out on the bed the formula of clothes he put in his rollaway for a four-day trip, and then neatly packed his bag. By the time he heard the back door open and close, it was 6:45 P.M. *Where were you?* he thought.

Sharon walked through the bedroom door and seemed half surprised to see Dan. It wasn't that she hadn't noticed his truck in the garage, it was that they had not spoken much lately. They were two people not know-ing that they were both avoiding the other.

"Oh sweetie, how are you? I had a client meeting this afternoon that ran late," she said.

Is she even putting any effort into lying anymore? That wasn't even a little bit convincing. No kiss, nothing. Dan tried to keep his bitter feelings off his face.

Sharon noticed the bag on the bed and asked, "Do you have a trip tomorrow? I thought you didn't fly until day after tomorrow, but you're packing?"

Dan turned his attention back to packing his rollaway. "Just thought I'd do it today, since I had no other plans. I'm going to catch the game tonight, but probably hit it early after that. I didn't sleep well on the last trip, and I'm still catching up."

"Why couldn't you sleep?" she asked.

Because I was up late fucking silly a real woman who actually enjoyed being with me.

"Just regular operational stuff. Flying late, then switching to morning flying, and then back. You know, routine scheduling torture." There was obvious annoyance in his voice, and Sharon's puzzled look told Dan that she wondered if it was directed at her, the airline, or both. Dan decided he didn't want to explain or be anywhere near Sharon. *I'll finish packing later.* He slowly started making his way to the bedroom door.

"Enjoy the game. I'm gonna shower, then relax in the bedroom with some TV." Sharon had begun to strip before Dan left the bedroom.

It was obvious to him she was keeping very fit. The thought did noth-ing less than anger Dan as he knew why she was doing it. *All these years, and now she puts in the effort for that asshole.* Dan had always kept in shape, but the events and the exercise he'd received in the last few days had leaned him a bit as well. *I hope she notices that, too.*

An hour later, Dan was in the living room on the couch in front of a baseball game being broadcast on his ridiculously large television. Dan had heard Sharon exiting the bedroom door, even though she was trying to be quiet. He immediately pretended to be asleep, and the scotch on the end table provided the evidence. Apparently, Sharon had decided that to keep up pretenses, she would seduce him tonight. She stopped briefly when she surveyed the situation, but Sharon was a woman who always got what she wanted. She had made up her mind. She kneeled in front of Dan and fished her hands into his baggy running shorts.

Hard to believe she is actually making me hard. I guess tonight is going to be one of my allowance nights. Sindee was right, I am going to enjoy this, but mostly because I'm going to be thinking of her the whole time. Dan reached out a hand and had just enough arm's length to switch off the lamp on the table, leaving only the kitchen night light to illuminate the scene. *That's better.*

19

Aside from talking to Sindee on the phone several times, Dan's last day off had been pretty uneventful. His life seemed to slip backward to the old life a little at a time, only to be jolted into his new existence by a text from Sindee, or a call on his other phone from Angelo.

Angelo had called only once, and then all he said was "You have mail." *Click.* Dan had a pretty good idea what he meant by that. Opening the email app on his phone, he saw an email from the travel agency with the subject line *Quote for Indianapolis getaway.* The body of the email had the header and footer of the travel agency and a price quote for airline tickets to Indianapolis and back. The times of the flights were the dates and times he was to arrive and depart Indy on his next trip. This was the confirmation Angelo spoke of.

That's odd. "Pack for the beach!" What the hell is that supposed to mean? Dan thought about it and decided he needed to take the hint. He added a pair of swim trunks to his overnight bag. When he woke the next morning to his alarms and got ready for work, his thoughts were on what lay ahead of him in Indianapolis.

. . .

Angelo was as much business on the phone as in person. "It's all set. You'll hear from the travel agent about where you'll go and when you need to be there to deliver the package. That's all you need to do. The instructions inside will tell the operator all he will need to know. You ask no questions, no small talk, don't even speak. Hand him the package; walk away. Understand? Okay."

Click

Very few people knew where Angelo lived, and he put in much effort to keep it that way. It was a large house, but not unlike the other houses in the neighborhood. Lavish enough to be comfortable, and obviously owned by someone of means, but not gaudy or designed to draw attention to itself. On the outside, it was very obviously a custom-built, fenced, and gated home, just like all the other homes. There were many features Angelo required when he had the place built; some of them more function than form. The drive around the house, with out-of-sight garage parking in the back, made for a very clean look from the curb. That layout, however, was way more about security than looks to Angelo. And of course, his IT guy had spent weeks at the place wiring it from top to bottom and all around the grounds.

His favorite room was his office: a room that made him feel in command as he ran business. Angelo's house layout was customize-designed to include that very large office fit for a Rockefeller. The desk was equally huge, and while it always had materials on it, he kept it neat. Four large windows—bullet-proof, of course, as were all the windows in the house—looked out upon his three acres of woods. Angelo made sure the window installer understood that he needed to be prepared to install "hurricane" windows. Angelo then purchased them and had them delivered to the build site.

Angelo surveyed the array of nine cell phones on his desk, carefully choosing the correct one. He dialed the only number in the memory. Dan, in his home, jumped a little when he heard the ringtone.

Dan spoke. "Hello. I was just walking out the door for the airport. As far as I know, everything is as I showed you."

Angelo's tone was serious. "Okay, that's good because we are on for tonight. Everything will happen just as I told you. One thing: remember, no talk. Not a word tonight spoken to anyone on this job. One last question. Do you bring a different pair of shoes with you?"

"Gotcha, boss. I'll remember. And yes, I have athletic shoes in my bag."

Click

Both men hung up their phones, then returned to very different lives. For Angelo, this was just one small, but important part of a very large operation. For Dan, he was now stepping back into the world of Captain Hatfield, whose singular focus was on the safe operation of one aircraft at a time. Both men were managers in a very real, yet totally different sense.

· · ·

The drive to the airport was just one in a long history of drives that ended at employee parking. Dan knew every pothole, every favorite speed trap location for the local cops, and the timing of every traffic light. But there was a quiet excitement in Dan for this particular drive, and there was something very new and very different about to happen on this trip.

Looking at his watch, he realized he had arrived at a parking space even earlier than he usually did. He hadn't yet turned off the ignition when he heard his phone text notifier. It was a special ringtone he had for texts from Sharon. Her text to him read, *I have a business trip tomorrow to San Antonio. Only be there a few days. Should be back before you.*

"Huh. Business trip, right," Dan said aloud. He texted her back. *Have fun. Go to the riverwalk.*

Sharon was taking advantage of Dan's days flying and Ed's days off. *Way ahead of you. Already booked a place on the riverwalk. Fly safe.*

Staying on the riverwalk, and it's a business trip? My ass, he thought. *And I'm the one that's ahead of you.*

That little exchange made up Dan's mind for him. He was wondering what to do with his extra time, but after that text, he suddenly decided calling Sindee was a good idea. She picked up on the second ring.

Dan could hear the smile in Sindee's voice as she spoke. "Ohhhhh baby, so nice to hear from you! I know you're flying today, so I didn't know if you'd have time. Where are you?"

"Sitting in my truck in employee parking. I have tinted windows and wish you were here right now."

Sindee's voice took on a sultriness at that thought. "I bet you do. I do too. I'm going to miss you. You'll be gone for four days?"

"That's right, we call it a 'four day.' I leave on the first day of the trip, and come home on the fourth, so I am in hotels the next three nights. From time to time, if you can be away from work, maybe we could arrange for you to come with me on some of the good overnights. Interested?"

The smile returned. "Absolutely! That sounds great. Just pick the place, and we'll make the plans. Where are you tonight?"

Dan brought to mind the hotel, location, and food options near the hotel, then gave it his rating. "Indianapolis, not that great of a layover, but it's okay. I'll look at the schedule. I'm going to miss you too, by the way, my sexy lover."

There was a slight pause before her response. What Dan didn't know was that, not having much experience with the kind of feelings she had for Dan growing in her, she was unsure what words to use next. The next question she asked sounded almost childlike and innocent to Dan. Innocence was not Sindee's dominant trait, but she was having a hard time sorting through this new attraction to Dan. "Dan, is it always going to feel like this, the way I feel right now, when you leave?"

"I think I feel exactly the same way you do right now, Sindee. And yes, I think so. I hope so, till the day I retire."

There was another pause. "You be safe, be careful. I like you a lot, Captain Hatfield."

"I will always. I like you a lot too. Can't wait to see you after this trip."

They both were a little taken aback by the sincere exchange. It wasn't the way Dan thought the conversation would go before it started, and he sensed the same from Sindee. Sindee's phone buzzed with an incoming call.

"Gotta go, Dan. Bye, lover!"

Before Dan could say his goodbye, Sindee had hung up to answer the call.

. . .

Angelo got right to business. "So, our friend is traveling this afternoon. Did you get a chance to talk to him today?"

Sindee said, "Just got off the phone with him."

"Okay, so what can you tell me about him?"

20

The sight of First Officer Mike Chelsea standing at the gate was a welcome one for Dan. He knew he was going to have a hard time concentrating on the flight to Indianapolis; having a competent first officer was a good thing at times like this. Mike was also a friend, so it was good all around. Dan decided the best thing to do was to immerse himself completely in the flying duties and try to forget about what lay ahead in Indianapolis.

Gotta focus and get my head in the game, he thought as he climbed into his seat in the cockpit and unpacked the necessary items from his flight bag. By the time he was done with all his preflight duties and welcomed the passengers on board the flight via the cabin public address system, he had almost forgotten the op. Almost. They had gotten the passengers boarded early, and the cockpit was ready to go, but they couldn't move because the rampers were still loading the bags.

With his brain throttled back now to neutral, his mind began to wander over the recent events that had him flying to Indy tonight. A few minutes later, when the flight attendant asked, "Is it okay to close the main cabin door?" she had to ask a second time. Dan hadn't even heard the first time, so he didn't understand the quizzical looks from her and Mike.

. . .

Dan's wandering mind had not gone unnoticed, so Mike decided to ask him about it. Mike thought he'd wait until they were at cruise altitude when there wasn't much to do. The last straw was the uncharacteristic lack of small talk from Dan all the way to cruise. "Everything okay over there? You have something on your mind you want to bounce off a friend?"

Mike had been a volunteer for a program with the pilot union that helps pilots who find themselves over their head with life problems. He had genuine concern. The suicide rate for airline pilots is many times higher than the national average.

"Nah, just got a couple of things going on that I am thinking my way through, coming up with a path. But nothing serious or life-threatening." Dan chuckled as he said it.

"Okay, well if you want to talk about something or run an idea past me, I'll give you my two cents at half price!"

That made them both smile.

. . .

The rest of the flight had been very routine, and Dan was glad it was uneventful. As a crew, the pilots and flight attendants walked to the hotel van pickup location together, and on this particular overnight, they were staying at the same hotel. Get the right group of flight attendants, and that's a good thing. The wrong group makes for long van rides. Again, Dan was delighted to find that these four flight attendants were upbeat, with good moods all around, and planning to go out of the hotel for dinner together. They even invited Dan and Mike. Mike jumped at it; Dan politely declined. "I have some business to do on the computer. Working on getting something going as a second revenue stream."

There were words of disappointment, congratulations on the business, and expressing maybe they could go out together tomorrow in Miami. The look Mike gave him said *You sure?* without actually saying it. Dan just gave him a nod.

Maybe twenty minutes later, Dan had signed the hotel check-in sheet, was given a room key, and was walking through the door of his room. Crewmembers usually pack clothes they can wear when they go out to get a bite to eat, or a few drinks. If the overnight is long enough, maybe a movie or shopping. It always depended on the amount of time, and what was near the hotel. It was May, and the weather was great, so Dan decided that after the uniform came off, it's shorts, a polo, and sneakers.

He was just hanging his uniform shirt in the wardrobe when there was a knock at his door, a standard three-tap, firm knock. Dan looked through the peephole and saw a twenty-something male wearing a base-ball cap and face mask, holding a pizza box with a bag on top. The bag looked like it had two food clamshells. *Pretty good cover, Angelo.*

He opened the door, and the guy looked over Dan's face carefully. When he was sure this was the right guy, he thrust out the pizza box and bag. Dan took what was offered, then took two steps back into the room, letting the door close itself.

There was some weight to the containers, but he would not describe them as heavy. Rather, just heavy enough to know there was something in them. Dan decided to get comfortable before he opened them and read his assignment. There was something about getting out of the uniform that felt so satisfying, a ritual that signaled the true end to the flying day. Dan couldn't help but notice that delaying the gratification of opening the package felt a bit like Christmas.

21

Dan had gotten as far as his underwear before he sat down on the bed with the package. He lifted both of the food clamshell containers out of the bag and sat them next to the pizza box. He opened them all and looked over the contents. They were packed neatly, and it was obvious that thought went into putting this together. He could see a single sheet of paper with computer-printed words at the bottom of the pizza box. He retrieved the paper and started reading it.

The paper had a bullet-point list of instructions.

"Unpack the packaging completely. In it you should find two pistol magazines, pistol, suppressor, a baseball cap, a face mask, a chest holster, a shirt, a pair of shorts, clear latex gloves, two hotel key cards marked A and B, computer USB thumb drive, $1,000 in cash, and a cloth bag."

Dan inventoried the goods in the package. It was exactly as the list described. The shirt was a black polo with *The Hightower* and logo embroidered on the right breast. He couldn't help but notice that the shirt was two sizes too big. *I guess, how else do you carry a suppressed pistol in shorts?*

"Change into the shorts, shirt, holster, mask, and cap provided. The athletic shoes from your bag are fine. Retrieve the pistol from the package and attach the suppressor. Insert one of the magazines provided in the package and charge the pistol. Place the loaded and ready pistol in the holster and conceal with the provided shirt. Place second loaded magazine in your front, left pocket."

Getting dressed? Piece of cake. Loading a pistol in a hotel room without putting a round through a wall? Priceless.

Dan very carefully went through the procedure of loading a weapon. After he had triple-checked that the gun was completely unloaded, he inserted a loaded magazine into the pistol, pulled the slide back and let go. The pistol was now loaded and ready to go. The barrel protruded from the front of the gun about an inch. Part of that last inch was threaded so that the suppressor could be screwed onto the front of it. He did just that, and then set the loaded pistol on the bed, and picked up the holster. It took a little bit of reasoning to figure it out, but Dan had it on in less than a minute and was adjusting it to his body.

The holster was a Denali holster. It had a strap that went around the mid-section of the body, and another that went over the shoulder to attach to the mid-section strap on the back. Dan understood the wisdom of choosing a Denali. Once the suppressor was threaded onto the end of the pistol barrel, the total length of the weapon was just over fourteen inches. Concealing a weapon that long in shorts would be difficult. The Denali rig holds the holster to the middle of the chest, usually pointing downward at a forty-five-degree angle. This holster was exactly that design, with two modifications. One was that the straps had elastic sections. This puzzled Dan at first, wondering if the holster would be secure. Then he noticed the holster had been modified not to cover the trigger. Usually, a holster would never be sold with no trigger cover, as the possibility of being able to trigger the weapon in the holster would be considered dangerous. This holster had been modified, post-sale, in order to give the shooter exactly that capability. With the elastic, the shooter would be able to aim and fire the pistol while still in its holster, albeit with limited range of motion. *That's cool, but that's gonna fuck up the shirt.*

Checking his look in the mirror, he then holstered the loaded weapon, and checked it again. It appeared the holster was properly adjusted. Putting the shirt on, Dan noticed it concealed the weapon well.

"Make yourself completely ready to leave the hotel. Read these instructions THOROUGHLY and memorize them before you leave your room. Do NOT leave your room with this paper. Wear the latex gloves until you are back in your room."

"Leave your room by the stairwell at your end of the hallway. Exit the door outside at the bottom of the stairwell. Turn right. Go around behind your hotel and use the alley behind the building to walk three blocks west to the back of the Hightower Hotel. There will be signs identifying it. Keep your head down as you cross the streets. There are no cameras in the alley that work, but there are cameras on the street."

"Use the key card marked 'A' to enter the door in the back labeled *Hightower Hotel Employees Only*. To your right will be a service elevator. There is no camera on that elevator. Take ONLY that elevator up and down. There will be employees and hotel guests you may see or see you from here on. Act normally, and don't draw attention. Go to the ninth floor to room 901: the corner suite. Time all of this so that you are at that door at 10:30 P.M."

Dan looked at his watch and did the reverse countdown he's done so many times before. This one he did out loud to make sure he got it right. "At the door at ten-thirty means at the elevator going up by ten-twenty-five. That would mean leaving the hotel about ten minutes prior for the three-block walk, or ten-fifteen. I'm on the fifth floor, so let's say five minutes to get from my room to the alley, so ten-ten. That sounds about right, so I'll leave the room at ten exactly to give myself a little cushion. It's nine-ten right now, so I have time to read the rest of the instructions and commit them to memory."

Dan went on to read the next line, then whispered, "Oh shit."

"This was supposed to be a dry run, and it still can be if you wish. But the target in room 901 is your first target, and if you wish to make your mission status a go, it is up to you. You will find on the thumb drive some background information on the target and images of his face. You do not have to decide until you are standing at the door to 901. You will use the key card marked 'B' to enter the room. You can enter and either complete the mission now or at a later date. He is a man of routine and will be in the shower at that moment today, tomorrow, or two weeks from now. After you leave the room, regardless of your decision, you will follow the next instructions EXACTLY."

Okay, I gotta take a second to process this. It only took a few seconds before he reached the logical conclusion. *Fuck it, I'm gonna do this sooner or later. Might as well be now. Let's see who this asshole is.*

The laptop Dan carried was in his extra bag, where he carried all his breakable stuff. It booted right up, and he inserted the thumb drive. There was a single PDF file on the thumb drive, and, with two clicks, it opened. At the top were a few pictures of someone who looked all bad at first glance. The words below described a sadistic killer who isn't afraid to target the families of those who have crossed his path. A prolific beater of women. Been an enforcer and a hitter for the mob for two decades but stepped on some connected toes when he tried carving out a territory for himself.

Salvatore Indofini. Sal the Fist, what a piece of shit. Yeah, this guy I can shoot. Okay, looks like I need to read the rest of the instructions.

"We have verified that he is there and will be alone at 10:30. If you key in, be prepared. He would have no problem ending your mission. The pistol, with that suppressor and ammunition is nearly silent. The noise it does make will not be heard through a wall or door.

"After you are sure the mission is complete, leave the room with your head down. There is a camera at the end of the hall. Enter the service elevator you used previously, return to your room the same way with no stops. If there is a problem, as an alternative to the service elevator, you may use the stairs and the bottom floor door. The 'B' key card opens both that door and the suite door.

"Once back in your room, place ALL items from the package in the cloth laundry bag. The packaging itself—pizza box, clamshells, plastic bag—are all clean, so you may leave them in your room. Last, take these instructions, tear them into small pieces, and flush them down the toilet. Make sure to scrub thoroughly in the shower using a washcloth in order to remove all gunshot residue and anything else. There will be another knock on your door at midnight. Answer it and give the messenger the laundry bag. The money is for you in case you need something or there are expenses. Keep it all."

Huh. I get a tip tonight.

22

It's go time. At precisely 10:00 P.M., Dan left his hotel room and headed down the stairwell. He kept hearing the words from the instructions in his head. The most important ones in his estimation were "act normally and don't draw attention." That was going to apply to every movement and every decision he made until he was back in his room.

There were very few people on the streets this time of night in this area of Indianapolis, and even fewer in the alley. Dan forced himself to walk at a normal pace, even though his heart rate was on a slow rise. Every step took him closer to a place where his life would change direction, substantially and permanently. And yet he wondered if that turn had already taken place, and if that change was behind him. "This was supposed to be a dry run, and it still can be if you wish..." was what the instructions said. But it wasn't really. Whether Dan went through with the mission or not, he was already in too deep to turn around.

Better to just go through with it. For a bunch of reasons. Remembering the locations of the cameras, Dan traversed the three cross streets with head down, looking straight ahead. He didn't even look for traffic, but there was barely any to see. He looked at his watch: 10:09 P.M. *I'm ahead of schedule.* His pace slowed a little, knowing he had to burn a little time on the way. *Better to spend the extra time in the alley in the dark rather than inside with people and cameras.*

A few minutes later, Dan was crossing the last street and looking at all the doors on his right. The third building was marked *The Hightower*

Hotel, and he found the door that was the employee entrance. Fishing the 'A' card out of his left back pocket, Dan was rewarded with a green light and a click when he inserted it in the door slot. He opened the door, and light flooded out into the dark alley. Dan stepped through the door and was looking down a long hallway that had a few passages to the left. On his immediate right was the service elevator. Dan was careful to keep his head down as he walked the short distance to the elevator door.

The doors on the elevator opened immediately upon pressing the button. At this time of night, hardly anyone would be using the service elevator. *They planned this meticulously.* Dan checked his watch again, it was 10:21 P.M. *Still a bit ahead of schedule.* He paused for a minute before pushing the "9" button. The heart in Dan's chest was definitely beating faster. The elevator rose the nine floors at a regular pace, but to him it seemed faster. At the ninth floor, the door opened, and Dan peered around the corner.

There was no one else in sight, and no camera outside the elevator door. Dan checked his watch again: 10:24 P.M. With a one-minute walk to the door, he had five minutes to kill. *Five minutes to kill. Literally.* At times like this, the minutes go by very slowly. He knew that if he held the doors open for too long, an alarm would sound. *Was that alarm just a local buzzer, or did it show in some security office too? Can't take that chance.* Dan let the doors close, and the elevator just stayed on nine. No one had called for the elevator on any other floor. *Okay, let's go for a little ride.* He pushed the "7" button, and the elevator descended two floors opening to the same layout as the ninth floor.

Dan's watch read 10:27 P.M. He let the elevator doors open and close a few times, and then pressed the "9" button again. The elevator doors closed, and it started to go up. At the eighth floor, the elevator stopped, and the doors opened. *Oh fuck*, he thought. Waiting for the elevator was a woman, and a large cart full of hotel linens. Dan moved to the opposite side of the elevator and looked away from the woman. He was relieved when he saw the "B" button illuminate. She was going to the basement but must have pushed the Up button on the eighth floor. When the doors opened on the ninth floor, Dan saw 10:29 P.M. on his watch. Dan was ready. *Perfect. Go time.*

Again keeping his head down, he walked off the elevator and turned right, the only direction he could go. When he got to the long hallway with room doors on either side, the signs indicated another right turn. It wasn't a long walk to the end of the hallway, and in less than a minute he was staring at the door at the end of the hallway. The ornate little sign next to the door bore the numbers "901." Dan had opened thousands of hotel doors in his time with the airlines. He knew from the look of the door it had an electronic lock that allowed a guest to open the door by the door handle for a short period of time after touching the key to the lock. If the door were not opened in a few seconds, the lock would re-engage. There was noise when the door unlocked, and unless opened carefully, the door handle sounded like a bank safe door opening.

This would require timing to be done properly. Dan lifted the front of his shirt and tucked it behind the holster; now his pistol was exposed and readily-available. He reached into his right back pocket and removed the "B" key card, holding it in his right hand. He paused for a moment and planned the actions he was about to take. Then Dan recalled *slow is smooth, smooth is fast.* It was something they used to say during his firearm training about drawing from the holster. In one, long, fluid sequence, he put his planned actions in motion. Dan touched the key card to the lock, was rewarded with the sound of the lock operating, then he slipped the card in his back pocket. As that was happening, his left hand already on the handle, he slowly pushed down the handle and disengaged the door latch, opening the door slightly. Key card back in his pocket, Dan's right hand went to the holstered pistol and removed it from the holster. With the door now unlatched, Dan's left hand pushed the door open a few inches as he rotated the pistol up, so it was now pointing at chest-level into the room. Dan was in the open doorway, pistol at ready position.

He froze for a second and listened. *Not a sound*, he thought, relieved. Keeping his pistol pointed in the room at the ready position, Dan slowly opened the door wide enough to step in. His heart was pounding. He could hear the sound of the shower running. Dan slowly scanned the room, making sure they were in fact, the only two people in the suite. Satisfied, he turned and carefully closed the door as silently as he could. Dan turned and moved in the direction of the bathroom. Dan took a long, deep breath, and tried to calm his nerves a bit.

Just as he got to the doorway, the water in the shower stopped. Dan stepped to his right, and stood against the door frame, out of sight of the man in the bathroom. Dan heard the large glass door open and bare feet take a few steps out of the shower. He brought the gun up to his eye level and placed his finger on the trigger. Gun high at the ready, Dan pivoted to the right, and pointed his gun right where he guessed Sal's head would be. He got it exactly right.

Sal looked at the gun first, then to Dan's masked face, and back to the gun. Sal had spent most of his life dishing out beatings and death to many people. Many. He had seen how people act when they realize this is probably their last moment alive, and it ran the gamut of reactions. What Dan saw was a man who knew he had arrived at a moment long overdue and accepted his fate.

Dan squeezed the trigger; the gun jumped in his hand but made surprisingly little noise. Sal fell backwards on the floor, moving fast enough that Dan didn't see the hole in Sal's forehead until he was a pile on the floor. There were movements to his body. Dan made up his mind about what to do next. *Probably involuntary, but I'm supposed to be sure.*

With his left foot, Dan rolled what was left of Sal the Fist on his back and put two more rounds in his chest. Dan holstered his weapon and turned to leave the suite. As he passed the living room on his way to the door, he noticed cash on the coffee table. Three stacks of hundred-dollar bills, wrapped in paper strips marked "$10,000." He thought about it for a second, then stuffed the bills into his pockets.

I guess I get a big tip today. Thanks, Sal. Enjoy hell.

23

Dan took a long look through the peephole on the door. Since it was the end suite, the view was of the entire length of hallway. Sal probably liked that. At that moment, Dan liked it too. There was a guest keying into his room about halfway down the hallway, just past the turn for the elevator. When the guest entered his room, and Dan heard the heavy door close, he opened the suite door silently. Dan gave one last pat down to his clothes, making sure all was right, and all was concealed. Satisfied, he walked out the suite door and slowly to the elevator.

The walk back to the crew hotel, the climbing of the six floors of stairs to his floor, and re-entering his room were all uneventful. By the time Dan opened his hotel room door, he was surprised to realize that his heart rate was pretty much normal. The walk back had given him some time to think, and something physical to do to cool down, the way a person does on a treadmill after a run.

Sitting on his bed, Dan took stock of himself, and the last hour of his life. He was questioning whether or not he could do that again, or even several more times. The reason he was questioning was because he had found the entire mission, all of it, surprisingly easy, and Dan wondered if he was missing something. *What if I had walked in, and Sal was on the couch? Or a girlfriend of Sal's? Would I have shot her too? Or tied her up? I'm going to have to put some thought to that.*

Dan decided to busy himself with finishing the instructions. He removed the magazine from his pistol carefully, worked the slide to eject the round still in the barrel, unthreaded the suppressor, and put everything in the pizza box. Dan tossed the pizza box, clamshells, and plastic bag in the corner of the room. Using the instruction sheet like a checklist, he put the items in the cloth bag in the order they were listed. Dan looked at his watch again, it was 11:19 P.M. With all the items in the bag, he pulled the drawstring on the top, then tied it in a knot to close it. A thought occurred to Dan. *Maybe I should put my shoes in there too.* He untied the knot, put his shoes inside the bag, and retied it.

It was 11:45 P.M. when Dan's other phone rang.

"Hey! Sooooo, how did the thing go?" It was Angelo, true to business, and wanting a quick debriefing.

"Mission complete," said Dan through a solemn smile.

"*Totally* complete?"

"Yes, sir, no need to revisit this issue." Dan was matter-of-fact.

"Nice going. I knew you were the right guy for this. Congratulations!" Angelo's words beamed like a proud father. He was good at sizing people up, and he clearly felt that Dan would come through.

Dan hadn't really looked at this like it was some kind of an accomplishment, something deserving a trophy. But Angelo's words and tone had him rethinking that feeling. His next words were sincere. "Thank you, big guy." He let out a barely audible sigh. "Can we meet again in a few days—same time, same place—and talk about a thing."

Dan assumed Angelo wanted a full debrief, and what place was better than Vincent's? "Sure, I'd like that. I have a few questions and a different thing I'd like to discuss. I'll be available Thursday." Dan knew his words about "a different thing" to discuss would intrigue Angelo, but he also knew that details were not for cell phones, and Angelo would have to wait.

"A new thing? Okay, Thursday it is."

"Okay, see you then, boss."

Click

Angelo hung up the phone, and a few minutes later there was the knock at the hotel room door. Dan went to the door, laundry bag in hand. He glanced at his phone; it said 11:50 P.M. *My guy is early.* Dan thought that was odd, considering the precision of the rest of the evening, but he opened the door. The man knocking on the door was Mike Chelsea.

"Hey man, I've been ringing your room, wanted to see if you wanted to get a beer. We're not out until late tomorrow, and there's a great little place a half-block from the hotel."

Dan made a note to himself to never open the door again without looking. "Sounds great, I just need fifteen minutes. I heard the phone, but I was taking one of my signature long showers. Give me just a few, and I'll knock on your door."

"Okay, room 648. Hurry up."

"Will do." Dan closed the door and mulled that over. *This thing is going to have lots of opportunities for mistakes, and I'm new to all of what is going on. It will always be better to never put myself in positions that require me to have to come up with an explanation suddenly.*

He stood there at the door, waiting for the knock he was expecting while still thinking things over. The knock at the door was at exactly midnight. Dan saw the messenger through the peephole, this time dressed in a shirt with a company name embroidered on it that matched the name on the laundry bag. He opened the door, and in the reverse of before, extended the bag to the messenger, who took it from Dan without a word. Dan nodded, as did the messenger, who turned to leave as Dan closed the door.

It took Dan maybe five minutes to dress for the hops meeting with Mike at whatever local joint Mike had lined up. He had already put on his shorts when he realized that all he had in the room for shoes was the dress shoes he wore with the pilot uniform. Dan chuckled, *Guess I need to break out the jeans, or I'm going to look like a German tourist.*

24

The rest of the trip was uneventful. The overnights in Miami and Charlotte were shorter than Indy, but still long enough that Dan was able to buy dinner and drinks for the whole crew in both cities. It was very generous of Captain Hatfield to do so, and they ate both nights at upscale locations. The crew was, to a person, very grateful for the outings, and they had a lot of laughs. Dan explained it as having been the recipient of a recent windfall, and he wanted to pass it along. As the crew kept thanking him, he kept hearing in his head, *Thanks, Sal!*

Angelo told Sindee that Dan would be busy in Indianapolis but gave her no other details. Sindee didn't call Dan on the other phone that night, but she did call on the Miami and Charlotte overnights. They both enjoyed the phone calls very much. Dan found that he was missing Sindee quite a bit. He would daydream a few times during the trip about taking her out of the life she was in and upgrading it considerably. It was one possible future, but not in the near term.

. . .

"Blue Sky 4565, Memphis Center. Contact Fort Worth Center on 135.35." It was Mike's turn to operate the radios while Dan flew the aircraft.

"Memphis, Blue Sky 4565, Fort Worth on 135.35. Good day." Mike turned to Dan. "God, I love to hear the words 'Fort Worth Center' on the last leg of a four-day trip!" Mike's words rang true with Dan, who looked at Mike and nodded agreement.

"*Fort Worth Center, Blue Sky 4565. Flight level 360, mostly smooth for the last hundred miles or so.*"

"*Blue Sky 4565, Fort Worth Center. I have holding pattern instructions for you. They are turning the airport around at DFW. Advise ready to copy the instructions.*"

"Well, fuck me silly. Figures. On the go home leg of a four day, we get a holding pattern on the way in to DFW." Mike was pissed. So was Dan, but apparently not as pissed as Mike, because Dan wasn't going to be able to see Sindee tonight and could not care less about seeing Sharon.

"It is what it is, Mike. Nothing we can do about it. All you can do is repeat to yourself over and over, 'we get paid by the minute, we get paid by the minute.'" Dan chuckled.

"Easy for you to say, Captain Hatfield. You get paid for your minute much more than I'm paid for mine, and some of my minutes tonight have a woman's name on them. A very interesting woman's name."

"Ah yes, the dog is on the hunt tonight, I see. Well, I'm sure this isn't going to hold us up for long. They are just changing runway configuration, and we have plenty of hold fuel. No chance we are diverting."

. . .

Even with the hold, Dan parked Blue Sky 4565 at gate A-27 only nineteen minutes late. Dan told Mike that as soon as they parked, Mike should pack up his bag and head out. Dan would take care of putting the aircraft to bed: making sure that all the switches, levers, knobs, and displays were in their proper position for leaving the aircraft. There were a significant number of tasks involved in getting a flight off the gate, and more after the aircraft is parked. While it was true that the pilots get paid by the minute, the pay minutes begin when the aircraft is pushed back, and end when the parking brake is set at the destination. All those preflight and postflight minutes while they were still working—those they did for free. Dan sending Mike off right away was a favor that Mike understood. But they were friends.

The captain from the inbound flight usually gives a quick brief to the captain about to take the airplane from him if they run into each other. Weather conditions, turbulence, mechanical condition of the airplane, and other topics can usually be communicated in a few pilot-speak sentences. As Dan walked up the jetbridge, dragging his bags behind him, the outbound pilots were walking toward the plane. Looking up, Dan saw a familiar face.

"Captain Ronkowski, pray do tell what force of nature managed to get you out from behind the Chief Pilot desk, dress you up like an airline pilot, and put you on an airplane? You're not going *flying*, are you?" Dan said. Pilots, cops, firefighters, sports teammates, and the like are known for the humorous trash talking they engage in with colleagues. Dan thought it would be a good method to conceal his true feelings for Ed.

"I'm fluent in sarcasm, Dan. That plane you just parked, *surely* it isn't still *flyable* after one leg with you at the controls, *is it?*" Ed said, keeping up the banter.

Dan faked a laugh. "No, Ed, I didn't break this particular one. You getting current?"

"Sort of. Some management stooge wants to help pilot manning by making the chiefs fly at least two trips a month and dressing it up as a 'see how things are working on the line' type of program. Turning us into reserve pilots. But at least the trips we fly we get to pick out of the open trips that have no captain assigned."

Dan was done with the banter. "Gotta go, Ed. Have fun reacquainting yourself with line operations. I'm going to rejoin my life, which is already in progress."

Ed just waved as he walked toward the main cabin door, oblivious that their decades-long friendship had already come to an end.

. . .

It was another ride home on autopilot, with the F150 almost steering itself. That was a good thing, because Dan had just slid into the driver's seat when the other phone rang. It was Sindee, who wanted to give him a tease about seeing her tomorrow. Dan let her know: same time, same place.

He was getting close to his house now, and he needed to hang up. That certainly wasn't the same as *wanting* to hang up. Measuring being trapped between the desire for Sindee and the dread of seeing Sharon, he decided to pull the truck over a few blocks short of his house. Sindee's gravity was stronger, and he wanted to extend the conversation.

"We've been on the phone a while, lover. Aren't you getting close to your house?" Sindee asked, her voice revealing a hint of sadness.

"Yeah, well, I wasn't ready to hang up yet, so I pulled over."

"You pulled over just to talk to me longer?" The cheery smokiness had returned to her voice.

"Yes, sweetheart. I miss you, and I am in no hurry to go home."

It would be another half hour before Dan put the truck in Drive and pulled away from the curb. *At least I have scotch and baseball to look forward to. I wonder if they miss me when I'm gone.*

Nothing else in that house does.

25

True to his word, Dan had been in his home all of about ten minutes when he sat down on the couch in front of the TV. He had a scotch in one hand, a remote in the other. He found a game still in its second inning; sometime around the sixth inning, Sharon came home. She had been out with the girls.

At least I know this one particular night she's not off fucking Ed.

By the time Dan climbed into bed, Sharon was doing her own passed-out routine, and Dan didn't care.

The next morning started well, with Sharon gone to the gym, and Dan enjoying another leisurely morning alone in his home. Sindee kept long night hours and usually slept until noon. He wanted badly to call her but didn't want to wreck her sleep. What he didn't know was that she was awake early that day to get ready to see Dan and didn't want to wake him either.

It was sort of déjà vu for Dan. The easy morning, the long shower, getting dressed, and heading out to Vincent's with the plan of a 12:50 P.M. arrival. At the calculated time, Dan was pulling out of the garage in his F-150 and heading toward Grapevine. There was nothing but antic-ipation in his mood. Talking to Angelo, settling some details, discussing Ed, and talking over the numbers. *Numbers!*

Dan had only gotten as far as backing the truck into the alley when he stopped the truck, putting it in PARK. He jumped out the door and quickly walked into the garage. He had a hiding place in the shop where he had stashed the money from Indy. After grabbing one of the three stacks of cash, he closed the lid on the old toolbox and slipped back into his running truck. *I almost forgot Angelo's tribute.*

Dan understood the Italian custom of giving tribute, so he was going to give Angelo his cut from the windfall in Sal's suite. *Don't know how that is going to go over. Could be good, could be bad. I don't know, but I think it's the right thing to do.*

Walking in at 12:51 P.M., Dan was greeted by Vincent at the maître d' stand. "Captain Hatfield, so nice to see you again. Mr. Genofi is already in your room where you may meet undisturbed."

"Thank you, Mr. Ricci, it is wonderful to be here again. The food last time was fabulous, and I'm looking forward to trying something else on the menu today."

"Please call me Vincent, Captain Hatfield. Try the Shrimp Farfalle Calabrese, it is new on the menu. I think you will like. Right this way."

Vincent led Dan to the same room, closed the same doors, and he sat down at the same table with the same man. More déjà vu.

"Aah, Captain Hatfield, nice to see you again." As Angelo issued his warm greeting, he glanced at the door to make sure it was closed. After shaking Dan's hand, the two sat down. An instant later, the same waiter from his previous visit appeared via the door in the wall.

Angelo ordered first. "The stuffed cannelloni with a shrimp cocktail, bread of course, and whatever wine Vincent suggests with our dinners."

Angelo turned to Dan and on cue, he ordered. "I'll have the Shrimp Farfalle Calabrese, the wedding soup, and water in addition to the wine."

"Very good." The waiter disappeared into the same door he came from, Angelo watching for the door to close.

Angelo jumped into business as if he'd been looking forward to it all day. "Okay, let's go over Indianapolis. Dan, I'm *proud* of you. I really mean that. Great job getting it done. I love any op that doesn't require my cleanup. Did you have any problems or questions?"

"Yes, Angelo. The mission was planned meticulously, and I appreciate that. But, let's say I walked into that room, and he had a girlfriend with him. What would..."

Angelo cut him off. "She'd have to go too. You shouldn't have a question about that by now. Of course, we try to limit collateral damage. Collateral damage, mistakes, problems, big mouths only create opportunity for problems down the road. Even if you walked into that suite and his mother was on the couch, they would both be standing in front of St. Peter holding hands. That's gotta be clear with you and me. Is that clear?"

"Crystal. Also, was it okay picking up that cash?"

"Was it okay?" Angelo laughed. "Why leave it there for the cops to swipe?"

"Okay, then I want to give you your tribute." Dan reached into his pocket and placed a stack of one-hundred-dollar bills on the table in front of Angelo. Angelo froze, and then his head tilted to the side slightly. A smile spread across his face as he glanced at the money, and then back at Dan.

"Dan, I'm touched, really. You surprised me in a good way, and I can see that we are going to go far." Angelo paused, smiling at Dan and clearly savoring the moment. "No, Dan, this is your first score. Following tradition, I give that tribute back to you. Take it and spend it on yourself in good health!"

Just then the waiter came in with the wine, water, soup, shrimp cocktail, and bread. When he had skillfully laid it all out on the table and disappeared, business resumed.

Angelo's demeanor changed as if he had suddenly remembered something memorable. His face morphed into a curious smile. "Flyboy, why were your *shoes* in the bag?"

"I had to turn over his body with my foot, and there could have been evidence on them. Plus, they were the only distinguishable thing I was wearing."

Angelo turned his laptop around so Dan could see what he was looking at. It was a story on the Indianapolis Star's website about the gang hit on a mob figure at a downtown hotel. The two pictures were grainy blowups from security camera footage showing the logo on the shirt and the shoes.

"You're a natural!" Angelo sat there for a moment, just smiling and shaking his head. Then the business face returned. "So, you said you wanted them both dead, your wife and the lowlife that's nailing her. I will start working on that, but I need information about him."

Dan leaned back from his soup, thoughtfully delivering his next words. "That's the new thing I wanted to talk to you about. He is one of the chief pilots at my airline, and it occurred to me that there are worse things that can happen to a pilot than a bullet to the head."

Angelo had initially been curious what Dan's new thing was, but now he was fully engaged. "Oh really? I know I'm not an airline pilot, but a bullet to the head would fuck my day all up. What are you thinking?"

"What if the pilot in question were to go to a hotel bar on an overnight, run into a very willing, very beautiful woman. Said woman goes back to his room, spikes his drink, maybe gets a little coke or weed or whatever in his system, then leaves him to himself. If that same woman was to phone in an anonymous tip to the police that she was concerned about the condition of the pilot she was with the night before—"

Excited, Angelo dove in. "They'd clip his wings if he ever got out of prison. And your wife will get to watch. Wow, that's cruel. I *love* it. So, I'm guessing the new thing is I line up that woman and those drugs?"

Dan nodded. "What would that cost?"

"A helluva lot less than a fatal car wreck, plus it removes any threat from connecting those two. I could probably arrange that for less than five K. You name the city; I'll start it in motion. Name the date and hotel, I'll make it happen." Angelo was completely on board to the point of obvious enthusiasm. Dan had delivered a solution to what Angelo saw as one of those opportunities for problems.

"I did some computer stalking this morning. He's flying a three-day trip with overnights in Miami and Cancun."

Angelo beamed. "Ha! Miami I could probably make happen this afternoon for a thousand."

"Perfect. Next Thursday, Skytrail Suites on South Beach. He gets in the hotel about 7:00 P.M. I have a pic of that douchebag on my phone."

"Text it to me. So now you only need to get your account to a hundred grand, and good news is, that hit on Sal paid better because it was high profile on a made guy. Payout was fifty thousand, so you're suddenly halfway there."

"That's good, that's real good, Angelo."

"Listen, you should be getting an email very soon with a destination. Get there as soon as you can. This is a rush job, and it's personal. The package will explain, but let's just say it's someone in the family, so I can't use any of my people, and I can't use people in the target city either. It pays twenty-five G's."

Just then the entrees arrived at the table. The two men had hardly touched the appetizers. The waiter again skillfully laid the table out, then disappeared into the kitchen.

"Okay, Angelo, when I get the email, I'll follow the procedure and get the overnight as soon as I can."

"Please do that for me, flyboy. You'll understand later why I appreciate any speed you can give this."

"Will do, Angelo, will do. If it's important to you, it's important to me."

The two men finished their dinner over small talk. Angelo told stories about his first hit, and some interesting stories about times when hits didn't go as planned. What he didn't do is ask Dan for any pilot stories. Dan had joined a fraternity with a limited membership, where some subjects can't be discussed outside the fraternity. Clearly, Angelo was now more comfortable talking about himself and the organization, and this was not lost on Dan.

At the conclusion of dinner, the men said their farewells, and Dan exited the room. He was very much looking forward to opening those doors and seeing Sindee across the room. He was not disappointed with Sindee's floor-length, flowing white dress. She was perfectly made up seated at a bar stool, fire-engine red four-inch heels at the end of silky crossed legs. Every man in the place had imagined themselves with her. Dan crushed them all by walking up to her and giving her a kiss on her deep red lips. "You look beautiful today. Truly stunning. I'll bet I can guess what you're wearing under that dress."

"Oh no, I bet you can't, but you're about to find out."

26

Dan had discovered quickly that crawling on the ground created more sound and took way more effort than just walking slowly in a crouch. By carefully placing each foot and lifting each foot, he was able to move nearly silently on what was mostly sand. He controlled his breathing so as to be able to hear as much as possible.

The activity in the camp had ceased almost completely. Dan guessed that that meant most or all of the soldiers were sleeping. No doubt someone would have drawn night watch duty, but if Dan was lucky, that guy was sleeping too. He continued to approach, and at about fifty feet, Dan paused in a crouch to survey the missile site and see if he was close enough to size up the assets that made up the camp. No such luck. There just wasn't enough ambient light to make out the bulk of the encampment. All he could see from that distance were dark outlines, then the sudden flicker of a lighter followed by the glow of a cigarette. *Pretty good light discipline. Moving around the camp will give me more intel on the layout.*

He slowly raised up from his crouch and turned ninety degrees to his right. At a low, slow, and methodical walk in an arc around the camp, he maintained his fifty-foot distance from whatever he could make out. Dan was beginning to feel like time was running out, and he didn't have an elegant plan for what he knew he needed to do when the inevitable sunrise came.

With a distance of maybe one hundred feet covered, something new came into his view. What was clearly an old school army tent was set up on the edge of the camp. Dan had been moving in an arc around the outside of the camp, which was set up roughly in a circle. If the soldiers had been maintaining complete light discipline, Dan probably wouldn't have made out the tent at all in the darkness. But at least a few of the men inside had some sort of illumination going. It wasn't bright by any means, but in the total darkness it was enough to make out some of its features.

He couldn't tell if it was square or rectangular, but the side he was looking at was roughly twenty-five feet long. *Even if that thing is rectangular, its plenty big enough for a dozen guys. I only counted seven, but I gotta assume there could be more.* It appeared that the tent had a single entrance facing the center of the camp. Dan knew that catching those guys sleeping would be a much better situation than a seven-to-one gunfight in the daylight.

While surveying the situation, and desperately searching his brain for a plan, a thought occurred to Dan. *If I were in command of this position, how would I allocate resources? How would I assign guard duty?* He surmised that with only seven men in that position, putting two men at a time on night patrol was not possible.

I would probably cut night duty in half, have one man on late duty, and then have an early morning shift that ends at daybreak when I would need all hands on deck. Seven guys is a pretty low number for what would need to be done to operate this position, and likely the missile guys aren't foot soldiers.

A plan began to gel in Dan's mind, but it wasn't concrete yet. He was moving again now, trying to get a different angle on the tent when two things occurred nearly simultaneously. He bumped into a sizeable rock, and his nose picked up a horrid smell. The rock was about sixteen inches high, flat on top and maybe a two-foot oval-shape from the feel of it. The smell told him immediately it was being used as a latrine. He hadn't smelled it before, as the breeze was taking the smell away from the camp.

They probably checked the prevailing wind before they chose that rock. *That's what I'd do.*

Moving away from the rock seemed like a good idea, so Dan retraced his last twenty-five steps, counting them as he went. When he got to twenty-five, with the stride he was taking, he estimated he was fifty feet from the rock. His attention was drawn to the sound of two men talking. Light was coming from the entrance of the tent, making visible the forms of two men having a friendly conversation in a language he didn't understand. After a short exchange of words, the man facing the tent tried to hand his AK-47 and battle vest to the man facing out of the tent doorway. The man in the doorway was holding a cup in his hand. Downing the rest of its contents, he disappeared in the tent long enough to put it away. When he reappeared, he took the rifle and the vest, and stepped into the darkness. Dan saw the first man give him a pat on the back as he went past him and into the tent.

Changing of the guard.

. . .

Abdul-Ahmad Brahimi got his first stripe just before they left the base to find a site in the desert for their SAMs. Being given a stripe of rank promoted him from Jundiun to Jundiun Awwal. That would be roughly equivalent to going from Private to Private First Class in the U.S. Army. That stripe gave Brahimi his choice of guard patrol that night. He chose the early morning shift, and to let Jundiun Awad handle the late-night shift. Brahimi preferred to try to sleep a little early, then get up before his shift and have a strong coffee.

Brahimi had risen as planned, rolled out of his cot, and made his coffee. He missed bitterly the coffee he drank in his home; a mixture of coffee, cinnamon, and other spices that was his personal recipe. All he had managed to bring with him was some cinnamon, which reminded him of his home coffee, but in a disappointing way. He was most of the way through his coffee when he decided to step out of the tent door and get a feel for the temperature and breeze. It was as he expected: chilly and just a light breeze.

With what felt like maybe a quarter of a cup left, he stood there and greeted Awad, who was obviously tired. Awad could hardly wait to get into his cot, and on seeing Brahimi, he offered him his rifle and battle vest.

"Just a moment, brother," Brahimi said to Awad. Brahimi downed the rest of the coffee, put his cup away in the tent, then stepped out to take the items from Awad. "All quiet out there tonight, my friend. Try to keep it that way. I need to sleep."

It was only half a joke by Awad, as he was completely exhausted. The officer in charge was a seemingly always angry man, who received his rank mostly because he came from a family of means and was not at all liked by the men in his charge. He had mustered his men late in the night to announce that a U.S. warplane had been gloriously shot down by a SAM battery, and the aircraft had crashed about five miles away. There was no way to tell where the pilot was, and so they should be on the lookout. To a man, they thought the officer was crazy, wasting their time forcing them in formation when Awad should be napping and the rest enjoying time without duties.

Yeah. A pilot with maybe a pistol is going to attack our position and capture our missiles? Idiot, Awad thought as he stepped out into the darkness, having loosely donned the battle vest, and slinging the rifle over his right shoulder. The battle vest offered no protection to the soldier but did allow one man to comfortably carry four extra rifle magazines, and four hand grenades. It could be loaded much more heavily, but in those early morning hours, that was the load it contained. He then went into the next part of his morning routine; walking in the direction of the rock that was now made necessary by the strong, disappointing coffee. In his pocket were a few wet wipes, a veritable luxury item that he had managed to bring with him.

. . .

Dan saw the exchange, then watched the soldier gear up and walk away from the tent. At first, backlit by the tent, it looked like the soldier was walking right at him. In his crouch, Dan's right hand found the hand-grip of the Beretta, and he flicked the safety off. He was about to unsnap the holster when he noticed that the movement of the soldier slowly changed to more of a left-to-right direction. Now that the soldier was shining a weak flashlight on the ground in front of him as he walked, it was obvious where he was going.

Of course. Coffee in this part of the world is strong. This could work out well.

27

The airport Crowne seemed as good a place as any, and that is exactly where Dan and Sindee headed. All heads were on Sindee as she glided out of Vincent's, just like they were all on her in the lobby of the Crowne. Dan paid with cash—he had plenty of that now—and he gave the guy at the front desk $100 to make sure someone else's name was on the room. Covering his tracks seemed like a good idea. He knew that being a separated or divorcing husband made him an automatic suspect in any foul play involving the wife. *I'm not going to give her any reason to divorce me, and no one is going to find out about Ed*, he thought.

That was the last thought Dan would have about Sharon for at least the next three hours. To both Dan and Sindee, the elevator ride to the tenth floor seemed to last forever. They decided to pass the time by kissing in a way that only reunited lovers do. When the elevator doors opened, they were still in each other's arms. An older hotel worker, certainly someone's mother, was standing there waiting to load her room-cleaning cart into the elevator. She smiled, her head tilting to the side as if she had just seen true love. The couple laughed through a hello and made their way to the room.

Dan first, and then Sindee, entered the room and walked past the king-sized bed to the window. While Dan took in the view, what he couldn't see on his right was Sindee unbuttoning the front of her dress. When she'd undone the proper number of buttons, her dress hit the floor, and Dan turned to take in that new view. He surveyed her form from the floor to her beautiful face, which was now looking at him from over her left shoulder. He gazed at the red heels, white stockings with a line up the back, white garter bustier, strapless on the top, and of course she still had the white ribbon in her hair. Missing was any kind of panties.

She is beautiful and she clearly prepared for this moment just for me. The thought, in more than a few different ways, further excited an already overly aroused Dan.

Dan stammered, "Wow, baby, just wow. I don't have words."

"You don't need words, flyboy. Just come over here and give me what *I* need."

. . .

Ed opened the hotel room door where he and Sharon had spent the morning and part of the afternoon. The airport Crown was their favorite meeting hotel because it was in between Sharon's neighborhood and the airport. As Chief Pilot, Ed would occasionally call the office to tell them he would be late in the morning, something he'd done after sleeping at Sharon's. But today was special. It was Ed's day off, so he and Sharon could enjoy themselves sneaking around behind Dan while he was in town. So, Sharon grabbed her gym bag early that morning to get in a "workout."

Their room was close to the elevator; Ed looked down the hallway both ways. All he saw was a beautiful, blonde woman in a floor-length, flowing dress disappearing behind a closing door. There was a maid pushing her cart onto the elevator. *Perfect timing*, he thought. He took a few steps and put his hand on the elevator door to hold it open. As Sharon entered the elevator, the doors closed behind her. Ed said "good afternoon" to the maid. She simply smiled at the couple, exactly the way she had just smiled at Dan and Sindee.

. . .

Nico peeled a one-hundred-dollar bill off a roll of bills, then put the bill on Angelo's desk. "I got your hundred right here, Angelo. No. Fucking. Way did I believe that guy would go through with it!"

Angelo collected the bill with a smile of victory. "You gotta trust me, Nico. You can't get to where I am without bein' a good, no, a *great* judge of character. We ain't in the business of making pizzas. If you figure a guy wrong, give him something important to do, you can get into real trouble."

Nico was one of Angelo's lieutenants, a trusted man in Angelo's operation. "I gotta hand it to you, Angelo. That was an amazing call. First fucking time, and he up and whacks Sal the Fist. I dunno, that's got to be some kind of outfit record!"

Nico was waiting in Angelo's office when he returned from lunch with Dan. Nico was the only person Angelo trusted enough to be let into his home when he was away. Nico was like family to Angelo, but that afternoon, they had business to discuss, and he had set a meeting with Angelo. Nico had bet Angelo one hundred dollars that Dan didn't have the balls to go through with the hit. When you owe the boss, you pay the boss. When they finished discussing that particular business, Angelo looked at Nico with a serious look that Nico immediately picked up on.

Angelo made direct eye contact. "I'll tell you one more thing about my flyboy, and this stays between you and me."

"Of course, Angelo, of course."

"He was walking out of Sal's suite, and there was thirty G's sitting all wrapped up nice and neat on the coffee table. He took it. Then, when he and I met at Vincent's not two hours ago, he slides ten G's in a wrapper across the table and says, 'here is your tribute.' That is what I mean by his character. Not only does he go through with it, see the money, take the money that I don't know about, but he offers tribute to me!" Nico noticed the gestures delivered by Angelo as he related his assessment of Dan. Clearly, Angelo felt as if he had stumbled onto something valuable.

Angelo let that sink in for a moment. After a pause, Nico offered his take. "Boss, that is *respect*. Real respect. I gotta say, I'm blown away. This guy, not even Italian, could be rare."

"He is rare, Nico. And he is mine."

. . .

"I think I'm going to stay in the room and get ready for work here. The outfit I wore today, it's new, and I bought it just for you." Sindee's voice was a mixture of emotion and satisfaction.

The two lovers were nose-to-nose in bed, still coming down from the high they were both feeling. After a brief silence, Dan spoke. "That's very sweet of you, and I love the ensemble. You are so very stunningly beautiful. I've been thinking, and I want to talk about the club. What would it take to replace your income from the club."

Sindee pursed her lips in a smile and said, "Oh, lover, I knew this moment would come. You want to take care of me. But I like making my own money, and I like the way I make it."

"Of course you do. But like most pilots, I would like some legitimate side business. I would like someone I trust to run it. And I want you in my life, I mean really in my life. That will be possible soon. I won't be able to support you completely just yet, but soon. Just want you to think about it."

"I will, Dan, I will. I... I'm... I don't know how to say this, but I think, I really want to be in your life too."

Dan visibly relaxed. "Okay, sweetheart. Let's talk about this later. For now, I just want to feel you in my arms for a few minutes more. You really bought that outfit just for me?"

Sindee beamed. "Of course! I must have tried on a dozen different combinations."

"Next time, I want to be there for that." The words could have been taken as Dan flirting, but his face and voice were serious.

Sindee's smile was ear to ear. "Of course, my lover. In the meantime, one more time, baby?"

"Oh, anything for you, beautiful."

◦ ◦ ◦

The goodbye in the room doorway was hard for the two of them, harder than ever before. Both of them came from backgrounds missing dimensions of love that most other people took for granted. Both of them had holes in their hearts that neither of them was even fully aware of nor had any idea how to fill. They weren't looking but had found each other, and their lives had begun to intertwine elegantly and passionately. What each did know was that both of their lives had changed direction, and that the new direction each took was a little scary, very exciting, and felt like suddenly discovering their location after being lost for a long time.

When Dan whispered "I love you" to Sindee, he knew he was baring the most vulnerable part of himself to her. So when Sindee whispered "I love you too" to Dan, both of them had a visible, relieved, joyous calm flow over them. The new direction of their lives was parallel—for now— but soon those lines would begin to draw closer.

28

The high-back chair at the desk in his office was something Dan purchased for himself. He spent quite a bit of money on it, but it was worth every penny to Dan. Most of his office time was spent paying bills or doing something work-related, which was enough of a pain in the ass already. No sense sitting in an uncomfortable chair doing it. When he eased into the chair this time, he booted up his desktop and checked his email. As Angelo had said, there was an email waiting for him from the travel agency.

The title read: *"Get away for a weekend in Colorado Springs!"*

"Okay, Colorado Springs it is." Dan opened a new browser window and looked over all the trips in "open time." The airport he was looking for has a three-letter code of COS, but he wasn't finding any trips open with that code. His airline operated several types of aircraft, and after a bit of digging he realized that his aircraft didn't do any overnights in Springs. There was, however, a three-day trip leaving in two days that overnighted in Denver, and it was a long overnight. The pilots were scheduled to be in the hotel for just over 20 hours. Springs wasn't even an hour away by car.

The necessary keystrokes were entered to indicate his desire to trade the present trip on his schedule with that one. A tap of the Enter key submitted the trade request, and the trip trade went through. Dan followed the protocol by inquiring about a ticket to Denver on the day of the overnight. He logged onto the travel agency website, then inputted the flight and hotel requests. That done, he went back to the travel email to see if it had any other clues in it. The last line caught his attention.

If your trip is in May, remember to dress warm, because it can still get cold there in the spring!

Dan heard the electronic lock on the back door opening. Sharon walked in carrying her gym bag. With the look and sound of someone mildly startled, she said "Hey, you're home. I was just working out. Whatcha doin'?"

"Just working with my schedule, trying to trade a few trips. I didn't like this next trip, so I traded for a three-day that leaves the day after tomorrow." Dan turned his attention back to the computer.

"I'm meeting friends for margaritas later. Probably gonna be a late night, so don't wait up. Amanda wants to go over her wedding plans with us."

Without taking his eyes off the computer screen, he said, "Okay, the Rangers are playing anyway. Gonna catch the game."

Wedding plans my ass. Ed is flying a trip tomorrow, and you want some action since he's going to be away. Dan heard the bedroom door close from his expensive chair. His focus returned to the task at hand, gaming out the situation as far as he had been informed. He tipped his chair all the way back and stared at the ceiling.

Colorado Springs? Not exactly a mob haven. Well, then again, how the fuck would I know? Those guys are probably in every big city. "In the family"? As in, his actual family, the crime family, or what? "Dress warm," so, maybe I will be outside. "Rush job," so, time critical. Angelo said the explanation would be in the package. For now, I guess I just pack my bag knowing I might be outside in the cold. Maybe...

Turning back to his computer, Dan called up the open time again. *If Angelo was wanting to get this done ASAP, maybe I should see if there are other Denver overnights in open time, just in case this one doesn't work out*. He hadn't noticed that the sky outside the window behind him had suddenly turned very dark. It was late afternoon in Texas, nearly pushing six, and in the spring, severe weather could literally grow up rapidly into tornado-producing thunderstorms in very short order. He had music playing on the speakers attached to his computer and had missed the first few rumbles of thunder. The loud boom of a close lightning strike made him jump a bit.

Hell, I didn't even know we were supposed to get weather today. It boomed again, and Dan's thoughts were distracted by the mental image of Sharon and Ed, illuminated in the flashes of lightning on the night his life changed. Each successive crash of thunder took his demeanor lower; it built toward a seething anger. The dark part of him wanted to walk into the bedroom and kill her right then and be done with it. The storm, which was now pouring rain on his house, was clearly a very active thunderstorm, and he knew he'd be hearing peals of thunder for an hour. Dan knew that replaying that night in his head right now was not a good thing.

Dan forcefully pushed his chair away from his desk. *Fuck it! This will all be done soon enough, I'll have Sindee, Ed will have nothing, and Sharon will be history. I'm done in the office. I'm going to pack my bag and grab a scotch on the way to the bedroom.*

There was a well-stocked bar in a room adjacent to the kitchen, able to handle a small party as is. But anyone looking at it for more than a few seconds would know the preferred liquor of the owner. There were three large bottles of daily drinking scotch. Five other bottles of twelve-, or twenty-four-year-old scotch varieties. Dan's choice for his first drink that evening would be an aged highland scotch. He poured a healthy amount into an iced glass and headed for the bedroom.

In the corner of the bedroom was Dan's rollaway suitcase, his overnight bag. He threw it on the chair, opened the main compartment, and unpacked the clothes from the previous trip. When it was ready to be packed, Dan put the clothing into it in the formula he used for a three-day trip. He considered digging some thermal underwear out of the closet, but then decided he would trust that his package would provide him anything he needed. *Guess I'm going to need new athletic shoes for my bag.*

Sharon finished her shower and walked into the bedroom naked. Dan acted as if he was absorbed in the task at hand, so he paid her no attention. That annoyed Sharon, who was working out daily to keep her body as sexually attractive as she could. Despite the fact that Ed saw her naked more than her husband did, the longer Dan ignored her, the more it pissed her off. She continued taking articles of clothing out of the dresser but put none of them on, waiting for some reaction. Sharon opened the bottom drawer of the dresser, rummaged through it for a long time, and acted as if she was looking for something. Her pose was bent at the waist, feet a foot apart; she swayed from left to right as she searched. Dan knew exactly what she was doing, so when Sharon turned to look at Dan, he had his back to her.

Sharon slammed the drawer closed and padded off into the walk-in closet. Dan could see from the stride that she was pissed. He chuckled, zipped his bag closed, and headed to the living room with the scotch in his right hand. He sat down on the couch, picked up the TV remote with his left, and powered up the TV. Practiced fingers had the sports channel on in less than a minute. *One last thing to do.* He placed the remote and the scotch on the end table, took his cell phone out of his front pocket, and before the batter was struck out, ordered some shoes for his bag, next day delivery.

29

There was a chair in Angelo's office, not unlike Dan's, and it, too, was comfortable because Angelo had to spend a considerable amount of time in it. It cost twice what Dan's cost, but to Angelo it was chump change. Angelo felt that the office and how it was appointed spoke to the character and power of the person who worked there. The head of any major corporation would find his office befitting and well-equipped.

Angelo was the head of a large organization; he was similar in many ways to a CEO in the private sector. Some of their business duties and tasks were similar, some very different. The business of organized crime required people who possessed a specialized skill set, training, and experience, just as a pharmaceutical company, or an insurance company would.

Nico was again in Angelo's office. They met regularly to discuss business in Angelo's office. He preferred face-to-face meetings when possible and secure. Angelo's IT guy had long ago made him understand just how vulnerable cell phones were to surveillance. He was also a voracious multi-tasker, a skill required for any person in his position to be successful. From his high-back chair, Angelo often asked questions without looking up from what he was studying at the moment. "Did you get a chance to work on that project I gave you, the thing you know with our new friend?"

"Uh, yeah, boss. My guy pretty much has her schedule and her patterns all figured out. She's banging that guy from the airport pretty regular. Oh yeah, about that. You might want to let our new friend know that he and his wife are using the same hotel for the same reason. Tell him the airport Crowne sooner or later will lead to an awkward moment in the lobby."

"No shit? *Both* of them?" Angelo laughed out loud.

"Per my guy. They missed each other by seconds."

"I'll tell him. What else you got?"

Nico continued. "They regularly meet at the hotel when Dan's in town—sometimes morning, sometimes night—and don't leave until late, like maybe eleven, if it's at night. I'm thinking mugging gone wrong in the parking lot for her. She parks in the back, cameras are not good back there, especially at night. We do her, take her purse, do it while fly-boy is on a trip, and the security video will show why she was there and who she was fucking."

Angelo sat back and thought it over. He liked to try to visualize all the angles. There was something about this he wasn't sure about. "Does she do anything else routinely?"

"She goes to this gym to work out pretty regular. Usually first thing, or in the early afternoon."

Angelo took a long pause to organize his thoughts and scrutinize the plan. "Okay, here's what I'm thinking. Flyboy is going to be paid up pretty soon. Maybe even in the next couple weeks. Doing her now at the hotel exposes that she's fuckin' some other guy. That guy becomes a loose end in this operation. We are set to take care of that guy in Miami in a few days. We do him right, he's out of the picture. However, now the wife is no longer going to the hotel. Let's take care of the guy first, then work up a carjacking gone wrong at the gym. How's the neighborhood around the gym?"

Nico's ability to recall fine detail quickly was one of the qualities that had gotten his high position in Angelo's organization. "Next to a Home Depot on one side, open field on the other, on a six-lane street. She parks her BMW a distance from the building, so the cameras won't show a lot of detail."

"Okay, work it up so we have someone to whack her in the lot, take the car, and we have our own witness to give the cops a statement. Have one of our guys, no make it a woman, get a gym membership there so she can be the 'officer, I saw the whole thing' for us. You see any holes in this, Nico?"

"No, sir, you know me. If I thought there was a hole in the plan, I wouldn't have brought it to you. I bring solutions. You got it, boss. I'll get everything in place in the next few days. You just tell me when, and I'll make it happen. You need me for whacking the boyfriend?"

"Oh no, Nico. Our new friend has something *way* worse for him. I got it covered."

Angelo's voice had taken on an ominous tone, and he could see that Nico was curious. One of the things that Angelo valued in Nico that made him a good lieutenant was that Nico knew not to ask questions about stuff he wasn't supposed to know.

"Thanks for reminding me, Nico. I gotta make a call about that. Can you go get a coffee or something while I do that?" That was Angelo telling Nico he needed privacy.

"Sure thing, boss." Nico stood up and headed toward the kitchen. He was rewarded by the sight of Angelo's housekeeper bent over the sink, doing some dishes. She saw Nico staring at her ass and smiled at him.

When Angelo was sure Nico was busy with what he found in the kitchen, he selected and picked up the right phone. "Looks like we're all set for that thing I asked you about. You ready for this? Okay great. I will get word right away when it's done. You and I can talk, uh, later. You'll get all the details. I'm sure you're curious about it right now, but for now, you know everything you need. Just understand this is important to me, *capiche?*"

Click.

Angelo nodded as he let out a long breath. *Dan is one cool customer, one cold motherfucker. Should I be thinking long-term about this guy?*

. . .

Nico stepped onto the back patio overlooking a sprawling backyard with woods behind, and he drew the cell phone from his back pocket. He scrolled down his Recent Calls and selected a number. Hearing it dial, he put the phone to his ear.

"Yeah?" One of Nico's men.

Nico didn't share his boss' distaste for cell phones. "Change of plans, from the boss. Set it up for the gym, carjacking gone wrong. Get one of your girls a gym membership there today, and I mean today, so when this happens, she can be a witness for the cops. Don't fuck this up; it's important."

"You got it, Nico, I'll make it happen. It will all be in place by this afternoon."

. . .

Only a few miles away, Dan was picking up some uniforms from the cleaners.

Big trip tomorrow.

A few miles from Dan, Ed was also at his dry cleaners picking up some of his uniforms. He didn't think it was a big trip for him, but he had no idea.

30

The routine that Dan followed for getting out the door for a trip was surprisingly similar to Ed's. But then, airline pilots in general have similar practices. The operation of a large aircraft like Dan's Boeing 737 is done using checklists. Dan had his own checklist for making sure he had everything he needed with him before he left the house on a trip. Checklist completed, he headed toward his truck. Ed completed his and headed toward his BMW. When each of them next returned to their homes, their lives would be very different.

Dan arrived at employee parking just like he had a thousand times before, as did Ed. They both unloaded their bags from their vehicles and walked toward the bus stop. It was some kind of fate that had them both walking up to the bus stop at the same time. It was some kind of irony that Dan knew more about Ed's trip than Ed did.

"Holy shit, is that Ed in a *pilot* uniform, dragging an overnight bag to the bus?" Dan's sarcasm was dripping.

"Yes, Captain Hatfield, I need to step down from the lofty perch of the chief pilot's office occasionally to fly in order to stay current on the airplane, but then you know that."

"So soon from the last one? Poor guy." Already knowing the answer, Dan asked, "Where are you off to?"

"Miami, then Charlotte."

You'll never see Charlotte, motherfucker. Enjoy the Miami-Dade lockup.

"Off to Tulsa and then Denver. Out of D Terminal." The D terminal bus pulled up to the bus stop, and Dan took hold of the handle of his bag, prepared to board the bus.

"I'm out of A Terminal. Take it easy, have a good trip, Dan."

"You too, Ed."

Dan dragged his bag onto the D terminal employee bus and found a seat. *What the fuck is the chance of that?* he thought as he sat down. *Running into that motherfucker, today of all days?*

Ed watched Dan drag his bag on the bus and he thought *What the fuck is the chance of running into Dan? It's almost sad how clueless he is. Almost.*

. . .

Walking up to his gate in D terminal, Dan was greeted by his entire crew. They were all ready to go, and Dan recognized a few familiar faces. He had flown with a few of the flight attendants before to be sure, and he had also done a few trips with the first officer. There were warm greetings all around, and Dan settled into the routine he was so familiar with.

A little later, Ed arrived at his gate. Only the first officer was there, who appeared a bit tentative since he noticed on the computer the letters next to Ed's name. He was going to be flying with one of the chief pilots. Ed was aware that this dynamic could be somewhat unnerving for whomever he was paired with. Any normal first officer, upon seeing the name of a chief pilot on their schedule, would be understandably nervous. Ed always tried to disarm that right away by bringing it up in the first encounter.

"Hey, I'm just getting in my currency flying, and since I don't fly all the time like you do, please try to keep me out of trouble, okay?"

It worked, and Ed's first officer said, "Okay, you got it." Too bad the FO wouldn't be around for Ed when the real trouble went down.

. . .

It was a short flight to Tulsa, and a long enough overnight that dinner or drinks was entirely possible. On the van ride to the hotel, the first officer asked Dan if he had plans. Dan was feeling like he didn't really want company that evening. He had a lot on his mind, pulling his thoughts in several directions, and the idea of just chilling in the room was appealing. "It's been, well, let's call it an interesting few days for me. How about we plan on doing something in Denver, on me. Tonight, I think, it's room service and Netflix for me."

"Okay, you got it, Cap. Denver it is."

. . .

"I'm going to be changed and downstairs fifteen minutes after we get rooms." Ed was still trying to fit in.

Ed's first officer was tempted by the statement but chose the path of least risk. "Oh, I have to call the wife, and then I have some bills to pay. I'll just see you at van time tomorrow."

Ed was not phased. "Okay, if you change your mind, drinks are on me."

"Thanks, captain, I appreciate it. Maybe in Charlotte."

"Yeah, Charlotte."

Not ten minutes after being handed a room key card, Ed was walking into the hotel bar. He noticed immediately the beautiful blonde sitting at the bar alone. She was looking at her phone, the same way everyone else in the bar was looking at their phones. What she was looking at was a picture of Ed.

. . .

This is going to be an easy grand. I do this right, I don't even need to screw him, she thought.

Ed took a seat at the bar that left one seat empty between him and the blonde. In front of her sat a glass that had been mostly empty for a half hour while she waited for Ed to arrive. It was an invitation to buy her a drink, a move she had used many times before. When the bartender asked him what he'd like, he took the bait.

"I'd like a bourbon on the rocks, and I'd *like* to buy this beautiful woman whatever she's drinking." Ed was doing his best to be smooth.

She flashed him a surprised smile, gave him a warm greeting and turned in her chair to face him. A few drinks later, she pulled out another move, switching chairs to sit right next to Ed. He took it as a good sign. She just needed to close the distance so she could surreptitiously dump a vial of liquid in his drink when he wasn't paying attention.

31

The first sensation that registered in Ed's brain the next morning was a pounding headache. His head hurt so badly, he almost couldn't believe it. He ran his hands over his skull, checking to make sure it was in one piece, then tried to recall his surroundings. Ed could not immediately remember what city he was in, something not at all uncommon for airline crewmembers as they travel. This time, however, it was chemically induced.

Ed was becoming aware that the room was very bright, meaning he hadn't closed the shades last night. He had a sudden, shocking thought. *Wait. What is the van time today?*

His key card was sitting on the table next to the TV, along with its little paper envelope. The van time is usually written on the key card, and Ed saw *12:25 van* neatly printed on the envelope. Next, Ed searched for his phone. Cell phones always have the correct local time on them; they are the trusted source of actual time in a business that requires hopping through multiple time zones. The phone was on the nightstand where he routinely left it before going to bed. *Oh my GOD, it's 12:03!*

Despite the debilitating headache, Ed knew if he was going to make van time he was going to have to hurry. His body went on autopilot, going through all the actions required to leave the hotel room and head to the airport van downstairs. Focusing on the urgent task at hand left his brain a little time to think, to try to reconstruct his evening, but he just couldn't seem to remember much. There was the hotel bar, the beautiful blonde, a few drinks, and nothing after that.

Ed entered the bathroom with shaver in hand and stared for a few seconds at the red, lace panties sitting on the vanity. *That would explain those. So, she was here, and maybe we did something. Why the FUCK can't I remember anything?!*

The hotel room morning routine was one Ed had accomplished hundreds, maybe a thousand times. Even in his present state, all that practice had him walking onto an elevator, dragging his bags behind him at 12:24 P.M. The rest of his crew were already in the van when he got there. It took some serious acting skills to play the part of a pilot who was alert, well-rested, and not the bearer of a skull-splitting headache. Ed searched his phone during the van ride for something, anything that may be a clue about the evening prior and when it ended.

The video from the bar camera that was evidence at his later trial would show that he left the bar when it closed at 2:05 A.M. Sadly, it wouldn't show the face of the woman he was with, who was not identified.

As they all got out of the van, Ed decided that a few sticks of gum might be a good idea, since he was no closer to remembering anything more than he did the moment he woke.

It wasn't an unusual sight at all and when he first saw them, Ed thought nothing of it. A couple of Miami-Dade police officers standing in the wide terminal hallway. Ed and his crew went through the crewmember checkpoint; as Ed passed, the security officer turned and pointed at him. The police officers had tactically positioned themselves inside the terminal at a location that allowed them to see the checkpoint and the security officer manning it. The flight attendant in line behind Ed thought the gesture was odd and out-of-the-ordinary.

It was. It's not every day that someone phones in a tip that they saw an airline pilot drinking heavily, and possibly doing drugs in a hotel bar until early morning. It was very helpful that the tipster had overheard the pilot say his name, and that she remembered the name he said. That and the physical description made it very easy to identify, detain, and arrest Ed at the airport. The police officers were not all that surprised to see the local news camera crew.

By the time Ed was taken to a holding cell, his airline had already informed the pilot union and all the news people calling for comment that Ed was a *former* employee and that he had been fired.

. . .

Sharon was a social media butterfly. Having a heavy social media appetite went hand-in-hand with her superficial nature. A few of those media platforms had areas dedicated to aviation and the airlines. Surfing those sites was a great way to pass the time while running on a treadmill or stationary biking. A headline caught her attention:

Airline pilot arrested in MIA had blood alcohol level three times legal limit—Blue Sky Airlines spokesman says he has been fired.

It took just a moment for Sharon to recall that Ed was overnighting in Miami. *Maybe he's helping handle it, but I doubt it since he is a chief in Dallas.* Someone commenting in the social media thread included a link to a local Miami news station. Sharon clicked the link, and there was a video box at the top. *Maybe I'll recognize him.*

With voiceover by a news anchor, the video clearly showed a pilot from the back, his hands being cuffed by the two officers at either side of him. One of the officers then took the pilot's hat from his head and handed it to another pilot. After a few seconds, all three men turned around to leave the terminal. The pilot had his head down; the officers were holding his arms to lead him out. As the trio got close to the news camera, the pilot looked right at it, surprised, and a look of horror spread across a face that Sharon recognized immediately.

She was shaken for a moment, trying not to fall off the still-moving treadmill. Tears immediately welled up in eyes that searched for the door of the gym. Sharon exited the gym quickly, leaving her prized gym bag laying on the floor next to her treadmill. She opened the unlocked door of her BMW and proceeded to scream and sob for the next hour before she could gain enough composure to re-enter the gym and retrieve her bag.

. . .

Dan woke that morning alert, well-rested, and free from any kind of headache. He was curious as to how Ed's morning was going. Tulsa is a time zone behind Miami, so the 8:30 A.M. he was looking at on his phone was 9:30 A.M. in Miami. Since Dan's van time was just after 10:00 A.M. in Tulsa, he decided he would get the news in Dallas, or after he landed in Denver.

For Dan, the routine of leaving the hotel would also be completely different from Ed's panic experience. It was a completely uneventful arrival at the airport, flight to DFW, then switch to a different airplane in Dallas. His first officer had just completed the preflight walk-around inspection of the exterior and was walking into the cockpit when Dan heard both his phone and his first officer's phone blow up with notifications.

"Holy fucking shit, Dan, one of our captains got arrested in Miami for DUI, *at the fucking terminal.*"

"Are you looking at a news article? Does it say who he is?" Dan was going to have to do a bit of acting.

"Holy shit. It's Ed Ronkowski from the DFW chief office!"

"Oh my God, I've known Ed for a long time, we go way back. He's a friend. Oh my God." Dan was acting to an audience of one.

"His life is over."

The poker skills of Dan now came into play. Hearing the first officer say that almost forced a smile onto Dan's face. Almost.

32

The flight from Dallas to Denver is not particularly long, and Dan knew that he was going to have a job to do when he got there. It's a two-hour flight that crossed a time zone, and therefore it gained an hour. So, the 2:00 P.M. Dallas departure arrived at around 3:00 P.M. Denver time. By 4:00 P.M. he'd be in a hotel room. Judging by Indianapolis, by 4:30 P.M. he'd be reading the package instructions. Even though they didn't leave the hotel until late afternoon the next day, from Angelo's description of it being a "rush job," Dan guessed he would be going to work on it in just a few hours.

Just like Indy, Dan heard the knock on his bedroom door while he was peeling off the uniform. Sporting a mask and ball cap, the man was standing outside Dan's door holding a full paper grocery bag stapled at the top. Dan silently took the bag, and the man left the same way. When the door closed, Dan set the extra locks on the door as a precaution and turned toward the bed.

Having no idea what's in the bag, Dan opened it carefully and emptied its contents on the bed one item at a time. Inside was thermal underwear, top and bottom. A jacket meant for cold temperatures. A light blue T-shirt, mask, and baseball cap. Last were the instructions. Dan got a sudden tinge of shock, as there were no pistol, magazines, or suppressor. *Did they forget something?*

Instructions in hand, Dan read aloud to himself.

"This will be an outside operation, and it is still cold here in the Denver area. Put on the thermal underwear first, then your long pants, the provided T-shirt, mask, hat, and jacket. At 5:00 P.M., an unmarked gray van will be parked outside the stairwell exit door. Plan it so you are walking out the door exactly at 5:00 P.M. The van will not wait."

I'm on the fourth floor, so I should leave the room about 4:56 P.M., Dan thought, planning the time carefully.

"Get in the van through the large door on the side. In the van, you will find all the other materials you will need. You will be changing into winter, woodland-style, camouflage hunting clothes. Boots will be there as well. You will be driven to a wooded area where you will exit the vehicle, with the backpack provided. In the right jacket pocket, you will find a compass. Proceed through the woods for about three-quarters of a mile on a heading of 225 degrees."

A field exercise it is.

"You will come to the edge of the woods in the backyard of a white, contemporary house with black roof, pool in the backyard, and jacuzzi to your right. The edge of the woods is a higher elevation, so you will be looking down on the pool. Wait for a man, six foot, two inches, approximately 180 pounds, and completely bald to exit the back door of the house. He will have a cocktail and a cigar, which he smokes on the back patio. Out of sight, remove the crossbow from the backpack. It will already be loaded and charged, on safety. It has an optical scope sight, recently accurized. Put a bolt from the crossbow in his chest. There will be two more bolts attached to the bow, but it's important to the op that you use only one. This will need to look like a stray arrow."

"Retrace your steps and call on your other phone to alert when you will be about five minutes from the drop-off point. Your driver will be alerted and will meet you exactly where you exited the van. Change back into your shirt, jacket, mask, and hat. When you get back to the hotel room, destroy the instructions, put the items in the bag and wait for retrieval."

Time check. 4:45 P.M.

Dan put down his cell phone, and changed into the clothes he would be wearing for the next twenty minutes or so. He didn't want to know too much about what was going on, but he was hoping that Angelo would at least give him a general reason why this guy so badly needed his chest ventilated. Fully dressed, he looked at himself in the mirror and was rewarded by the nondescript look of almost any middle-aged, American, white guy. With the short haircut and the baseball cap, no one would be able to tell what color his hair was.

4:56, time to go.

Dan was thirty seconds early and the van was just pulling up. The side door was unlocked. Dan climbed in, glancing at the driver as he closed the door. He was pretty sure the driver was also the package delivery person, but it didn't really matter. What mattered was the clothing neatly piled on one of the back seats, and the matching woodland winter camo backpack on the floor, leaning on the seat. Not knowing how long he had, Dan started to disrobe right away. *Nice of the driver to make it warm in here.*

Changed in less than five minutes, Dan was tying his boots when the van pulled onto the highway. He guessed there would be plenty of time, so he reached down and opened the zipper on the backpack. Hearing the sound it made, the driver held up a single finger and wagged it, signaling Dan that taking the weapon out of the bag in the van was not a good idea. *Yeah, well, it's a crossbow. How difficult to operate could it be?* He had opened it just enough to see that it was, in fact, ready to fire with a bolt loaded. From just the glance, he could see it was a compound-crossbow, and it looked like a sophisticated one.

About an hour south, almost to Colorado Springs, the van turned off the highway. In just a few minutes, they were driving on a twisting, two-lane road that soon turned into all woodlands. The driver held up two fingers, which Dan assumed meant two minutes. Reviewing the instructions again in his head, he reached into the front right coat pocket and found the compass. Dan zipped up the jacket all the way, put on the backpack, and then the thin but warm Nomex gloves. Last was the elastic ski mask and the warm jacket hood over his head. Dan was ready to bail out of the van.

As the van started to slow, Dan looked out the window for landmarks. He took a mental picture of the bridge fifty yards down the road, and the road sign the driver had stopped nearby. He exited the van, which sped off immediately, and started walking toward the woods with compass in hand. When he got about twenty-five yards into the woods, he knelt and took a bearing from his compass. There were still patches of snow in the woods, and the temperature was in the high thirties. The combination of warm clothes and the walk kept Dan warm for the three-quarter-mile trek.

Just as the instructions said, he saw the woods opening up in front of him about fifty yards ahead. Dan approached the opening, careful to remain unseen. As the terrain dropped off steeply, he got on his hands and knees and crawled up to the edge to survey the landscape below. He had come out of the woods maybe fifty yards to the left of the backyard of a house that perfectly fit the description. The approach was good, as no other houses had a view of his position. Dan backed up into the woods enough that he could move to his right, and not be seen by anyone in the house. He found a good spot at the crest of the hill, which had some brush and what certainly had been a large snowdrift during the winter. Dan removed the crossbow from the bag, and low-crawled to the edge. *Perfect.*

He had just started to feel cold after laying there in wait for maybe a half hour. Dan was looking to the left, trying to figure out exactly where he exited the woods, when he heard a door close. The bald man, tumbler in one hand, and a cigar in the other, took a seat. He set the drink on the table to his right and retrieved a torch lighter from his left pants pocket. Dan had a very clear view through the optical sight on the crossbow.

The planner for this hit was as meticulous as Indy and had used internet maps to determine the range at which Dan would be firing. Not taking wind into account, the reticle crosshairs had been set to exactly where the bolt would be going. Dan's heart was pounding now, and he hadn't even considered the wind. There wasn't any. The man torched his cigar, then looked at the end. Satisfied, he took a thick drag on it and the cloud of smoke verified he had it properly lit. He leaned back in the chair, pocketed the lighter, and took another big drag. Dan let his breath out slowly and squeezed the trigger.

The crossbow leapt in his hands but not as much as he expected. It did make some noise as it fired, but it wouldn't have made any difference to the man on the receiving end. The impact of the bolt in his chest felt like something heavy had been thrown at him and hit him hard. So hard, it knocked the breath out of him, and he was unable to take another. Shock and surprise turned into panic when he saw, and then touched, the end of an arrow sticking three inches out of his chest. He tried to get up but was unable to, as the arrow had exited his back and was sticking into the chair. Dan watched his convulsions quickly growing smaller, until there was no movement.

What Dan didn't know was that the man was home alone because the last beating he delivered to his wife sent her to the hospital. He had no one to call out to, and no one to help him, a situation his vicious temper caused. Dan crawled back to the backpack, loaded the crossbow in it, and started off through the woods to the pickup point. When he first glimpsed the road, he called Angelo on the other phone, and told him he was two minutes from pickup point.

Angelo's voice was all anticipation. "Is it done?"

"Oh yeah. Exactly as per the instructions. Exactly."

"Good job. You'll understand soon."

Click.

. . .

"Is it done? Good job, you'll understand soon." Angelo hung up the phone. *That fuck is never going to lay a hand on my sister again.*

Nico was in Angelo's office; they were drinking wine. "Was that the call? How'd he do? Flyboy came through again?"

"Yeah, left him sitting in a chair by the pool with a serious puncture wound taking the life from him. I looked at the forecast. It's gonna be below freezing there tonight. Who knows when they'll find him, or if they will even be able to determine when he caught the arrow?" Angelo's face had a look of anger and satisfaction. It was a look displaying vengeance.

"That must be a relief, boss. How is your sister doing?"

Angelo's face softened at the mention of his only sister. "They say full recovery, but its gonna take some time. Won't be eating solid food for at least a month. I think we are as clean on this as we are with Sal. This arrangement with Dan is a good one. That thing in Miami, that's done?"

"Oh, it was a beautiful thing, boss. Cameras at the airport too. My guy watching the wife saw her completely lose her shit at the gym. Found out right there on a treadmill."

Angelo was comfortable with retribution. "Good for her."

33

Moving closer to the road, Dan crouched near some brush. He was taking up a concealed position while he waited for the van. Anyone driving by at the speed limit of forty miles per hour would never see him in that camo outfit. He was there maybe two minutes when he heard a vehicle approaching. Looking through the brush, he made out the van as it turned the corner and came to a rapid stop right in front of him. When he stood, he saw surprise on the face of the driver, who had not seen him. Dan jumped in, and they took off.

Now Dan knew he had plenty of time, but it was warm in the van, so he changed his clothes immediately. He unzipped the jacket and the driver held up a large trash bag, which Dan took and filled with all of the clothing. By the time they got to the highway, Dan was in his casual outfit. The driver held up a second bag and pointed at the backpack. Dan put both bags under the bench-style seat in the back of the van and stretched out on the seat. Glancing at the time on his phone, he realized he'd be back at the hotel in plenty of time to have dinner and a few beers with his first officer.

Closing his eyes, he saw in his mind the man losing his life to the arrow in his chest. *Angelo went to a lot of trouble to make this happen. I'm sure there's a good reason, but I'm not going to dwell on it. I'll find out soon enough, maybe at Vincent's day after tomorrow.*

The exertion of the mile-and-a-half trek through snowy woods caught up with him, and he dozed off. He didn't feel the van come to a stop in the hotel parking lot. The driver shook him awake, and Dan recognized the stairwell door in the windshield. Patting his right rear pants pocket, he felt his key card, the piece of plastic that would open the stairs door. Five minutes after he entered his room, there was the familiar knock. Dan checked the peephole and opened the door. Once the door had closed, his exchange was complete. Now Dan was free to rejoin his other life.

* * *

"What did you do with your afternoon, boss?" Dan's first officer was interested to hear if his captain had made any discoveries about how to better enjoy a Denver layover. Flight crews looked for things to do at every layover city, and they like to pass on their intel to other crewmembers.

Dan, however, took that opportunity to take a drink from his beer, and chose his words carefully. "Oh, I just had some business to take care of, nothing worth talking about. You have anything going on the side? Second income stream?"

Dan's first officer was a young man in his early thirties. "No, not really, but I think I need to get something going. I got lots of time, though."

"Everyone says that, but who knows how much time you have, or when this industry is going to stumble. On September tenth in 2001, the airlines were doing well. Same thing January of 2020. Both times something came out of nowhere, and pilots got furloughed."

The junior pilot smiled widely and said, "I was in fifth grade when September eleven happened."

Dan felt old. "Fuck off, I wasn't! Yeah, okay, you have *potentially* a long time, but why not start early?"

The waitress walked up and started distributing food from a large tray. "Two more beers?"

Dan quickly injected, "Absolutely. And I get the check, okay?"

"Sure thing, sweetheart!"

"Thanks, Dan, I appreciate it."

. . .

"Dan! I'm so glad you called!"

"I missed you, baby. You miss me too?"

"I miss every part of you, lover. Some parts more than others." Sindee's voice left no doubt that she was sincere or exactly what parts she was talking about.

"Been mostly routine. I'm looking forward to coming home tomorrow. I don't get in early enough to see you. Angelo's orders: don't break routine, right?"

Sindee's voice again left no doubt that she was disappointed, hoping Dan could work something out. "You sure we can't get together, just real quick? Maybe your flight will be *late*."

"Unfortunately, Sharon has learned how to check on my flights. There are sites on the internet that track flights, and I've always told her my schedule before. If she checks and I tell her it was late, it breaks routine."

Sindee let out a heavy sigh. "I know, I know. I was just thinking a quickie might be fun. Will you be meeting at the usual place day after tomorrow?"

"Yes, baby, and then we can go to our usual place. How about that?"

"That sounds great, flyboy. In the meantime, you want to see what I look like right now?" It was a question Sindee was asking, but she already knew the answer.

Dan didn't even get an answer out and his phone was ringing with a video call. He would get a good night's sleep, but it wouldn't start for a half hour or so.

. . .

Sharon couldn't stop crying. Ed had been allowed to call her from jail, and he was obviously distraught. She had no idea how to help him with getting a defense attorney in Miami, but that was where he was going to need one. She asked what had happened, how it was possible, but Ed deflected saying he "couldn't talk" where he was. She was starting to get the feeling there was more to the story, something she wasn't going to like to hear.

She hung up, promising to help him. But what could she do? How could she possibly help? How was she going to keep all this from Dan. Sharon sunk to the carpet and began to sob again. Ed was in jail five states away with no one to help him, and all Sharon could think about was how much this had hurt her.

34

It was a blessing that Dan's flight didn't get into DFW until just after nine P.M. Seeing Sharon at the house was going to be awkward; it was just the amount of awkward that was in question. Ed was done. It would be lucky for him if he got home at nine P.M. four to six years from now. What Dan hoped would not happen would be Sharon realizing that Ed was gone and try to patch things up between them. For her, Ed was either going to be a way of getting more attention, or a gravy train to replace Dan. Dan knew it would be obvious in the first five minutes which direction things were going to go.

Dan was surprised when he came home to an empty house. *Oh, this is good. I don't give a fuuuck where she is; I'm just glad she's not here.* He dragged his bags into the bedroom and followed his standard routine: overnight bag in the corner of the bedroom, uniform off, all the parts of his uniform insignia and accessories put in his hat, and shirt/pants in the dry cleaner's bag. Now in a polo and comfortable shorts, and it was the living room in his sights. Well, by way of the bar anyway.

Gotta be a baseball game on tonight. I miss football. Dan set down his drink on the end table and fell into the sofa.

. . .

Sharon had made a few phone calls, trying to figure out how to line up an attorney for Ed, but was getting nowhere. *I'm just going to get him connected with someone, and then step out of the whole mess. I'm sitting in my car making phone calls, for fuck's sake. I can't even go home, not like this!* She was too absorbed in herself to realize the irony of what she said. The internet search engine came up with another criminal defense attorney phone number, which she dialed. With a promise from him to visit Ed in jail, Sharon felt her work was done, and she headed home.

. . .

No sooner had Dan pressed the power button on the remote, he heard the electronic lock on the back door turn. *Fuck. Ah well, here we go.*

"You're home. I didn't know you were coming home today." It was one of Sharon's standard lies. The demeaning comment was just one of many ways that Sharon tried to diminish Dan's status in their relationship while elevating hers. It said in a very real way: "You aren't important enough to even care to know when you are coming home." He had heard it many times, and many times there were unmistakable signs that she did actually know he was finishing his trip. Dan knew she had the ability to stalk his trips on the computer, and she had been doing it for years. She always knew, but since she had been seeing Ed, that job went to him. She walked into the living room so that Dan could see her.

Dan looked up and faked a look of concern. "Where you been? Wow, your eyes are red. You okay?"

It was unlike Sharon not to check her look in a mirror at least once an hour. She hadn't realized that the crying had taken its toll. "Oh! My allergies are killing me. I'm going to go take something for it right now."

"Okay." Dan heard a quality in her voice that he sensed was Sharon wavering and lacking in focus. His concern spiked that Sharon would see her relationship with Ed falling apart and decide to try to fix their marriage. *Maybe she is already feeling lost and is trying to decide. Maybe not. I dunno.* But Dan wasn't taking any chances. He walked into the bedroom; Sharon's eyes tracked him as he headed to the closet. Coming back with athletic shoes in hand, he sat on the bed to put them on. "Dave texted me. Reminded me about poker at his house tonight. I forgot. Don't wait up. You know how late poker can go."

Sharon, who had started taking off her clothes as soon as he walked into the room, was speechless. Mostly naked, she stood there and watched him walk out without saying another word.

. . .

She heard the back door of the house open, then close. Sharon had never *felt* so alone in her life but was now *actually* alone. She felt as if every bit of solid ground beneath her feet had been suddenly replaced with complete uncertainty. *What the hell am I going to do? Is Ed just gone? Can I make things right with Dan? Do I even want to?*

She sank to the carpet as if the weight of the situation forced her knees to buckle. Not having any idea what direction her life was taking, she thought, *I don't deserve this*, and the tears welled up again.

. . .

Not two blocks from home, Dan felt his other phone vibrate in his pocket. It was Angelo. "Tomorrow, regular spot and time?"

"You got it, boss. See you then."

Click.

I'm going to have to put some thought into the meeting, make sure we cover what we need to, thought Dan. He couldn't have known at that point in time, but Angelo was thinking the same thing.

. . .

"Dan Hatfield?"

His actual phone had rung, and he recognized it as a Blue Sky number. "Yes?"

"It's Kyle Davis, VP of Flight, how are you?"

"Doing well, Captain Davis, and yourself?"

"Well, we have been better. I will get right to the point. We have an opening in the DFW Chief Pilot's office we would like to fill sooner rather than later."

Dan sold his reaction. "Yeah, I heard about that. I've known Ed for years. It was very surprising."

Davis continued, "I'm calling because you are on a short list of names of pilots we are asking to consider filling his position."

Dan made up his mind easily. *There's no way, not with everything going on, and being home every night is really not appealing.* He sold his reaction to the offer as well. "Sir, I'm honored that you called, and I certainly will consider it. I just have some personal business right now that might make it a difficult choice."

"Give it some thought, Dan, and get back to me as soon as you can. We are looking to fill it soon, and the window may close if you take too long."

Dan lied, "Okay, will do, and thank you again for thinking of me. Have a good one." Dan didn't need time to think about it. By the time a pilot makes captain at an airline, they all know the details of the job of a chief pilot. Many aren't interested in the realities of the job: less pay, not flying much, discipline of fellow pilots, and the management responsibilities. Dan wasn't having it, and his mind was already made up.

"You too, Dan." Davis hung up the phone.

Take Ed's old job? Hell, he tried to take one of mine. But, nope. I could never work in the chief pilot's office. I'm not the management type.

35

Vincent Ricci greeted all of his patrons by name when he could, but friends of Angelo were on a higher level. They were greeted like royalty. "Good afternoon! So nice to see you again, Captain Hatfield. Mr. Genofi is right this way."

Dan was starting to get the impression that one of Vincent Ricci's jobs was to stash him out of sight as soon as he got to Vincent's. *Probably a good idea*, he thought.

"So nice to be here again. I could get used to this place. It grows on you. In fact, I believe it's grown on me a little already." As Vincent looked over his shoulder, Dan patted his belly, and they both had a laugh.

The pair approached the heavy mahogany doors, which Vincent opened, and then closed behind Dan's entrance. A smiling Angelo was already seated, laptop computer at one hand, and big glass of red wine at the other. They greeted each other warmly with first names, like old friends would. Or members of the same club. Dan noticed that Angelo's world was feeling far less foreign and far more familiar to him.

Dan was excited to hear the details—what would be called in the Air Force the "After Action" report—regarding the last op. "How did I do in Colorado? Was everything up to your specifications?"

"Flyboy, I knew you were the man for the job. I'm assuming at this point all went well."

Dan was surprised by the answer. "*Assuming?* What do you mean?"

"Well, sources informed me that they only started lookin' for him today. He had a few days off, so I knew he would be home. His wife is in the hospital, so he's home alone. You saw the place, it's out in the woods with no one looking at the backyard. It's still cold. Hell, for all we know right now, the animals found him and left him a mess. Well, even more of a mess than havin' a big fuckin' arrow sticking out of his chest, anyway." Angelo snickered at the idea.

"So, he's out there still? Huh. Well, he does have a big fuckin' arrow in his chest. I'm sure he didn't walk away. I completed the task just as instructed. So, Angelo, what can you tell me about the target? I don't want to know too much, but—"

"But why the production? Why the trouble to make it look like a poacher's arrow? Use an out-of-town guy? I did tell you it was a rush and that I'd fill you in. So, here's the deal. That *stronzo* motherfucker is married to my sister. He used to live nearby here in Texas, worked for a legitimate business. Seemed at first to be a good guy, which was fine with me. I didn't want my sister marrying someone in the outfit. Then came the opportunity in Colorado. Big pay raise, nice house in the woods. I stop hearing from my sister for a time, so I call her. She breaks down, tells me how he has a mean temper, is hitting her. I call him—*I warn him*—make him understand how important she is to me." Angelo's eyes narrowed, displaying the anger he was clearly feeling.

There was a long pause in the explanation, as Angelo knew the story already, and was getting to a part that was hard to tell. Just then the waiter came in. Dan noticed Angelo had his hand on the signal button. Angelo wanted that pause.

"What can I get for you today, Captain?" said the waiter, hands behind his back.

"Ask the chef what his favorite dish is, and that is what I'd like. Also, some of that bread with garlic oil, and a glass of whatever Angelo is drinking. Thank you." Dan looked at the waiter and then at Angelo.

"Mr. Genofi has already made his selections." The waiter turned and disappeared into the wall.

"Things settled down for a little while. I'm finally starting to think that maybe he understands, maybe it will be okay. Then I get a call from a Colorado area code to a number of mine almost no one has. It's a doctor. He tells me she asked him to call because she can't speak. That *pezzo di merda* broke her jaw and her cheekbone."

The rage flowed from his eyes, and his voice practically turned into a hiss. Then his demeanor changed almost instantly to an expression of righteousness. "And then you came along. You corrected the problem. So, you understand the whys now. You probably suspect, and you're right, that I chose a plausible accident that was the most horrible fuckin' way to go that I could think of."

"How is your sister?" said Dan, with obvious concern.

Again Angelo's demeanor changed, this time to that of a pleasantly surprised friend. "Thank you for asking, Dan. Under the circumstances, she is doing well. I'm told a full recovery will happen, no change in appearance—amazing what the right surgeons can do—and it won't be too long before physical therapy and solid food happen."

The waiter signaled, and then brought out a large tray with lunch and all the accessories. In almost no time at all, he was back in the kitchen with an empty tray.

"That book is closed now, good Captain. Wanna open another one?" The playful smirk was back on his face.

"Sure, what do you have, boss?"

"Lemme give you an update on your wife. It's all set, ready to pull the trigger on that situation anytime. So, if you can come through for me again in the next week or so, we can close that book, too."

"No details, Angelo. It's easier to look surprised if you are surprised. When we decide it's a go, I don't even want to know the day."

Angelo nodded. "Sure, yeah, good thinkin'. One last thing. You and your wife have more in common than you know. You share the same favorite place to get laid."

Angelo laughed while Dan took a second to think it out. "Wait. She and Ed were using the *airport Crowne*?" Dan's mind immediately went to scenes of walking through the lobby of that hotel, and how badly it would have gone for all of them if the two couples ran into each other.

Angelo's face was in a smirk now. "Yup. From now on, it's maybe conjugal visits at the Dade Correction Center." Another laugh, this time from both of them.

Smiling and nodding, Dan said, "That frees the Crowne up for me, and I have a pretty good feeling I'll be there in an hour or so. Enough about her. You said, 'come through for you next week or so'?"

"Yeah, this one's gonna be a bit, well, *different*." The way Angelo hung that last word intrigued Dan.

"Different? In what way were the first two similar?"

"The ending, flyboy. The end was the same."

"Okay, yeah. I'm sure it will be well-planned and within my capabilities." Dan said with confidence.

"Dan, we are just only scratching the surface of your capabilities."

Angelo raised his glass, and Dan toasted. "Here's to capabilities!"

. . .

Dan wasn't interested in dessert or coffee. His after-dinner aperitif was sitting at a barstool, sipping an old-fashioned. He promised Angelo he would keep an eye on his email, said his goodbyes, and was opening those mahogany doors as if he was tearing into a Christmas present. He was not disappointed. Sindee was in a very tight, very short, almost certainly latex, strapless dress that made no attempt whatsoever to reach the tops of thigh-high lace stockings. The view ended at the floor with burgundy, four-inch heels.

Makeup and hair were impeccable. Most women would look like a prostitute in that outfit—Sindee pulled it off with her gorgeous smile and easy-going, confident demeanor. When they made eye contact, Sindee's smile changed from anticipation to that of a predator eyeing her prey.

He closed the distance between them slowly, carefully, looking her up and down as he walked. He wanted her to see him doing it. She did, and when his gaze found her face again, that smile was a bit wider. He wanted her to see him taking her in slowly, enjoying each glance the way a person savors every bite of a rich dessert. Her arms opened when he was only a few feet away, and Dan felt her melt into his.

"I missed you, flyboy. I really did. Let's go *right now*." The last two words were more breath than sound.

36

Jundiun Awwal Brahimi had a single purpose in mind, driving his steps at a quickening pace. He needed to close the distance to the rock and drop his pants before something tragic happened. Water was limited, a resupply run wasn't scheduled for a few days, and there wasn't a shower at the camp, of course. The noise Brahimi was making obliterated any sound Dan made moving to his new position. Dan's plan was to take up a position behind the latrine area, while keeping the darkness behind him and the tent light that was backlighting the enemy soldier.

The plan was working so far, but a new obstacle emerged in the reality of the moment when Dan got roughly to his desired approach line. Seven men, military rations, strong coffee, and a camp that had been there for ten-plus days equaled a latrine area that was impressive in its smell. *What the fuck are these guys eating?* It was nearly overpowering, but Dan tried to put it out of his head. As he approached, he saw the soldier take off the rifle, battle vest, his helmet and even his jacket, and place them in a neat pile about four feet from the rock. Shining the light all around the rock to make sure he was the only life out there, he stood on the rock and dropped his pants, facing the camp. Dan was only about ten feet from him and approaching.

The survival knife was in Dan's right hand, and he was approaching slightly from the left, slowly and carefully. There were noises being made, but none of them by Dan, and he wanted to keep it that way. The man continued to use his flashlight on the ground, not realizing that that was wrecking his night vision. He never saw Dan approach to within arm's reach.

Dan had been visualizing the moment as he approached, practicing the movements in his head several times. The soldier was sweeping his flashlight around the rock, starting by turning to the right. Dan took that last step, grabbed him by the hair with his left hand while simultaneously burying the knife in the soldier's throat with his right. It sunk into the front of his throat all the way to the guard and came out the back of his neck. Using the knife for leverage, Dan pulled the soldier forward, twisted and removed the knife as they both fell to the desert floor. Dan held the man's face in the sand until he stopped moving. Looking to his right, he saw the flashlight laying on the rock, still shining, right where the soldier dropped it.

The soldier hadn't made a sound, and if there had been enough light, Dan would have seen a look of unbelievable shock and surprise on his face. Dan couldn't see it, but he could feel a large amount of warm blood on his right hand and arm. Dan quickly felt the soldier's pockets to see if he had anything Dan could use. He pulled a wad of something out of a front pocket that by feel and smell immediately told him they were wet wipes. *Well, at least they will get put to good use*, he thought as he tried to get some of the blood off his hand.

Nothing more of value was found in a quick search, so Dan dragged the body a fair distance from the rock. There was no telling when the rock would get another visitor. He carefully shaded the flashlight so it wouldn't be easily seen from the camp and found his way back to the pile of belongings on the ground. That's when the rest of the plan fell into place. He donned the jacket, helmet, and battle vest, checking its contents by feel. Four magazines for the AK, and the vest felt heavy enough that they could be full. Four cheap Russian hand grenades of a style that Dan had seen a picture of, but never operated.

It's a hand grenade. Pull the pin, throw it at something you don't like, find some cover. Pretty simple, he thought.

All that was left on the ground was the AK. Turning away from the camp, he picked up the rifle, and illuminated it briefly. It looked to be in good shape, and Dan familiarized himself with the safety location and magazine release. *If this works out like I want it to, I'll be fighting in the dark. I'm gonna need to be able to operate everything by feel.*

His plan was pretty simple. He was going to stroll back into camp, wearing the jacket, vest, and helmet of the dead soldier. AK over his shoulder, flashlight at his feet, but not looking at it. The last part of his plan had to be determined once he got inside the camp and was approaching the tent. *Gotta figure out what I'm going to use for cover after I toss these grenades in that tent.*

Dan had gotten past the first vehicle and found another near the front of the tent that would be perfect cover from the explosions of the grenades. Dan's heart sank as he detected the faint sound of something way off in the distance. It was the unmistakable sound of rotor blades of a helicopter.

37

"I *love* the beds they have here at the Crowne. They are the perfect balance between comfort and firmness for getting into the right rhythm. And you *dooo* have good rhythm, flyboy." Sindee's voice and the way she used it were as seductive as everything else about her.

Sindee, lying next to Dan, stretched her arms and legs out straight on the bed. Then she brought her knees up, and spread her stockinged legs wide, taking a very provocative pose. Dan took it for the invitation it was, and shortly, Sindee was being treated to more of the rhythm she had just complimented.

. . .

Now sweaty and catching their breath, the two were laying on that comfortable bed, Sindee in Dan's arms. Sindee had been quiet for a few minutes, so Dan thought she was just enjoying the moment. Sindee moved on the bed, creating enough space to allow her to be able to make eye contact with Dan. He saw an uncharacteristic look of seriousness on her face. Dan mentally braced for whatever it was Sindee was about to say. The concern on Dan's face matched Sindee's.

"Dan, at first what we had was just sex, and it was good. Great, really. But it's grown into something else, something deeper. I told you I love you, and it's true, I have fallen for you. It's not something I've felt much of in my life, and it's exciting." Sindee smiled briefly, then continued. "But it didn't start that way for either of us. That first time we met, I did something that I feel guilty about now. I have something I have to tell you, and I hope you understand why I did what I did and why I'm telling you now."

Sindee paused, so Dan jumped in. He saw the tentative look on her face, and he sensed she was feeling like she was in completely unfamiliar territory. Dan took her right hand in his hands, trying to reassure her with both physical contact and words. "Baby, I agree with everything you just said, and I hope that you know I love you, too. Tell me."

Sindee breathed in a deep lungful, then let it all out before she spoke. "Angelo planned on some kind of business with you, and I don't want to know what it is. But it was important enough that he paid me to keep an eye on you, to report to him how you were doing, what you were doing. Even asked me for information like clothing and shoe sizes. He would ask me questions when he came to the club or would call me on the phone. Please, Dan, I wasn't trying to hurt you, and I never really told him anything confidential. Why he would ask me things like what kind of mood you were in, I don't know, but that wasn't me betraying you, right?"

Dan thought for a moment, relieved that what was on Sindee's mind was something of mild importance, and that it was Sindee showing her true, deep feelings for him. The reasons for Angelo's questions were easily understood, and not at all betrayal. Dan thought carefully about his next words, and after a pause, studied Sindee's face. He could clearly see that the suspense was killing her. "No, baby, of *course* not. I don't feel upset in any way. Angelo was just checking on me because he's a detail guy, that's how he's gotten to where he is. You answer any questions he asks, honestly, and keep up the routine. Remember, no changes in routine."

There was a visible reaction of relief in her face and body to his words. Dan saw it and realized that this must have been bothering her for some time. It was also another clear sign that her feelings for him were real.

Dan rolled over and kissed her on the cheek, touching her neck with his right hand. "I love you, sweetheart."

"I love you too, flyboy."

. . .

Driving home, Dan was pondering all that Sindee had said, in between playing mental movies of everything she had done in that room at the Crowne. *Angelo must have planned everything after our first meeting. That guy plans every fucking detail. I need to never forget that.*

The drive home was an exercise in autopilot driving, and in no time, he was pulling into his garage. An empty garage. *Works for me*, he thought. Dan entered the house, went to the bedroom, and scanned for the gym bag. Also gone.

I think a nice, long shower sounds about right. Better get in before she gets home.

. . .

Sharon had gone to the gym and gotten as far as the parking lot. She certainly intended to go inside and work out, thinking that a good hard workout is what she needed. Car parked, she was about to turn off the engine when her phone rang. *Area code 305? That's Miami*, she thought.

"Hello?"

"Hello, Sharon, this is Kelly Tasker, the attorney you phoned a few days ago. I wanted to give you a quick update on where we stand."

"Did you see him in jail?" she asked, with an anxious voice.

"No, Sharon, there is no need for that yet. I'm compiling information and shaping up how this case should be handled. The police have given me everything they have so far. They haven't questioned him yet, and they won't without me present. I think I will be in a position to see him tomorrow."

Still anxious, Sharon asked quickly, "You said you had an update for me. What have you found out?"

"Sharon, remember, everything you tell me is confidential, and it's very important that you be as honest with me as you can."

After a pause, Sharon said, "Okay."

"Do you know of or have you ever seen Ed use any kind of drugs?"

Sharon was flabbergasted. "Drugs?! No, of course not. Ed gets random drug and alcohol testing at work. Why are you asking me that?"

"His blood toxicology, which he consented to, showed marijuana and cocaine. Also, his blood alcohol level was just over three times the legal limit to fly. I've been thinking, and I have two theories. Either he was able to keep from getting tested using his position as chief pilot, or this is all a setup."

Just when Sharon thought she had heard the worst of the report, Tasker took it in a direction that was even worse. "Setup? Who would do that? *How?*"

"Well, the um, security footage in the hotel bar where he was staying shows him spending time with a woman, and then leaving with her very late. An inspection of his room turned up a pair of women's underwear, along with some cocaine residue on a table."

Like a lightning bolt, Sharon felt a shock go through her entire body. She tried desperately to make all the puzzle pieces before her fit together, but she just couldn't. She wanted to speak, but there were no words she could find to express how she was feeling. Sharon tried to find the right direction to go next with the conversation and found that all of the options before her were bad ones. Tasker knew full well that that information was going to be extremely difficult for Sharon to swallow, and assumed he'd need to give her time to process it. He was right.

"It doesn't make sense. None of it makes sense. I don't understand, I don't understand!" Sharon's voice raised to a pitch that was almost a scream. Any way the information was digested, the end was awful. Ed was either a secret drug-using pilot and a womanizer, or he fell prey to a woman who drugged him and set him up. That simply did not sound likely. Sharon knew and understood pilots. Neither of those scenarios sounded even possible. The least likely scenario to her was the first, and she didn't consider it a possibility at all. *But who would want to do a thing like that to him? I would know if he was using drugs. He's a pilot, and no, he is not with other women. He loves me! But why would someone want to destroy him like that?* The thoughts were spinning around her head, as were questions she badly wanted answered. "What does all this mean? I mean, is he going to be found guilty? Is he going to prison and for how long?"

"The process is just starting, Sharon, but I want you to be prepared. It doesn't look good for Ed. We may have to accept a plea deal, and I would imagine that would include substantial jail time. A best guess would be five years, maybe more."

Sharon gasped, and then sucked in a few violent breaths.

"Sharon, we will get to the bottom of this, and figure it all out. In the meantime, take care of yourself, and trust that Ed is safe where he is and in good legal hands."

Between sobs, she managed, "Thank you, Mr. Tasker. Call or text anytime."

"I will. Goodbye."

Sharon just hung up the phone and fell apart, sobbing loudly. In her mind, just hearing the news about Ed's arrest had changed her life direction as far as it could go. The phone call from the attorney had changed it further. The possibility that someone set him up to fall that hard made so little sense to her. Sharon knew that the facts in front of her were truth that made up a story, but missing details were what tied them together. The thought that maybe it was true, maybe Ed took drugs or was with another woman, began to creep into her head. As hard as she fought it, there it was, and it was as unmistakable as it was unthinkable. Anger added to the spectrum of emotions she felt, and the weight of those emotions crushed her. Sharon didn't know her exact location on the map of time, but she knew with certainty that all directions to go from there were bad. Her demeanor changed to that of resignation and doom. Her deep sobbing would have been heard outside the car if someone were there.

In fact, someone was there watching her. He picked up his phone to report to Nico.

38

It was early when Dan woke in the bed next to Sharon. He had to piece together his evening prior. He'd been parked in his usual spot on the couch, catching a baseball game, lubricating his brain with a twelve-year-old scotch when Sharon walked through the back door of the house. She didn't say much, but she had that beloved gym bag over her shoulder and looked the kind of disheveled one got from working out. She went straight to the shower, and from there, bed.

As he walked into the kitchen to start a pot of coffee, he felt his other phone vibrate. *I'll call him back,* he thought when he looked at the incoming call and saw it was Angelo. Dan thought up an excuse to go to the garage, and headed that way, phone in pocket.

"There you are, flyboy. How are you?" Angelo's good mood came out in his voice.

"I'm good, but I'm calling you from the garage. She's home. What's up?" Dan was in a half-whisper.

"I was hoping we could meet today. I want to give you a little information about the next, uh thing, we got goin' on. I was thinking my place, whenever you are free today. I'm at home all day."

Dan thought for a moment. "Okay, around ten? Is that a good time for you?"

"Yea, perfect. I'll have the travel agency send you an Airbnb ad with the address."

"See you then, boss."

Click.

Dan noticed something about Angelo. It was subtle, but it spoke to Angelo's stature in the organization that he never said "goodbye" on a telephone call. He just hung up. It was as if he was saying, "The call is over when I make it over." Dan smirked at the thought.

When Dan returned to the house, Sharon was just walking out of the bedroom in business attire. She poured herself a coffee in a travel mug, got it to just the right blend of sweetener and cream, and snapped on the lid.

"I have a new client meeting this morning. There are other designers being interviewed, and it's a big job. Wish me luck!" she said.

There was an almost total lack of sincerity in the request, just Sharon's usual façade. Dan picked up on that. "Good luck!" At least he acted enthusiastic. Keeping up appearances...

· · ·

The navigation app on Dan's phone guided him to the right address. He was impressed with the Northlake neighborhood, and not at all surprised to see that Angelo's estate was the nicest he had driven past. He hadn't seen them all yet; if he had, he would still conclude that it was the nicest. Most of the houses in the subdivision had electric gates to prevent unwanted vehicle access. Dan noticed that Angelo's gate was reinforced—heavily.

He pulled up to the video intercom, and before he could say a word, the gate began to open. No doubt some kind of sensor had alerted Angelo to Dan's arrival, and he was right on time. When the gate had fully opened, Dan could see circles on the ground behind the gate that were clearly an even more impressive line of defense. The circles were the tops of concrete-filled heavy steel tubes, hydraulically-actuated, but when not needed retracted into the ground, flush with the surface and nearly invisible. They extend to a height of four feet and will stop a fast-moving truck. Four of them spanned the gate opening.

Dan's other phone rang. "Pull around behind the house, out of sight." *Click.*

He couldn't see it from the street, but the back of the house had a large parking area in front of a five-car garage. He parked nearest to the back door, got out, and took in the scene. Perfectly manicured landscaping surrounded a large diving pool with a spillover jacuzzi. Plenty of outdoor furniture and fixtures, a covered seating area with outdoor kitchen and three TVs. Angelo emerged from the back door.

"This place is fantastic, boss. How many people live here?"

Angelo displayed a proud smile. "Just me full time, but I do like to entertain when I can. I'll have to tell you sometime some of the names that have attended my get-togethers. You'd probably be surprised."

"Maybe so, but you're a very connected guy, Angelo."

Angelo held the door, and they moved inside. "Thank you, captain. Welcome to my home." The house opened up into a large dining area attached to an enormous kitchen. There was a wine room the size of a walk-in closet, and several other doors, undoubtedly pantries and storage. They passed through a hallway to the front of the house. The front room opened into a cavernous area with living room, formal dining room, and Angelo's office. Dan liked the office most of all, as it was furnished with beautiful cabinetry, a huge desk, and a large bar in the corner.

"All this for just you, huh? How do you manage?"

Angelo laughed. "I'm going to be on the next episode of *Lifestyles of the Rich and INfamous.*"

Dan laughed. Angelo pointed to one of the four nicely upholstered chairs in front of the desk while he sank into the captain's chair behind the desk. Once they were both seated, Angelo drew in a deep breath and let it out as he went over the details in his head. In a few seconds, when he felt like he had collected his thoughts, he nodded his head and said, "Okay."

After a small pause, Angelo continued. "You're going to get the specifics for the next op from the instructions in the package, the night of the op. But, I wanted to give you an overview myself so that this thing goes smoothly. Of course, conversations like the one we are having right now are always face-to-face. First, I want to let you know that there are almost certainly going to be two targets on this, and I wanted to let you know that now. The main target has a bodyguard everywhere he goes. You will need to drop him first, but I got that all worked out. On a side note, this will pay more than what we talked about, so we will be more than even when this is done, and I'll owe you. This one pays a hundred G's."

Dan was riveted. "Okay, so how high-level is the target? I can't help but notice, even you don't have a bodyguard everywhere you go. But then, this place is a fortress."

Angelo was curious about what Dan had noticed. "How so? What makes you say that?" Angelo wanted to measure Dan's detail observation skills.

"Well, reinforced electric gate, driveway sensors, hydraulic driveway barriers, cameras everywhere, bulletproof glass in your office, reinforced entry door in the back, and I'm sure the front is the same. I haven't seen your safe room yet, but I'd bet six month's salary you have one."

Angelo laughed, happily surprised that Dan, too, was a detail guy. "You don't miss much, flyboy. Bet your *ass* I have a safe room. Tornados, assassins, crazy girlfriends, whatever. It *works*. So, let's keep going. The target works hard to keep a low profile, and that's very important to him. It's also important to the op. Our current government has a wide-open border to the south. One of the drug cartels has taken that as an invitation to go past trafficking and right into trying to stake out territories of their own in the U.S. El Paso belongs to me. Your target would disagree.

You are going to show them what happens when you disagree with me. What we are going to do is make him and his bodyguard vanish, disappear, poof. He won't be the only target, and there will be targets south of the border as well. But he is the only part of the larger op involving you, and he is the most important. Think of him as the Mexican me."

"Oh fuck." Dan felt the weight of that last statement.

"Exactly right, captain. Exactly right. Your role will take place in a club where the owner is a friend of mine and is helping, but not officially. Target has a thing for a dancer in the club, visits regularly. You will be in a position where you can strike quickly and unexpectedly. I have a cleanup crew that will immediately handle the situation, and you will be done."

"You know, Angelo, if he is the Mexican you, they will send others... and more of them."

Angelo nodded. "Another time, I would agree with you. But like I said, I have more messages to send that same night, and I have assets that cover the border for me as well. Like you said, I'm connected."

"Wait, but, Angelo, I can't guarantee I can get an El Paso overnight on any particular night."

"Ah yes, captain, but the entire operation is waiting for you to get an El Paso overnight. When you do, all of the other triggers get pulled, literally, on the same night you go."

Dan let out a deep breath. "Okay, Angelo, I'll let you know when."

39

As the garage door slowly opened, Dan made out the fact that Sharon's BMW was parked inside.

Great. I can't wait to sell that piece of shit. BMW drivers...

Walking in the back door, he was greeted by a woman with her arms folded. Sharon clearly had something on her mind, and Dan could see it. *What the fuck now?* Dan didn't have the patience for an argument with Sharon.

She said in an obvious complaining tone, "Where were you? Your phone was off. It seems like we haven't seen each other in a week."

So the fuck what? I don't want to see you now. Dan had his best poker face on. Her very presence in the house was a reminder of the night he caught her screwing Ed. Dan had known he might have to have some excuses lined up to explain moments like this. He chose quickly from his list. "I was at the headquarters building. They wanted to meet with me. They want me to consider taking Ed's old position."

"You don't even seem upset about Ed. I mean, you've been friends since college. Aren't you the littlest bit concerned about him?"

"Maybe initially." Dan shrugged. "But you do the crime, you do the time. I thought he was smarter than that. They are going to need to fill that Chief Pilot slot soon. Ed won't be in it any time soon. Probably, never."

Dan added the last two words in order to end a conversation that was going in a direction he had no desire to go.

. . .

It worked. "Probably never" was too much for Sharon, and she reflexively turned away from Dan so he couldn't see her face. She had allowed herself to imagine life with Ed; much of her alone time was spent daydreaming about what it would be like to be living with Ed after Dan was out of the picture. She had even been looking up local divorce attorneys. Now that was all over. Ed was in jail, headed for conviction and prison. Now Dan might be taking his job in the Chief Pilot's office? That was too much. And how could Dan be so matter-of-fact about Ed's arrest. It's like they weren't friends. Not even a call to Ed in jail.

"What did you tell them?" Sharon asked while walking toward the bedroom.

As Sharon got to the bedroom door, Dan replied. "I told them I would think about it, but I'm not really considering it. You have to be part asshole to work in the Chief Pilot's office."

Dan meant it as the dig that it was, but she had no idea, and that was lost on Sharon. Too upset to continue the conversation, she headed for the shower. She didn't need one, but it would be a good place to cry and think. That's what she needed most right then, and she was sobbing before the water got warm. She'd never felt so alone.

Standing under the showerhead for about 10 minutes, she came to a decision. *I need some time. I need some SPACE! I need to see Ed.*

Sharon began formulating the trip, and how she would explain it to Dan. A sudden trip to Miami, even though she flies for free, required some sort of plausible explanation. She wasn't ready to leave Dan, or even close to being able to. A few reasonable scenarios bounced around her thoughts as she measured each one for believability and concealability. The water had been running for forty minutes when she finally began to apply soap. Plan complete, lines rehearsed, she was ready to talk to Dan.

Sharon was about to turn off the water when she had a sudden thought about timing. She realized it was going to take a few days to set everything up, especially visitation with Ed. *Wait, maybe I should wait a few days. I don't want him to have too much time to think about it before I go. Right now, he knows nothing, and I don't want him questioning why I'm going. Wait, wait, how do I know* he's *not cheating on me? He's been gone a lot, and sure isn't interested in fucking me. I'll just wait a few days and tell him right before I go.*

. . .

"She's been in there a long time. Just as well. Dan's office shared a wall with the master bath, so he could clearly hear the water running through the pipes. He was sitting at his desk, checking the open trips in the next few weeks, looking for an El Paso overnight. There were a few flights a day to El Paso from Blue Sky's Dallas hub, so Dan knew he'd find one, it was just a matter of when.

After looking at a few El Paso overnights, Dan settled on one. It was a long El Paso overnight that would give him plenty of time to get the job done. *We get to the hotel at about 2:00 P.M., leave the next day at 3:00 P.M., perfect.* He put in the trip trade request, and it went right through. Dan had started a big operation moving forward, and he would play one crucial part.

Dan logged onto the travel website and put in all his requests for the flights and hotel in El Paso. When he hit the *Submit* button, he was nodding at his computer screen. *I'll bet they are watching for my requests.*

. . .

Angelo heard one of his phones buzzing on his office desk. Determining it was the travel agency phone, he looked at it with anticipation.

"Day after tomorrow, *Madon'*. I got phone calls to make!" he said out loud.

Feeling the gravity of what was about to start, Angelo looked out his big office windows and let out a breath. This would be the biggest op he had ever orchestrated and by far. It encompassed so many people and locations, so many tasks, Angelo did something he would normally never do. He had outlined the op on a single piece of paper, laying it out in a coded framework. That paper was sitting in front of him on the desk, and he studied it one last time. Satisfied, he then began selecting phones carefully, and sent numerous coded messages. It was a go. Many more short phone calls, all spoken in code, took the next hour. Angelo didn't use the shredder at his feet to destroy the diagram when he was finished with the phones. He took it to the kitchen sink and torched it with his favorite cigar lighter.

. . .

Sharon exited the bathroom and looked out on the living room from the bedroom door. What she saw was Dan, on the couch, scotch in hand, channel surfing. He was looking for a ball game to watch, and he was there for the evening. As quiet as she tried to be, he could still hear her. He never reacted to her presence, and she retreated to the bedroom and the TV she would fall asleep to.

Dan texted Sindee on his phone. *I miss u, baby, I love u! I wish I could see you tonight!*

. . .

Sindee felt the phone buzz in the little handbag that she always carried in the club. She was sitting with a middle-aged, unhappily married type that she had wrapped around her little finger. She looked at the text and just melted. *I love you too, baby. I don't know how much longer I can do this.*

. . .

Dan put his phone back in his pocket. *I don't know how much longer I can do this.*

40

The trip Dan had traded into was an easy three-day trip. The first day was just one flight to El Paso, then to the hotel. The second day had him going to Phoenix, and from there to Denver for the overnight. The last day was long: flying from Denver to Los Angeles, then back to Dallas and done.

The day before the trip was pretty routine. The *new* routine. In the late morning, Dan put his golf clubs in the back of the truck, with Sharon watching. Then he drove to the airport Crowne and met Sindee for "a round of golf." By late afternoon, he was back home and found Sharon and the gym bag gone. Dan grilled himself a ribeye, poured a healthy scotch, and enjoyed his favorite cut of beef for dinner.

The show time for the trip was not very early, about 11:00 A.M., but Dan always preferred to get ready the night before. After dinner, he packed his bag for a three-day trip, put together his uniform shirt with all its accessories, selected a pair of uniform pants, and hung them all on the dresser. *Okay, I'm ready for tomorrow.*

He took in and let go a lungful of air, thinking about whether or not he was really ready for tomorrow. Dan was staring at his uniform when he was startled by Sharon walking in the bedroom door. He had jazz playing on the living room sound system and had not heard the door. She tossed the gym bag in its usual space.

"Have a trip tomorrow?" It was more of an observation than a real question.

"Yeah, an easy three-day. El Paso and Denver. Good workout?" Dan was keeping up appearances. He couldn't care less how good the workout was. He wasn't the motivation, and Ed wasn't going to enjoy it any time soon.

"Pretty good, yeah." Sharon had just started to peel off her spandex workout attire when Dan walked past her, headed to the living room.

. . .

Dan exited the bedroom and only a minute later she heard the music stop, followed by the television. *I'm not going to beg him*, she thought to herself defiantly. Sharon took off the rest of her clothes, threw them into the hamper and walked naked over to the nightstand. She found her favorite waterproof toy and headed to the shower.

. . .

Less than sixteen hours later, Captain Hatfield was at the controls of his 737, making the short flight from Dallas to El Paso International Airport. Being a short flight, it was high-workload with little time for chit chat with the first officer. He had made the flight many times, but this time it was with a newly hired first officer who had not. That made it an even higher workload for Dan, so he was relieved to be setting the parking brake and shutting down the engines when they parked in El Paso.

"Parking Checklist, complete. Jeez, that DFW–El Paso leg is all work, no time!"

Dan reassured the Blue Sky new hire. "You'll get used to it, Julio. You did just fine."

"Thanks, cap. Hey listen, I have family in El Paso that's going to pick me up at the hotel, so I won't be any fun on this overnight. Maybe we can do dinner in Denver?"

Perfect. One of Dan's issues just solved itself. "Sure, sounds great."

Thirty minutes later, Dan was signing in at the front desk of their downtown hotel. If the layover was short, the hotel was usually something very close to the airport. But long layover hotels were routinely nicer, and a farther distance from the airport. Dan liked this hotel as it was very nice, and the restaurant in the lobby was good. It had good beds, and a good workout room. As soon as his room door closed, he checked the time: 2:35 P.M.

Ten minutes later, he got the knock. A man in a mask and baseball cap was visible in the peephole. He had on a T-shirt boldly displaying the name of a food delivery service and was holding two brown paper bags. Dan opened the door. Wordlessly, the bags were exchanged. Dan opened each one on the bed, carefully setting out its contents.

In one bag he found a black polo with the name of a club embroidered on the left breast, black slacks, a black belt, black shoes, and a blue and green Hawaiian-style shirt that looked oversized for Dan. The second bag contained a mask, a ballcap, large plastic garbage bag, the instructions, and a smaller paper package containing pistol, loaded magazines, and a suppressor. There was also a thumb drive. Dan pulled his notebook computer from his bag, put it on the desk, and powered it up. He inserted the drive into the socket on the notebook and picked up the instructions.

"Dress in all the clothing provided, including the Hawaiian shirt over the black polo. Be ready for a pickup at the exterior exit from the stairwell at the end of the hall, closest to your door, at exactly 8:00 P.M. Carry the loaded pistol, suppressor attached, and extra magazine in one of the paper bags. Open the thumb drive on your laptop computer now."

Dan had already done that. All that was on it was a single file containing pictures of two men, from a few different angles.

"The man in the first picture, completely bald and holding a drink, is your primary target. He is never armed and will not be tonight. The other man pictured, the one holding the rifle, is his bodyguard, who is always armed and is always at the side of the primary target. You will have to eliminate him first, and then the primary target."

He took a minute and studied the photos. *They look like serious assholes. That bodyguard is huge. He has the look of prior military. So, this is the Mexican cartel version of Angelo?*

"The driver will take you to the back door of a strip club. The only camera in or around the club takes video of people entering and exiting the front door. You will enter the club and go straight to the bathroom where you will place your brown bag in the stall with the *Out of Order* sign on it. Remove the Hawaiian shirt and place it in the bag. For the night, you are the men's room attendant. The normal attendant, who the target is familiar with, is named Chino. When asked, you will say you heard he had some family emergency, but you don't know."

Men's room attendant? What the fuck, well, okay. I guess it's a cover that gets me inside and alone with asshole number one.

"The target normally arrives about 10:00 P.M. and stays until 1:00 A.M. or later. Expect him to make a few visits to the men's room with his bodyguard, who will stand by the door. On his second trip to the men's room, regardless of what time it is, as he enters you will pick up the toilet plunger near the sink and enter the *Out of Order* stall. Use the plunger as you retrieve the pistol. As you come out of the stall, take out the bodyguard first, and you must assume that he is wearing body armor. Then take out the primary. Disassemble your pistol, leave it, the suppressor, and magazines in a bathroom sink. Put on your Hawaiian shirt, make sure you have hat and mask on. Exit the bathroom, go straight to the back door, and a car will be waiting to take you back to the hotel. There is a cleanup crew that will be on site and handle everything else. Their signal is you leaving. Back at your room, place all provided package contents in the plastic bag and wait for their retrieval. Wash your hands thoroughly.

Then go about your routine. After you have read these instructions again and memorized them, destroy them as you have previously."

Dan did exactly that, reading slowly and visualizing everything as he did. *The bodyguard is going to be the tricky part. He has to be hit hard and fast, several times. Then, asshole number one.* It was now 3:05 P.M., hours before he had to be ready. Not wanting there to be any surprises, he put on all the clothing provided. "How the fuck did they know my shoe size? Ah, right, Sindee giving him my intel," he said out loud as he chuckled.

He understood that Angelo was not a man to leave anything to chance if he could help it. Dan just didn't quite yet have an appreciation of the depths to which Angelo was capable. Angelo's IT guy had Dan's phone cloned ten minutes after he stepped into Vincent's the first time. Of course, they already captured everything that happened on his other phone. Dan's laptop got owned the first time he put a thumb drive into it. The browser history of a notebook can betray so much about a person, and Angelo had seen it all.

Room service was called, and a light meal ordered. He pulled his pilot uniform shirt on to answer the door and pay for his meal. Dan had always just paid for room service when it was delivered. Putting meals on his room charges meant possibly standing in a line the next morning to settle them, and then being late for the van. He had a new reason now. A credit card charge at the front desk was an electronic footprint. Cash at the door of his room was not. Dan passed the time by eating, channel surfing, and going over the plan in his head numerous times, looking for problem areas and rehearsing his moves. By 7:45 P.M., he was fully dressed, pistol converted, and stored in a paper bag sitting by the door. Ten minutes later he was exiting his room, bag in hand. He felt the excitement building.

41

The car pulled up at 8:00 P.M. exactly. Dan had been standing outside waiting for less than a minute. He opened the front passenger door and got in. The driver just looked straight ahead and started the car rolling. Neither man said a word.

The drive to the club was short, maybe ten minutes by Dan's estimation, the club being in the downtown area. The driver chose to take a route past the front of the club first. Dan recognized the name and logo as that embroidered on his shirt. Two right turns later, the car was pulling slowly down a dark, dirty alley. It stopped in front of a completely unmarked door, where the driver nodded to Dan. *This must be it. Showtime.*

He had barely closed the car door when the driver gave it some gas and drove away. The unmarked door was unlocked, and Dan walked in. The music that he could hear through the door in the alley was booming inside the club. Dan realized the instructions gave him no layout of the club, but he guessed the bathroom would be in the back of the club near the back door. *Good guess.* He saw the *Men* sign immediately to his left when got a few steps inside, and never broke stride walking to the bathroom. No one in the club even noticed him enter, except the owner, who was watching the door.

Inside the bathroom, Dan started making a detailed note of the layout, and then superimposed his visualizations of the task on what he could now see. Sinks were on the left, close to the door. The table for the attendant was across from the sinks, and there were five urinals on the left wall of the rectangular room. Five toilet stalls were on the right wall, the closest to the door displaying an *Out of Order* sign. On the floor under the table were cleaning supplies and a plunger.

Dan followed the instructions, and within a few minutes, he was seated at the table, in uniform. He checked his watch: 8:17 P.M. *Time to start my new career. I hope the tips are good.* There was a conspicuously empty tip jar sitting on the table. Over the next half hour or so, about fifteen men used the bathroom, some of them back for a second time. All of them had small bills, and all of them tipped Dan for his service of handing them paper towels and allowing them to choose from the many bottles of inexpensive cologne. *Huh. A bunch of beer drinking men with pockets full of small bills. Pretty good racket for whoever it is that's taking the night off*, he thought, looking at the jar now full of dollar bills.

It was past 10:00 P.M., and Dan assumed the pair had already walked in. He couldn't see the bodyguard parking the sedan in a wide spot of the alley. Dan also couldn't see the two men come in the same back door that he had used. He hadn't expected to see the target or his bodyguard for at least a half hour, but the target had wine with his dinner and arrived at the club in need of the bathroom. Dan made it a habit not to look up immediately when someone walked in, so as not give away the fact that he was actually waiting for someone. So, he didn't notice who they were until he saw a pair of expensive shoes come to a stop in front of him.

The target walked in expecting to see Chino, but this was obviously not his build. When he walked up to Dan, he stopped. Dan glanced up just in time to see the target look his bodyguard in the eyes, then look back down at Dan. The target was too important a guy to talk to a man working in a bathroom.

"Where's the regular guy? Who, are *you?*" The bodyguard's booming voice was as intimidating as his stature.

"I dunno. You mean Chino, I guess? Owner said he had a family emergency." Dan kept his voice low, and tried to sound like a guy who was unenthusiastic about his present situation.

"And you are...?" The bodyguard's voice had a quality that said he usually gets his questions answered.

"Dalton, just filling in. I've done odd work for the owner before. Nothing as odd as *this* though."

The target laughed, and so the bodyguard did as well. The target stepped over to the urinals, while the bodyguard shifted sideways, so that he could put a boot against the bottom of the door. Dan noticed the move and thought, *I guess this guy is too important to piss next to a stranger.*

The target washed his hands, then stood in front of Dalton, who handed him a few paper towels. Throwing them in the trash, he reached into his pocket, and peeled a bill off of a roll of money. As he placed it in the tip jar, he said, "Nice to meet you, *Dalton.*"

"*Con mucho gusto, maestro.*" Dan's greeting in Spanish put the hint of a smile on the target's face. "*Y gracias mucho.*" Dan said as he glanced at the tip jar. The moment the target started to turn toward the door, the bodyguard swiftly went through it, and held it open. Dan then took a good look at the tip jar: the target had put a hundred in it. *Hey, the tips are good. See you in a half hour.*

Forty minutes, and about twenty customers later, the door swung open, and it's the bodyguard and his asset. As the target passed, Dan stood, and retrieved the plunger from below the table. He didn't look directly, but he saw the movement out of the corner of his eye. The bodyguard took a more ready posture. When Dan made a right turn into the *Out of Order* stall, the bodyguard relaxed a bit. Dan closed the stall door behind himself, and while plunging with his left hand, he retrieved his pistol with his right. The noise of plunging water could be heard above the club music.

The target finished faster than Dan had anticipated and was walking past the stall as Dan was about to exit. It was different than Dan had envisioned, but he realized it was even better. *I can use this to my advantage.* He held the plunger out in front of him, high and visible, as if trying not to let it drip on his shoes. Low on his right side, and shielded by the target's body, was the gun in Dan's hand. The bodyguard was much taller, allowing Dan to raise the gun, and have it aimed at the bodyguard's head before it could be seen. The target turned toward the sink, and Dan put two fast rounds in the bodyguard's face. He fell to the floor a lifeless heap.

The target froze for just a second. He didn't look at the bodyguard. He had heard suppressed subsonic ammunition being fired many times, and already understood what the fate was of his friend and protector. Dan turned the gun on the target, who looked like he was about to make a break for the door. When he saw the 240-pound man on the floor blocking it, his shoulders sank, and he let out a heavy sigh. The target put up his hand and opened his mouth to say something. Dan put three rounds in his chest, and he fell to the floor with a heavy groan. The target was writhing on the ground, clutching his chest. He was moving much more vigorously than Dan expected a dying man to be able.

Dan moved closer to give the target another few shots. When he was within a few steps of the curled-up man, the target lunged at Dan's legs and brought Dan to his knees. Dan ended the struggle by shooting the man through the top of the head. The target's body went limp immediately. Dan rolled him over and ripped open his shirt. *Body armor, fuck. That lightweight, expensive, executive shit. Well, I guess he could afford it. It almost saved him. Almost.*

Following the instructions, he unloaded and disassembled the pistol into a sink. *Hat on, mask on, shirt on, check. Time to go,* thought Dan, going through the instructions like an airplane checklist. Dan pulled the bodyguard out of the way and exited the bathroom. He turned toward the door after noticing that the two men sitting at a table closest to the bathroom got on their feet simultaneously when they saw Dan. When Dan exited the back door, the car was just pulling up. Dan got in, and they were off immediately toward the hotel.

. . .

Back at the club, the cleanup men went to work. Body bags had been pre-placed under the table, out of sight. Even though the bags had handles, and one of the bags was noticeably larger than the other, maneuvering the enormous bodyguard into the bag, and out the window took every bit of strength they had. Two men in the alley dragged the bags over to the target's sedan, and again with much difficulty, got the two bodies in the trunk. By the time the trunk was loaded, a garbage bag with the evidence and the cleaning supplies for the blood in the bathroom was tossed out the window. It went into the trunk as well. The cleaners exited the club by the back door and climbed into the cab of the tow truck the alley men were driving. The target's sedan was quickly hooked up, and they were all off-scene in minutes. A late-night tow from downtown was a common sight that no one would notice.

One of the men in the tow truck asked the others, "I still can't believe someone tipped that fuckin' bathroom guy a hundred bucks. Did you guys see that shit?"

42

A few times during the drive, Dan caught the driver looking him up and down. He would have only been given a few details about Dan to keep the information compartmentalized. But people talk. *He must have heard something.* Dan thought the driver was showing a bit more interest in his passenger than a guy would if he thought it was just a drop-off and pickup.

In the same amount of time it took to get to the club, the car was pulling up to the pickup spot at the hotel. As his hand went to the door handle, Dan could hear the driver take in a breath, as if he wanted to say something. Dan cut him off by holding up a finger, reminding him of what he'd been told: no questions, no conversation, not a word. The man nodded, and Dan got out of the car. Dan thought, *Better this way. Less of a chance that someone says something they shouldn't.*

It wasn't until he was climbing the stairs that he noticed something about himself. He stopped and held out a hand horizontally—it was rock steady. His heart was only elevated by climbing the stairs. *I guess I found something besides flying I'm good at.* But it was more than that. What he had sensed from the driver was something he couldn't quite put his finger on. Then he realized what it was. *Respect. He was showing me respect.* He had *heard something. I'm glad he kept his mouth shut.*

When Dan entered his room, there wasn't another person in the hallway. The door closing behind him was a reassuring sound that announced he had completed the task, and all that was left was his own cleanup. The plastic garbage bag was laying on the bed, and he walked over to it, stripping off his clothes as he went. Dan noticed the blood on his shoes. *I'm glad they provided the shoes this time, or I'd be going to the bar in my work shoes again.* The whole outfit, shoes, and all other items went into the bag. The laptop was still sitting on the bed; he'd left it there intentionally as a reminder to toss the thumb drive into the bag.

One step into the bathroom for a needed shower, Dan heard the knock on the door. He checked the peephole, and it was a hotel employee. He paused for a moment and measured what he saw. *Is this a good cover, or bad timing? Only hotel employee I've seen with a baseball cap. It's gotta be the pickup guy.* Dan opened the door, and the two stared at each other for a few seconds. The man then said, "Package." Dan was holding it behind the door, out of sight from the hall. He handed the man the package, and the man walked away.

· · ·

Metal World was a scrapyard in El Paso that had done well for itself for a few reasons. Being near the railroad tracks and laying their own rail spur had enhanced their ability over the last four decades to move a lot of scrap as cheaply as possible. When they started forty years ago, the Toccino family was a father-and-sons business, doing everything by hand. Now they were a sprawling yard that ran three city blocks along the tracks. They scrapped anything.

Literally.

One of the more expensive pieces of equipment that Papa Toccino invested in was a car crusher. It was a lot of money, but it had paid for itself many times over. It had the ability to take any auto and crush it into a cube shape, impossibly small compared to what the auto looked like before it met The Beast. Cubes could be stacked onto railroad cars, and transported directly to a smelter, who would melt the cubes down into a liquid that could then be separated and sold. Papa smiled many times at the thought that he took cars obtained for free and turned them into money.

The "specials," though, they were the real deal. People he knew, people who were connected, would tell them they were bringing him a car, and they needed it taken care of. They paid well enough that it really didn't matter what the day or time was—when they called, a Toccino began warming up The Beast. The tow truck with the target's car showed up at Metal World just after midnight with a single driver. He had dropped the others off after the job and picked up the envelope for the Toccinos.

The eldest son, Ralph Toccino, was the one who came to the yard after they got the call that a special was on the way. With The Beast ready to go, he was glad to see the truck. *I could be back in bed in a half hour*, he estimated. Metal World opened early. Ralph heard Papa in his head, saying what he always said about specials: "nobody asks questions, we get paid, it's none of our concern." Ralph looked at the car and thought, *What a shame, crushing that nice sedan. Ah well...*

In less than two minutes, Ralph had deftly, skillfully loaded the car into The Beast, and it worked its magic. Even though the lighting wasn't great—The Beast usually ate during the day—Ralph maneuvered the loader skillfully and set the cube on the stack of cubes near the tracks. When he got out of the cab of the loader, Ralph was handed an envelope by the tow driver. Ralph turned to The Beast to shut it down, and the driver climbed into the tow truck. Every car, when crushed, leaked a half dozen fluids. The Beast was designed to collect these fluids into a tank recessed into the ground on the side of the crushing bay. With a special, there were other fluids that leaked out, and they were the kind the Toccinos didn't want to leave for others to see. As Ralph got up close to his pet, he looked in the car bay and let out a huge sigh.

"From the look of that, there musta been more than one in that special. Bed's gonna have to wait a little while. If I don't hose out The Beast, Papa will have my ass."

. . .

Dan soaked in his hotel room shower for an hour, decompressing. That is the process of just relaxing, going over your day in your head, processing it all, then filing it away. He wanted to thoroughly assess the evening and get it out of his head before he climbed into bed and called Sindee. He knew exactly what they would both be doing thirty seconds after he called. And he knew it didn't matter where she was, she would be joining him in missing each other.

He took a detour on the way to his pillow and turned on the TV. He thought maybe the local stations will have some kind of news about the big operation Angelo was unfolding that night. Dan took in the news for a few minutes. *Spring chili cookoff at Gannett Park to support the homeless shelter? Yeah, not really hard-hitting news.* Dan turned off the TV and picked up his phone in one motion. He had her dialed before his head hit the pillow.

. . .

Angelo had gotten the confirmation call about Dan's op over an hour ago, and he was getting many more as the evening went on. Then he noticed on his computer monitor that Dan had just dialed Sindee. *Go get 'er, flyboy.* Angelo thought it was nice to have a little laugh in the middle of what was an otherwise stressful night. By the end of that night, as light was beginning to leak into the office windows, Angelo finally hit the bed. *Everyone scored, tonight. Everyone. Moving in on my territory was greedy. I made it expensive,* he thought with satisfaction as he dozed off to get a few hours of sleep.

. . .

Phones were ringing all over southern Texas and Northern Mexico— ringing that went mostly unanswered. The ones that were answered all had bad news to report. The calls were coming from two places. A huge estate in rural Mexico; a fortress really. The other was from inside a house in El Paso, Texas, that by appearances was a single-family home in an upscale neighborhood. It was really a front for the CIA. Someone was seriously disrupting the operation they both shared. When the phone in the El Paso home was dialed again, the call was answered by the man in the office of the Mexican estate.

"*Digame*, secret agent man. What. The FUCK IS GOING ON!" The sentence ended in a full-throated yell.

"Carlos, *tranquilo*. We will find out *what* and find out *who* is fucking things up. I will let you know when I know something, and you can take care of things on your end. I will take care of things up here. Call me if you find out anything, I'll do the same."

"*Hermano*, it is not enough that the actors in this play tonight die. The leaders need to *tambien*. Whatever organization is—is—is—who are you, and *WHAT* are you doing in here?!" The voice on the phone, in the last five seconds, added prideful indignation to vicious anger.

"Carlos?"

"No, NO!" Now, deep fear rattled Carlos's voice. Over the phone, Agent John Bayan also heard three suppressed gunshots, and the phone hit the floor. The moaning of a man dying was heard, then the call slipped into silence.

"Carlos?!"

The silence continued and was then followed by the sound of the phone being picked up off the floor. Two men listened for a sound from the other side of the call.

"Carlos?"

"No Carlos here no more."

43

The next morning, Dan awoke well-rested. Sindee had done a good job putting him to bed, albeit on the phone. He didn't have to show at the airport until the early afternoon, so breakfast and even a workout was possible. Dan wondered for a moment if his new life should be affecting him more. *Nah, why should it? So far, I've just been taking out the trash.*

. . .

The rest of the trip was uneventful. It was a day later, and Dan was driving home from employee parking, looking forward to a scotch, and a baseball game. Sharon was not on his anticipation list. A few houses from his own, he touched the garage door opener button. It was mostly up when he turned into the driveway and the sight of her garaged BMW assaulted him.

Dragging his bags behind him, Dan walked into the bedroom and stopped at the sight of two suitcases on the floor by the bed. He could hear Sharon in the master bath.

Dan announced, "Hey."

Sharon shouted from the bathroom. "You're home. Hey, I was thinking of taking a few days, maybe a week, to go to Miami and reconnect with an old high school girlfriend. We found each other on social media, and she invited me to spend some time at her place in Florida. Beach, shopping, girl time, you know?"

"Sounds good." He actually meant that, a few days alone at home. "Looks like you're packed already."

"Yes, in fact I've listed for a flight tonight. That okay?" The way she asked made it obvious to Dan that she wasn't seeking permission, but to see if there was any objection from Dan.

It's fuckin' great! he thought.

"Uh, yeah, if you like. Have a blast." Dan was actually excited at the news. He would be free to see Sindee for the next week and spend some real time with her. *Hell, I may even call in sick for the next trip.*

Dan surprised her when he walked into the bathroom naked. He'd been going through his routine as they spoke, and a long shower was *high* on his anticipation list. He climbed into the shower without so much as touching Sharon. She continued to perfect her makeup, pretending to act as if she wasn't offended by his slight of her.

. . .

Sharon waited until the water had been running five minutes or so. *He'll be in there forty-five minutes.* She picked up her cell phone and went to her email app. Ed had limited access to emails in jail, so it might be tomorrow when he sees it, but she wanted him to know she was coming to Miami. Two minutes later, she was back to her makeup. *If I hurry, I can be out the door before he's out of the shower.*

. . .

By the time Dan was toweling off, there was no Sharon in the bathroom. Stepping out into the bedroom, he saw the suitcases gone as well. *This is working out well,* he thought. Dan shouted, "Sharon?" and the silence that followed felt very good to Dan. *My house to myself.* He walked around the house to make sure Sharon was, in fact, gone. Back in the bedroom, Dan retrieved his other phone from his bag and dialed Sindee.

"Hey, baby, you're back in town, right?" Sindee's voice betrayed the smile on her face. She was beaming to be hearing from Dan.

"Yes, my lover. I just got out of the shower." Dan knew when he said it, he would get a response.

"Just? I'd like to *see* that. Look in the mirror and tell me what you see, flyboy."

"I see a man in love with a woman, and that man is visibly excited by the sound of her voice."

Sindee paused. She was at work, and in pure predator mode, but Dan's words had stopped that persona cold and tugged at her heart. "You are so sweet, my captain, and also so sexy."

"And you are the genuine article, sweetheart. I'm a very lucky man. Sounds like you're at the club."

"I am, and it's really dead here tonight."

Dan had an idea.

. . .

As Dan pulled his truck into the parking lot of the club, he had the distinct feeling of returning to the scene of a crime. It wasn't all that long ago that Dan had met Sindee for the first time, and the sight of the club's front door, and the hotel it shared a parking lot with brought back a flood of memories. By the time his shadow was darkening the club door, Dan's excitement reached a high peak at the idea of seeing Sindee.

Sindee was on the stage as he walked in, killing a booming rock song with a routine on the pole. The crowd in the club did look pretty light, and most were at the stage fixated on Sindee. She was graceful, fluid, and devastatingly sexual in the way she moved and the poses she took. The men were continuously stuffing dollar bills in her G-string, already loaded with cash. There was even a couple at the stage, with the woman occasionally handing Sindee bills.

She had her back to the door when it opened, so she didn't see Dan right away. He stood there watching her work. *She really* does *enjoy her job*, he thought. Sindee gave her complete attention to each person at the stage, one at a time, and whenever someone tipped her. She enjoyed the attention and enjoyed giving it back. It wasn't until Dan sat down at a table near the stage that she saw him, and made smoldering eye contact with him while flashing her big, crooked smile.

As soon as her set was over, she made quick apologies to three different men, each interested in a lap dance, and walked over to Dan's table. She bent at the waist and gave him a long, soulful kiss.

"How late are you working?"

Sindee's already smiling face widened. "I can leave anytime, baby. The other dancers would probably love to see me hitting the door. I'm the only one doing well tonight."

"Well, if you're doing well..."

She cut him off. "I thought I was doing well until *you* walked in! I'm going to freshen up, change, and let the manager know I'm done. I'll be back in a few minutes." The excitement in her voice was obvious and genuine.

"Why don't we get a room next door for old time's sake?" Dan asked.

She stood, looked him in the eyes, nodded, smiled that incredible smile, and spun around to face the dressing room door. Normally, she would walk slowly and sensuously through the club, smiling at patrons as she went. In this case, the anticipation of an unexpected meeting with Dan moved her feet with purpose, so she beelined it straight to the dressing room door.

. . .

The dressing room announcement that she was leaving was met with several insincere pleas to stay. Sindee was well-liked by the other dancers, but they also all understood that her leaving meant everyone's income potential just went up. The manager was there to hear her announcement, so Sindee thought she'd be back at Dan's table quickly. One of the dancers, someone Sindee would consider a friend, had seen her kiss Dan, which made her curious.

"Who was that fuckin' hottie I saw you kiss, girl? If he has money, I'd let him fuck me on a table in the club!"

"He and I have a good thing going right now. It also doesn't hurt that he is great in the sack, and he's an airline pilot."

Stunned, her friend sat there staring at Sindee. "Get the fuck out of here! Girl, I wouldn't leave him sitting out there alone in this place for ten seconds."

Unconcerned, Sindee flipped her hair as she gathered her belongings. "I've got nothing to worry about, girlfriend. See you later." Sindee blew her friend a kiss and spun away.

Ten minutes later, the couple stood in front of the hotel desk. Dan remembered the number of the room they first rented, so he requested it. "It's *our* room now, baby." Dan kissed her on the lips, then took the key card from the desk staffer's hand.

. . .

Sindee was thinking out loud. "The paint is peeling in the corner. I don't think this place would get any five-star ratings on any travel sites." She chuckled a little as she folded herself into Dan's arms, their two bodies interconnected across the bed like pieces of a puzzle. Sindee had never felt with any other man the feelings she had for Dan. Though he was quiet and his eyes were closed when she made the remark, he obviously was awake, as he pulled her closer upon her observation. He peeked up at the ceiling, then returned her chuckle before burying his face in her neck.

DEPARTURES

"Five stars? I don't think this place could earn one thumb down, but right now, it's my favorite place on earth," Dan said.

"Lover, I want to talk about something, but I'm not sure how to say this." Sindee's voice had a tone that Dan had not heard before. She could see this by Dan's sudden alert expression and tense body language as he created a space between them by pulling away. She had wanted to bring this up with Dan for some time but had been afraid to do so. This new look of concern on Dan's face made her even more afraid that she had just made a big mistake.

"It's okay, baby. What's going on? Talk to me."

That was unexpected. Dan's look of concern was not for him, but for her. This gave her the confidence she needed to open up to him.

"You are the first man I've ever had these feelings for. I feel like I'm losing my footing with you. I'm used to being in control, being the aggressor with men. I've always been the one who was desired by the other. But now, with you... I know you love me. I know you desire me. But... I also have all those same feelings for you, and I'm afraid, I guess, because for the first time in my life, I feel like I'm going in a direction where I could get hurt. I mean... I *want* to go in that direction, it's just..."

"What is it, baby?"

Her eyes met his. A tear rolled down her cheek.

"Oh, baby, what's wrong?"

"Nothing's wrong, my captain. And everything." She grabbed his hands. "I love you, Dan Hatfield, and it scares me."

Dan took all this in, never breaking eye contact with Sindee. The look on his face was a mix of apprehension and love. "Baby, I love you, and my heart swells to hear you say the same to me. I'm not going to hurt you. I would never."

"It isn't that I'm afraid you will hurt me. I have had contact with many men that enjoy hurting women. There is none of that in you. I'm

207

not afraid of you hurting me, I'm afraid of being in the position of allowing someone to be able to. That first night we met, you told me a lot
about your past, told me things that made me understand right there
and then what kind of man you are, and what made you the man you
are. I think it would be good for us if I told you the same about me, right
now." Sindee felt as if she was crossing a stream, stepping delicately from
rock to rock.

Dan's head tilted to the side. "Wait, what? I don't recall telling you
my life's history that night."

"You can thank the scotch for that. It was later in the evening, but
you told me all about Sharon, how you met her, how she was never
happy. You talked about your childhood and your father, your mother
dying, the group homes, all of it. I've thought a lot about what you said
and what we have in common. What I think brought us together so
quickly and so completely is that we both grew up without love and have
lived our lives without real love in them. Until now." Sindee felt like she'd
made her way halfway across the stream now, still standing on solid rock
and ready to go the rest of the way. Dan was speechless, still a look of
apprehension, like he wasn't sure where this was going, but clearly, he
wanted to hear it.

Sindee continued, "The dressing room at the club is filled with stories of childhood trauma, abusive fathers, creepy uncles, shit like that.
That isn't my story. I have nothing like that in my past. But like you, there
was little love in my house growing up. My father was eighteen when he
got to Vietnam in 1968, and it changed him, at least that's what I was
told. He was forty-five when he finally gave in to my mother and made
me. He didn't want kids and couldn't get his head out of the jungle. He
was distant and unreachable. I didn't know any different when I was little. When I was ten in 2006, he died of cancer. By then, my mother had
been beaten down emotionally by all of it, and she pretty much checked

out. I grew up quickly. By the time I was in high school, I was more of a roommate than daughter to my mother. I had to take care of myself, and sometimes I had to take care of her. I tried out for cheerleading to feel like part of a team, not to feel so alone, and that was where I discovered my good looks and how exciting it felt to be desired. Shortly thereafter, I discovered sex. One of the other cheerleaders showed me some internet porn, and what I saw was a woman who was clearly enjoying herself. I wanted that. Since that moment, I have enjoyed being the object of desire, I *love* to turn men on, and I love to fuck."

Sindee paused, feeling like the jump to the next stone in the stream was a big leap. "And now there's you. I love all of those things with you, but for the first time I'm feeling something else. Something more, something bigger. A small part of me doesn't want the rest of my life to change, and I think that is out of fear. Most of me wants to be yours and yours alone, until we are in a nursing home."

"Jesus, Sindee, what makes you think you won't still be driving all the men in the nursing home nuts?" They both laughed. "I understand what you are saying, and I feel honored that you shared it with me. I'm in an odd situation here too. I thought Sharon was the one, but I misjudged that relationship from the beginning, because it was my first time. This is your first time *and* my first time with open eyes. I love everything about you, even your desire to make every man on the planet think thoughts they wouldn't talk about at a Thanksgiving table. I believe you are mine; I know you are mine. Anyone who heard you say what you just said would know that's true. I love you, Sindee, and I know you love me."

Sindee's face broke into a slow, wide, beaming smile that was full of love. Her eyes blinked slowly once, and then the smile changed to her predator face. Sindee's hands started sliding all over Dan's body, and finally settled on something that interested her.

44

The other phone rang at just after 9:00 A.M. The pair had already been awake for a half hour or so but had not yet gotten out of bed. There was enough light leaking through the narrow space between the drawn curtains for Dan to see where the phone was sitting on the nightstand. He answered it.

"Hello, boss." Dan tried sounding as if he hadn't just been woken up by Sindee in a wonderful way.

Angelo, all business as usual. "Hey, I'd like to meet with you today. This afternoon, my place."

"Sure, sounds good. I'll be there about 1:00 P.M."

Click.

Sindee rolled over. "One, huh? That still gives me a few hours to play sexy flight attendant for my hot pilot."

"That sounds great, sweetheart. I've never had a flight attendant do to me what you are already doing to me."

. . .

Looking at his watch, Angelo chuckled at the sound of the front gate alarm. It was almost exactly 1:00 P.M. He liked people who had attention to detail and followed through on their word. Those were two of the bare minimum qualifications a person had to have, in order for Angelo to employ them in any substantial way. Of course, there were others. But

Angelo was sizing Dan up, measuring him with every interaction, and he was consistently and pleasantly surprised with what he saw in Dan.

Standing in the doorway at the back of the house wearing a warm smile, Angelo looked like he was greeting the arrival of an old friend. It had taken Dan the same amount of time to drive around to the back of the house as it did for the owner to walk from the office to the back door. Dan returned the smile when he rounded the front of the truck and saw Angelo standing there.

"Captain! Good to see you!"

"Hey, boss, good to see you too." Dan closed the distance between them and shook the offered, outstretched hand.

"C'mon inside. You want a coffee or something? My housekeeper is here. She can get you whatever you like."

The pair was walking through the kitchen, and Dan caught sight of a woman at the sink. Even with the casual attire of jeans and designer top, he could see that she was an uncommonly beautiful woman. Angelo caught Dan's discovery and noted the look on his face. *I'll explain that in the office.*

"Coffee sounds great, boss. If the coffee is good, I prefer it black, and I'm guessing the coffee here is *very* good."

"Good guess, flyboy. Hey, sweetheart, can you bring us two coffees to the office?"

With a smile, the housekeeper said, "Of course, sir. Right away."

The pair walked through the house to the office, and they took their respective positions. There were few places Angelo felt as comfortable and as in control as when he was seated in that very expensive, comfortable, high-backed office chair. Dan could see it immediately. Angelo looked like a ship captain at the helm.

"Sooo... you did good in El Paso. Real good. In fact, it was a very, *very* successful night on both sides of the border. Remember your concern about more coming? There will be no more coming. We cut the head off the snake that night, and it seems the other snakes were happy to feast on what was left. The other cartels looted the entire leaderless operation. You took out the number two man, who was setting up shop in America based in El Paso. The number one we took out south of the border. The other cartels jumped on assets, territories, and employees who were only too happy to work for someone when they found they were suddenly out of a job. There's fighting going on all over Mexico right now, and my sources tell me they are now spooked about crossing the border. The cartels that are still looking to do business north of the border..."

Dan stepped in. "Are now talking to you, ready to set up in your shop."

Angelo was once again impressed with Dan's insight. "Yeah, talking to me. I've been putting all the pieces in place for months on this one, but the whole op was necessary. They made it necessary. I can't have them taking over up here, so they forced my hand. I might as well get something out of it for my operation. I took invaders and turned them into customers."

Dan was obviously impressed with Angelo's business mind. "You said you were going to make them disappear. That's part of making sure no one wanted the job opening the number two left. I'm curious. Something this high-profile in your world would require something foolproof and permanent. What did you do?"

Angelo thought for a moment. He decided that if Dan were going to go further, he would need to be brought closer into the circle of trust. "We have a friend who owns a scrap metal business in that area, and we ask him occasionally to crush and dispose of a vehicle for us when necessary. It's this huge hydraulic press that crushes a car into a, uh, a sorta metal cube. The cubes then get railroaded to a furnace that melts them down. Let's just say no one checks the trunk or the backseat before they crush the cars I send. That is not the only way we have of making sure a body never is found, but that was the El Paso op."

Dan nodded his head. "Wow. Smart. Permanent."

The housekeeper walked in at that moment with two large cups of coffee, setting one in front of each man without a word. Both thanked her, and she walked out giving each man a smile. Angelo saw Dan looking her up and down again. When they made eye contact, Angelo explained, "She's the daughter of a friend, nothing more. I'll tell you her back story some other time. And yes, captain, permanent. Not the only method. Spend some time, think of where you'd bury a body that it would *never* be found or disturbed, and you'll probably be able to guess a few other methods. Anyway, I have a few questions to ask you. We are putting a fine point on the reason that brought you and me together. Does your beloved ever carry a gun? Mace? Is there anything we would need to know about her habits? Think like a hitter."

. . .

When Angelo asked the first question, Dan started formulating an answer, but the last four words Angelo said to him resonated within Dan. There was a long breath and a long pause as Dan thought, *Think like a hitter? I guess that's what I am now, and this is Angelo saying it. He's not asking me to pretend to be someone else; he's asking for expertise I already have.*

Dan felt as if he had been promoted. When he finally gave his answer, he tried hard to seem thoughtful and level-headed. "Not that I can think of, and nothing you couldn't learn by tailing her. And no, she hates guns."

Angelo nodded. "Okay good. You think of anything, let me know."

. . .

John Bayan had been a field agent for the CIA for the last eighteen years. Aggressive, intelligent, and meticulous, Bayan had settled into the Mexican drug cartels as his niche. He spent the first few years trying to get close to the leadership of a few cartels, and finally worked up the chain of the Villareal cartel. The next seven years of his life was spent working the partnership between Villareal and the CIA. A quiet partnership between the two that had been lucrative for the CIA, and personally for Bayan. Through Bayan's contacts, the Villareal cartel had the latest intel on anti-drug operations and technology, as well as the location of assets conducting interdiction efforts. Villareal drugs flowed, other cartels were intercepted, and Bayan was paid well. As was the CIA. The CIA take was over a billion dollars. Bayan had managed to skim millions.

And then, just like that, it all went up in smoke. The head of the Villareal cartel along with his family and the entire upper management structure were murdered in a single night. The number two man, Bayan's American-side asset, simply disappeared with his trusted bodyguard. When word got out, which it did with amazing speed, the other cartels swooped in on the Villareal assets, personnel, and territories. For years, the Villareal had enjoyed unrelenting success. Enough that it had gained the attention, and also the anger, of all of the other cartels. They all knew something wasn't right. The opportunity to swallow them up was all the invitation the other cartels needed. Villareal simultaneously became a cautionary tale and a history lesson in one night.

Seven fucking years. SEVEN! Bayan has superiors, and they were asking some very pointed questions for which Bayan had no good answers. He needed info, and he needed it fast. The only lead he had was the tracker he installed on the car of his guy in El Paso. The signal of that tracker ended abruptly the night his guy disappeared, and the location was Metal World scrap yard. This was his only lead, and he needed a way to snoop around Metal World without looking conspicuous. A pickup truck with scrap metal in the bed took a few hours to put together, but it would be his "in." Bayan needed to be low profile on this.

. . .

I don't believe I've ever seen that truck before. Even at seventy-five, Papa Toccino was as sharp as a straight razor. Scrappers were regulars mostly, and the guy he was looking at and his truck were new to Metal World. An old pickup truck with very little in the back. It didn't make sense, so Papa approached the truck. One guy, who was driving the truck, rolled his window down as Papa walked up to the door.

Papa said with a friendly smile, "Can I help you?"

"Yeah." Gun came into view so only Papa could see it. "Come around the truck and get in the passenger side. Or, I can go inside the office building and kill everyone inside. I'm guessing there are people in there you care about."

Papa had been to Korea where he saw combat for two years, was wounded twice, and earned a Silver Star, so he didn't scare easily. But there *were* people in that building that meant everything to him. He opened the passenger door and climbed into the pickup truck. Before the evening was over, Papa told Bayan everything he knew about the specials he scrapped, and Bayan promised to leave his family alone.

. . .

Bayan called a tow company to hook up the pickup truck and deliver it to Metal World. The owner, Bayan, sold it to Metal World for $60, calculated from the weight of the metal it would yield. Papa was behind the seat under a tarp when the truck was loaded into The Beast. Bayan rode away in the passenger seat of a sedan, with a new lead. *Seven fucking years.*

45

"Make the meeting three-thirty. Don't come earlier."

The text popped up on Nico's phone just in time. He was just turning into Angelo's subdivision for the three o'clock meeting. Angelo could trust that Nico didn't need to know why, he just needed to respect what Angelo told him. He turned away from the house and toward the community park, where he'd spend the time in his car doing business on the phone. "You got it, three-thirty."

Angelo, with reluctance, "You know, I could bullshit all afternoon with you about flying, but I have a meeting at three-thirty that I have got to take."

"Sure thing, Angelo, I'll get out of your hair. At some point though, we need to talk about our future from here. You and me, and also Sindee."

"Yeah, I was thinking the same thing." One of Angelo's phones rang, and he immediately picked it up. "I gotta take this, I'll be in touch." Angelo's face showed the importance of the call.

"I'll find my way out."

Angelo let it ring until he was sure Dan was at the back door, then he answered it. "Yeah?"

It was Angelo's information guy. Angelo met this man more than twenty years ago, a very personable, outgoing guy who was blessed with a photographic memory. He carried a half dozen cell phones with no contacts saved on any of them. In Angelo's organization, his job was to create contacts, friendships, develop snitches and informants anywhere, and in any way he could. Angelo only knew him as "PG" and didn't even know what that stood for. He remembered the letters by assigning them with his own invention as standing for "People Guy."

PG got right to business, as Angelo was not someone who liked to waste time. "Okay, sir, I've been on the phone since seven this morning and have a lot to tell you. Some good, some bad. Do you have the time?"

"Of course, PG, give it all to me, leave nothing out." Angelo noticed on the security feed that Dan was pulling out of his front driveway. Time on the monitor was 3:20 P.M.

"South of the border, Villareal is gone, just gone. You know how the other cartels felt about Villareal, and they jumped on everything Villareal owned. There were firefights at first over assets and territories, but those have stopped because *no one* from Villareal is defending anything anymore. They are all defecting or dead. North of the border, my sources say they are pretty much paralyzed. There's no one to give them orders, north or south, and they are hearing what is happening in Mexico. Their guy didn't die, he *disappeared*, and they know if someone can do that to him, they could get to anyone."

"That all sounds good so far." Angelo was nodding, waiting for the part of the briefing that wasn't good.

"Yes, sir, but there's something else going on, and I'm not sure what it is. You know there were always rumors about Villareal being connected with maybe U.S. intelligence. We talked about that before. But I was never really able to connect those dots. If it's true, there are going to be some pissed-off people out there now that Villareal is a ghost. So, we had something happen that may be connected. I have to ask you a question. Is Metal World involved in this op?"

That gave Angelo a jolt. "Yes. What makes you ask that?"

"Papa Toccino is missing, but the family may have figured out what happened. They looked over the yard security footage and saw him getting into an old pickup truck with a single driver. No one had ever seen the truck before. Two hours later, same truck is towed into the yard, sold, and crushed. Location on Papa's cell phone shows it was almost certainly in the truck when it was crushed, and they found reason to believe a person was in the truck as well. Ralph was the one who loaded the truck. He's a mess, the whole family is. Mr. Genofi, sir, know that I'm shaking *every* tree on this one, but it is feeling more and more like intelligence, like maybe CIA."

"PG, I understand business, and I understand loss. This just got very personal. Papa Toccino and my uncle served together in Korea. I've known his family since I was a kid. Whoever did this knew exactly what he was doing to that family. I will back any bribe money, anything at all you need to get what we need to know." Angelo was seething. The Toccinos were family.

"I will find out, sir. I understand. Last, I have the intel file you requested on Sharon Hatfield. Would you like me to send it? I was able to get the Miami jail visitation footage as well."

"Yeah, send it right now if you can. I'm meeting someone right now about that subject." The security feed showed Nico pulling up to the front gate camera.

"You got it, sir, uploading it now. I will be in touch. G'day."
Click.

Nico knew the rule was that if the back door was unlocked, just let yourself in, and so he did. He nodded and smiled at the housekeeper in the kitchen on his way to the office. He saw immediately that something was very wrong by the look on Angelo's face.

"Boss, what's wrong?"

Angelo shook it off and went right to business. "Let's put the fine details together about the Sharon hit, get that worked out, and then I'll tell you all about the call I just got." Angelo opened the digital file PG just sent and started looking it over with Nico.

"I'm changing direction on this. I want to try something new that our Mobile Mechanic ran past me a few days ago."

They spent the next half hour gaming out all the details of how things would go down. Nico was as focused as he could be, but he knew Angelo well enough to know that something was far from right, and he was dying to find out what it was.

"Okay, boss, I think we've covered all the angles. So can you tell me what is bothering you?"

"Someone killed a friend, Nico, and it's bad. We are going hunting."

. . .

Dan saw the car parked in the alley behind his house as he pulled up to the garage. He couldn't make out the driver through the tinted windows. Thinking nothing of it, he hit the garage remote to open the door. "What the fuck?" he shouted when the car pulled into the garage next to his truck. Dan grabbed the pistol, which he kept on a magnetic mount in the truck, with his right hand, then rolled down the passenger window with his left. The driver rolled down their window just enough to show a face—that of Sindee. They both laughed, and Dan showed her the gun in his hand. Sindee wasn't fazed at all by the sight, and in fact was smiling in a way that gave Dan the impression she knew something he didn't.

He shut off the truck, hit the garage remote to close the door, and walked up to Sindee's window. She had rolled it all the way down, and now that he was standing in front of it, he was greeted by the sight of a completely naked Sindee behind the wheel.

Dan was shaking his head and smiling as he said, "I was going to say that you are breaking routine by coming here; now I realize you are shattering it. What I *am* going to say is that you can't walk into the house like that."

Sindee turned in her seat and lay back, putting one foot on the dash and the other on the driver seat headrest.

"Maybe we'll just have to stay here in the garage. See anything you like?"

Dan opened the driver's side door of her car and answered her question without speaking a word.

. . .

Agent Bayan was trying to see all sides of the problem and game it out. "It's not going to be difficult to find out who did this. We stepped on someone's toes, someone connected, upper-echelon. He's smart, careful. The metal guy didn't know a name, or he was tough enough not to give it up. We need to grab someone who does know a name. I had the security cameras at the metal yard hacked, so no need to sit on the place. We wait to see who shows up sniffing around, and we grab that guy."

Like Angelo, Bayan preferred to work out of his home office, and the operative he was talking to just nodded. In another room of his house, filled with computers, monitor screens, and other tech, a man was watching the Metal World security camera feed. Sooner or later, someone would visit, someone out of the ordinary. Metal World was the connection to whomever had destroyed the operation.

. . .

An assistant booked the ticket to El Paso for Nico, and with today's tech, the boarding pass coded symbol was texted to his phone. Paper tickets are so yesterday. The same arrangements were made for a rental car there, the assistant knowing already what kind of car he would like. Nico actually preferred mini-vans or SUVs. They were nothing flashy, something that blended in, and something that didn't look like an out-of-town mob guy would drive. Less than four hours later, Nico was throwing his bag on the passenger seat of a late model SUV in the El Paso airport rental car garage.

46

"New Castle 9, Pegasus 7. Uh, we have a good look at the entire area, and your flight of three are the only aircraft operating within one-hundred miles right now. I'm sure your map analysis came to the same conclusion ours did. There should be nothing but desert and one pilot out there in the surrounding twenty-five miles. Anything but that pilot should be considered hostile. As far as I see, you are mission status Marble, over."

"Pegasus 7, this is New Castle 9 flight of three. Agree completely with your last, and we appreciate you watching our backs. We will monitor your frequency. Switching to tactical frequency now, we are mission status Marble."

Marble was the radio code word meaning that this particular mission, rescuing the downed F-16 pilot, was a go, and New Castle 9 should proceed with the rescue operation. New Castle 9 flight consisted of one MH-53J Pave Low helicopter and two MH-64 Apache gunship helicopters for protection. The two pilots in the heavy Pave Low, and the pilot in each Apache, were wearing night vision equipment, allowing them to fly in total darkness. Clear nights in the desert with a star-filled sky made the pilots' jobs easier.

"Hacksaw 1, Hacksaw 2, New Castle 9. Pegasus says we are clear of aircraft for one hundred, nothing but desert for twenty-five. Anything except the pilot is to be considered hostile. Report any contacts or visuals. Our present heading is directly to the pilot's location, over."

"New Castle 9, Hacksaw 1 copy."

"New Castle 9, Hacksaw 2 copy."

The three helicopters flew low and as fast as they could go in the moonless night. They were spread out, with the Pave Low in the middle, flanked by an Apache on each side at a distance of about two hundred feet. Radio discipline would be strict from this moment on in the mission. Only necessary communication would happen until they had picked up the F-16 pilot and were in safe airspace. In the back of the Pave Low, there were two medics and a full trauma kit in case the pilot had injuries. Also in the Pave Low, there were three gunners manning machine guns on swing mounts: one on each side, and one on the back of the helicopter on a retractable ramp.

The Apaches carried an array of weapons. They could be loaded with rockets, guided missiles, and a host of other ordnance. The Apache also had a forward gun that was connected electronically to the helmet of the gunner, who sat in front of the pilot. When the gunner turned his head, the gun went with him. He merely needed to put the gunsight in front of his eye on something and squeeze the trigger.

"New Castle 9, flight party in ten."

New Castle 9 then switched to the Pegasus frequency and broadcast the same message. The helicopters were ten minutes from the pickup area that the GPS tracker was transmitting. The flight was traveling at just under 180 miles per hour, just under the maximum speed of the Apaches. The Pave Low was capable of two hundred miles per hour, but the Pave Low pilots wanted to keep their guns in their holsters, flying right next to them. The Pave Low pilots, in fact everyone aboard that helicopter, were grateful for the protection, and they all hoped the Apaches were an unnecessary precaution.

Moving at 180 miles per hour translates to three miles every minute, and that meant they were roughly thirty miles from the F-16 pilot. At the low altitude they were flying, less than fifty feet, their sound would not give them away until they were much closer. They always assumed, and it was almost always true, that the sound of rotor blades is the happiest sound in the world for a downed pilot. Downed pilots all said that after rescue. It was a sound that meant safety, going home, and not being captured. Captured pilots made it onto the news, displayed by the enemy as a trophy. Or killed. Or both. All equally bad in the eyes of a pilot.

The thirty miles was going by fast.

"New Castle 9 flight, party in five."

. . .

There's no way they could have known, or even guessed, that the F-16 pilot on the ground was in a position of dreading that sound. But that was the position Dan found himself in when he first made out the fleeting sound of rotor blades cutting through the night air. He froze for a second, holding his breath to make sure that he was, in fact, hearing rotors. It was so faint, Dan knew that with any noise at all happening inside of the heavy canvas tent, it would be a little while before anyone besides Dan heard the sound. But he knew that was not going to last, and he knew he needed to act fast.

Dan focused his resolve. *Time for you fuckers to die.*

47

The virtual meeting with leadership was tense, and Bayan sensed they were holding back a big issue to discuss. After one subject wrapped up, a long, uncomfortable pause followed.

Finally, the program director spoke. "Let's discuss the direction we are going to take now." Bayan knew they were about to broach the main issue, so he was eager for the director to continue. "It took over seven years to cultivate a relationship deep into the Villareal cartel, and it turned out to be very beneficial to our organization and our program. That said, the new head of counterintelligence feels that programs such as ours with Villareal present a... liability for the Agency. He considers these recent events as fortuitous for us. A perfect ending to the situation. He'd like us to look into interdicting the fentanyl flow into Mexico, and he thinks our section would be perfect to spearhead the effort, as we already have so much intel and contacts in Mexico and with the cartels. John, what do you think?"

Bayan almost missed the question. He was fuming. *Seven fucking years of my life, and now that extra money is gone. There is* no *money in interdicting drug shipments from China.*

"John? Thoughts?"

Bayan shook off the seething inner anger and tried to redirect. "Yes, well, over the last seven years I, we, have made extensive inroads into the cartels. Villareal is gone, to be sure, but most of the contacts we made were absorbed into other cartels as they swooped in on what was left of

Villareal. That now gives us limited access into several cartels. I will begin developing a new structure and create a work package for everyone."

"Great, as soon as you can. Carol, can you put together the financials?" With the director's attention elsewhere, Bayan tuned him out to listen to his tech assistant. The man had walked into Bayan's office, staying off the meeting camera on purpose, and nodded at Bayan's keyboard. Bayan muted the meeting and nodded at the man.

He reported, "Sir, I think what you're waiting for arrived. Out of town, dressed like an off-duty gangster, and driving a rental."

Bayan looked at a completely bored agent who had been sitting in the corner of the office during the meeting. He finally perked up when Bayan said, "Let's go."

. . .

Bayan's tech guy had been able to read the license plate, and he noted the direction the SUV went when it left Metal World. Bayan took an educated guess where the vehicle was going. The hotels in El Paso were bunched up in a few locations, and the airport hotels seemed to be the most logical choice. They started with the most expensive hotels first. No self-respecting made guy would stay at a motor lodge. They only had to drive through three hotel parking lots before they found the SUV. Bayan called the tech guy and related the name of the hotel. While he was still on the phone, the tech guy had compromised the hotel's reservation system, and he gave Bayan a name and room number.

"The guy's gotta eat, and it's about lunchtime. He'll go out soon. Tech hacked the hotel computer, so we got the guy's name and room number. If he doesn't come out soon, we'll go in."

"He just ordered room service." The text on Bayan's phone from the tech guy made up his mind about the next move. He didn't need to tell his assisting agent that he had decided to go up to the room. Threading a suppressor on the end of his pistol told the other agent all he needed to know.

. . .

Nico was tired and had phone calls to make. He chose to order room service. The trip to Metal World had been a solid gut punch. Nico reported to Angelo, then started the process of looking at all sides of this issue, trying to figure out the next move. The knock on his door brought Nico out of a state of deep thought and into looking forward to a meal. *It ain't Vincent's, but it's here.* Nico saw a man holding a large room service tray when he checked the door's peephole. He opened the door and asked the man to take the tray all the way to the bedroom of the suite. The room service delivery man, dressed like a restaurant waiter, placed the tray on the bed. Nico tipped him with a twenty. It was gratefully accepted by a man clearly not used to being tipped.

After the delivery man left, Nico sat on the bed next to the tray. As he lifted the metal covers off the plates, his lunch was suddenly interrupted by the sound of his door being kicked in. Nico had heard the sound many times, and violent entry was never a good thing for the people inside. His bed was two rooms away from the entry door of the suite. The distance gave him just enough time to activate the emergency signal on his phone and dial Angelo. The phone was back on the nightstand when the two armed men entered the bedroom. Nico didn't have a gun; he didn't think he'd need one.

Bayan, gun in hand, looked at Nico, then to the food on the tray, then back to Nico. "Well, well. If you can talk and eat at the same time, feel free to eat that while you tell me *all* about who you work for, where I can find him, and how he's connected. You know... *everything.*" Bayan said the last word through clenched teeth. He left a pause to let it sink in. It was clear to Bayan by Nico's demeanor that he was one cool customer.

Nico was still chewing his food, and hadn't otherwise moved, even though he was looking down the barrel of a suppressed pistol. Bayan relaxed a bit and changed the direction of the conversation. "I can tell just by looking at you that you are familiar with giving and receiving pain. I'm sure you guessed the same about me. Everyone breaks sooner or later."

Nico never lost eye contact, set the fork and knife on the tray, and began stalling to give the boss time to send help. "I'm in the scrap metal business and have no fucking idea what you're talking about."

. . .

Angelo heard the sound of a suppressed pistol shot, heard Nico yelp in pain, then the man's voice again. "That's just a scratch. Start talking." Bayan was trying to sound tough.

It took half a second for Angelo to decide which phone of the dozen splayed across his desk was the one to call his contact in El Paso. The phone was answered on the first ring, and Angelo pleaded for a crew to get to Nico's hotel, armed heavy and ready for anything. The request was granted without question; this man had known Angelo a long time and had *never* heard him like this. Four men with assault rifles were in a car in under two minutes.

"They're ten minutes out, Angelo. That place ain't far away. We're going to get your guy and take care of who did this!"

"Be smart. Tell three of them to head up to the room but leave one guy in the parking lot. Tell him to take the tracker off his car and put it on their car. Tell the three to rough the assholes up, make it look good, but let them go. We need to find out who these fucks are, and where they operate from."

"Damn, Angelo, that's why you're the man. That's smart. I'll pass it on to the crew."

Click.

Angelo closed his eyes, thinking of his friend, his most trusted soldier. *Cavalry is coming. They'll be there in ten minutes, Nico! Hold on!*

. . .

Sindee and Dan had slept in. It turned out that Sindee had clothes in the car after all, so about an hour after they had parked in the garage, Sindee was able to travel appropriately to the house. Dan woke first and spent several moments just looking at Sindee's beautiful face. When Sindee opened her eyes, Dan was laying there staring into them. He clearly had something on his mind.

Sindee lightly touched Dan's face with her fingertips. "Tell me what you're thinking, lover."

"I'm fast-forwarding six months to a time when it will be every morning that I wake in a bed with you. To when I can roll over, look into those eyes, climb on top of you, and make you suck in a deep breath of ecstasy."

"Oh, Dan, do that to me *right now*," she whispered.

. . .

An hour later, the two were in the shower, enjoying the feeling of warm soap and water being applied by another person. Sindee's face changed. She had been thinking things over, and her thoughts had turned into several unanswered questions. She wasn't sure where the line was about what she should know and what she shouldn't. She didn't even know exactly what questions to ask, but she knew that the subject needed to be handled if they were to have a real future together.

"We are in love, Dan. Deep, and if this is going to go any further, and I very much want it to, we need to be open with each another. I don't need to know everything, but I'm concerned about whatever your business with Angelo is."

Sindee could see the thoughtful look on Dan's face and heard the caution in his voice as he answered. "Sweetheart, first, I agree that we shouldn't be keeping secrets from each other, and I want to be in love with all of Sindee as much as you want to be in love with all of Dan. But... I won't put you in any dangerous situations with the cops *or* the robbers. You know as well as I do, information can be dangerous." Sindee started to speak, but Dan put a finger on her lips. "So, I will tell you, yes, I do some work for Angelo. No, it is not particularly dangerous. No, I'm not going to speak any more specifically than that."

Sindee paused while she tried to digest what Dan had said. After a few seconds of silence, she spoke. "You said in six months we would be together every morning. How can you know that? Are you planning on that quick of a divorce?"

"I've been planning it since the night I caught her fucking someone I thought was a friend." The disgust in Dan's voice was palpable.

He spent the next ten minutes going into detail about what happened, and how he ended up in the hotel with her that first night. What Dan couldn't remember was that he had told Sindee most of the story on the night they met. Yet she listened to him tell it all, as the story this time had far more detail and far less club music and scotch drowning it out. He then told her the "sad" tale about Ed.

Dan finished with the punchline, "In fact, she flew to Miami and is down there right now visiting that asshole in jail. *Bitch!*"

"Okay, yeah, you need to divorce that."

. . .

The conversation had caught Dan off guard and took a serious turn when Sindee asked about Angelo. He wanted to be honest with her and answer all of her questions, but he realized immediately the danger in doing so. The moment she asked about his business with Angelo, he thought, *Oh fuck. Telling her anything specific would just put her in jeopardy. Cops could grill her, and Angelo would see her as a liability. He has already made it clear what happens to loose ends. How would she handle what I'm doing for Angelo, and how would she handle what he's doing for me?*

By the time Dan finished the story about Sharon, he felt as if he'd dodged a bullet. It was handled, for now, but he was concerned that it would come back as an issue in the future. *I am always going to need to be careful not to put Sindee in harm's way.*

48

The three men approached Nico's hotel room door quickly but quietly. It would be obvious to anyone who saw them that it was military training they were observing. The man on point noticed that the door had been kicked in. He let his assault rifle hang on its sling so that with both hands he could silently communicate with the others using hand signals. *"Door broken. We all go in silently. I go right, you go left, you go in the middle. Look for hostiles. Subdue silently."* Just as they all nodded in agreement, they heard Nico yelp in pain. One last hand signal. *"Let's go."*

The three executed that plan quickly and quietly. The thing that had saved Nico—his room was a suite—made the plan much easier to execute. The two men interrogating Nico had their backs to the three men entering the bedroom doorway, their assault rifles leveled at the interrogators' heads. When they turned to see what Nico was looking at, they froze. The point man spoke in a quiet, commanding tone.

"Hands in the air. Do not make a sound. You fucked up, but not badly enough, yet, to be killed. Give me an excuse, you'll be dead as DaVinci. On my right, go check them for weapons. On my left, sweep the room."

Point kept his rifle trained on the man doing the interrogating when they walked in, guessing correctly that Bayan was in charge. The man to point's right leaned his rifle against the wall, unsheathed an impressive knife with his right hand, and approached the two men. With the knife in one hand, he frisked thoroughly with his left. "Move and you get this in the balls." The words were sincere; even a little enthusiastic.

The left-hand man held his rifle at ready while he went around the room in a circle and noted all the contents. On the dresser were two identical pistols. They looked government issue. He announced, "Guns on the dresser, two."

"Take them apart, put the barrels in your pocket." Bayan was now guessing correctly that point was the team leader, something that he displayed by maintaining his eye contact on the point man. Everyone in the room knew that taking the barrels served multiple purposes and left no doubt that the men were professionals. The man sweeping the room made it around to Nico, and cut him out of the duct tape, and the chair. The right-hand man had returned the knife to its sheath and picked up his rifle. Point never moved.

With Bayan and his assistant guarded by his two wingmen, Point motioned for Nico to join him in the living area. Once they were out of earshot of Bayan and his man, Point said, "Boss says we let them go so we can track them and roll them all the way up. He said we can tune them up a bit though, so go give them as good as you got, and then we chase them out. We have a guy putting a tracker on their vehicle right now."

. . .

Nico processed the info and realized the wisdom of Angelo's plan. *Boss has always done me well; he'll do it now, too.*

Point re-entered the bedroom and relieved one of his men. "Left, go see to our brother in the living room, and give him your gloves." The man on the left went into the living room, took off his tactical gloves, and detached a small trauma kit from his belt. Nico's gunshot wound actually was just a surface wound, but they didn't know that until they took a closer look at what was bleeding. With obvious medical training, the man had Nico's wound sterilized, cleaned, and dressed quickly. Left picked up his tactical gloves from the floor and handed them to Nico.

Nico put on the gloves; they felt good on his hands. *Time to show that asshole how right he was about my ability to pass out a beating.*

Ten minutes later, two bruised and bleeding men were running to their car in the parking lot. They jumped in and took off quickly. It took a few minutes for Nico to pack, and within ten minutes, the four men were exiting the back stairwell door. The parking lot man was standing there waiting for them.

Point asked, "Did you get the tracker on the car?"

"Oh yeah. I picked it out right away. Black sedan, parked by the door you just came out of, crooked across a walkway. Had to be them. And get this." He held up his cell phone to show a picture of a license plate. "It's got government plates."

Nico looked at Point and said, "I gotta phone this in to the boss, right away."

"Me too." said Point.

. . .

"It seems that we left a loose end the day we imploded the cartel." Angelo's voice on the phone was a mixture of concern and puzzlement. *First Papa Toccino, and now Nico. What kind of shit did we step in here?* "But Nico, I am tremendously relieved to hear your voice. We will catch up on all this later. I have calls to make, but know that when the time comes, I will put you in place to erase this problem if you would like."

"Boss, it is an honor to work for a man of your vision, and yes, I would like. Thank you, truly."

Click.

Angelo hung up that phone and selected a different one. "Hey, you know how I suggested the other day we meet? I'd like that to happen soon. Are you busy this evening?"

Dan, after a brief pause. "No boss, I'm free."

"Go to where we first met, get a room first. You'll want it, I'm sure, but not until after we meet."

Dan didn't question the request. "Consider it done."

Click.

Hanging up, Angelo had many things on his mind, and he was trying to make sure he analyzed all of them properly. He was in a transition stage with Dan, and wanted to make sure he handled it with care and planning, like an agent would handle a college ballplayer going to the pros. Dan presented an opportunity for Angelo's organization, one that was unique and effective. It also was not lost on Angelo that the stakes in his game in El Paso just went up.

Who the hell did those two guys think they were, showing up to take down Nico, driving a car with government fucking plates. He did not work well with unknowns, and this is what those men were to Angelo.

Angelo picked up a different phone and reached out to his IT guy. "I've got some data I'm sending you. I know it's not much, but I'd like to see if you can find out anything about it." After hanging up the phone, he put an email together. The text was a few notes about what had happened in El Paso, and attached were the picture of the car and another of the government license plate. As he clicked SEND, he thought, *Let's see how good you are.*

Feeling pretty confident that he would be able to sign Dan to his team tonight, Angelo decided to put another part of his plan in motion. He selected the proper phone from the line of them on his desk. "I need specific information about the make, model, and year of target car, and it needs to be accurate. Run the VIN. I need specific location info that I can forward to the mobile mechanic."

The email he received two minutes later told him all he needed to know. Angelo selected another phone and, from its contact list, dialed "Mobile Mechanic."

"I'm forwarding you the information for the vehicle I need to be fixed as we discussed last week. Get it done today. Text me confirmation when it's done."

Click.

Angelo knew from the jail visitation video that Sharon planned to stay in Florida two more days, but he liked to have his To Do list as short as possible.

. . .

The little van with the logo "Mobile Mechanic" drove slowly through the garage at A Terminal, DFW airport, looking for a specific BMW. The driver spotted several BMWs before he found *his* BMW, confirmed with the license plate number. Luckily, the spot next to it was empty. Working quickly, he unlocked the driver's side door of the BMW, opened the hood, and disabled the alarm. He then went back to the van and retrieved a few tools he had laid out in anticipation of this job.

Tools in hand, he slid under the back of the car and tapped the fuel tank, noting it felt mostly full. Locating the fuel pump, he loosened all but one of the bolts securing the fuel pump to the fuel tank. He also loosened a few fuel fittings so that even a minor rear end collision would have fuel spewing out all over the ground under the car. Satisfied with his work, he put the tools back in the van and retrieved a device that was designed to plug into the car's computer system.

Knowing exactly where to look under the hood, he had it plugged in quickly. He then pressed a button on it and let it do its work. The programming was above his head, but he had a guy that could reprogram a car's computer to do things, all kinds of things. In this case, the system was being programmed to send a continuous relock signal to the door locks once the doors were closed and the engine started.

Once all the tools were back in the van and the hood of the BMW closed, the mechanic retrieved a five-gallon red can from the van. He topped off the gas tank with high-octane fuel normally used for racing. The mobile mechanic was driving away just five minutes after he had parked next to the BMW, and no one had seen him come or go. The security camera on that level had been disabled an hour before he arrived.

49

Dan's usual room at the hotel was available, so he booked it. He took that as a sign of good luck. The guy at the front desk started to tell Dan how to get to the room when Dan interrupted him. "I've stayed here before. I'm going next door to the club first, then I'll head to the room."

The man chuckled. "You seem pretty sure of yourself."

Dan decided to have a bit of fun with him. "I'll bet you the price of the room that before the night is over, I'll be heading up to the room with the hottest dancer in that club."

The man laughed. "You're on. And I hope I lose."

With a smile and a nod, Dan turned to the door and straight to the club. As Dan was paying his cover charge, he made a bet with himself. *If I were a made mob guy, where would I be sitting? Back right corner of the floor, darkest spot possible, view of the door and stage, obstructed view of me.* Dan walked through the door and made immediate eye contact with Angelo.

• • •

Fuckin' guy knew right *where I'd be sitting. He's a natural.* Dan continued to impress the made guy, who had been doing for decades what looked like came naturally to Dan. As Dan walked up to the table, he was greeted warmly by Angelo, who was in the company of two very attractive women.

"I know that Sindee fell hard for you, flyboy, and I wish the two of you all the best. You are the genuine article. I want Sindee to be happy. So, I'm conducting job interviews right now for the position of Angelo's New Angel. What do you think?" Angelo's face was that of a kid getting the first glimpse of the tree on Christmas morning.

Angelo gave both girls a look, then smiling, looked back at Dan. Dan looked them over carefully. "Well, I'd say they are neck and neck in the swimsuit competition. I guess we will have to see how well they do in the talent part of the show." They all laughed, then the blonde slid to her knees under the table. With the talent competition started, Dan asked, "Where's Sindee?"

All Angelo could manage was a motion toward the dressing room door. The brunette who was now waiting her turn nodded at Dan, then she headed toward the dressing room. Sindee and the brunette emerged seconds later. Surveying the entire scene, Sindee noticed a window of opportunity. "Angelo said you were coming to meet him, but he looks, uh, *busy*. How about a lap dance?" The way she said it, no man would refuse.

. . .

On the way to the private area, Sindee had an idea. "Go inside, make yourself comfortable on the couch, and I'll be right back."

Dan did as instructed. His night vision was kicking in, so he was able to make out a couch, a reclining chair, and a small table in the middle of a room with a curtained entrance. A moment later, Sindee parted the curtain with another blonde, beautiful woman in tow. "He wants a lap dance. Give him one like he is your lover. He tips well."

As a new song started, the blonde removed her top and her bottom. She moved over to Dan and Sindee began giving the blonde detailed instructions. It was as if Sindee was touching Dan with someone else's body. All of the club rules were being broken. Sindee was clearly enjoying what was going on, and she was signaling to Dan that it was okay for him to enjoy it too. When the song was over, Dan was as hot as he'd been in his entire life. Sindee took Dan's wallet, gave the blonde a hundred, and waived her off. Sindee took the next two songs to finish what the blonde had started. It took a third song to recover his breathing to a normal rate.

His head still swimming, Dan parted the curtain and headed toward Angelo's table with Sindee on his arm. When they took two seats at the table, Dan noted that it appeared a winner had been declared. The blonde was there under Angelo's arm and the brunette was gone. "Captain! Did you receive a proper attitude adjustment?"

Dan blew out a full breath and said, "Let's just say I'm ready to talk about whatever you would like to talk about."

Angelo was cordial in his request to his new angel and Sindee. "Okay, girls. As beautiful as you are, please give us the table. I promise you both, you will be back later."

Dan spoke directly to Sindee. "Lover, that was... I don't know how to describe what that was, but I loved it, and I love you. You are amazing. Please give me and Angelo a little while, and I will give you the rest of the night."

Sindee stood, leaned in, and put her bare breasts right in his face. "Sounds good, my lover, and I'm glad you liked that. I have a few other ideas that I'd..."

Dan laughed and cut her off. "Oh my God, I want to hear them, just later. Right now, I need to concentrate."

They all laughed, and the girls made their exit, walking in the direction of the dressing room. Dan's eyes were only on Sindee. Just before entering the door, Sindee stopped, and looked over her shoulder to find Dan still gazing at her. She smiled and blew him a kiss before disappearing through the door.

Angelo led the conversation. "I meant what I said, Dan, I am very happy for the two of you. I like Sindee, but mostly for that raw sexual energy she has. Otherwise, I am not the right guy for her. You're perfect for her."

Dan was glad to hear that from Angelo, but there were things on his mind that he wanted to make sure he had an understanding with Angelo. "Thanks, Angelo, really, thanks. In the interest of time, I think I can cut to the chase on a few items. I am interested in continuing our business arrangement, with a few conditions. There is an excitement about it that I like, and the money is good. Speaking of the money, my fee is going to increase substantially. I have a service unlike, I'm guessing, anyone else can provide. Also, I want your word on Sindee's status. She is no longer a stripper; she is my love and is not to *ever* be seen as a liability. She and I have an understanding: I don't tell her details, so she knows nothing that could be seen as affecting you. No matter what happens to me, she is not to be seen as a loose end."

Angelo laughed and said, "Damn, flyboy, slow down. Okay, welcome aboard. The organization wants your continued involvement, and you have already proven your worth. Second, I'm impressed, *yet again*, by you asking to up your fee. That takes balls, but you're right. You're worth it, so every contract will be negotiated, and you will be seen as a professional. Last, enough said about Sindee. I like her, and I like you. Both of you already have an elevated status. If you say you don't talk to Sindee, I believe you, and the future will happen as you say. Let's just say the words out loud so there's no misunderstanding: are we totally clear between you and me right now?"

"I believe we are, Angelo."

"I believe so too, good captain. So, I have the next order of business to move on to. I don't have anything specific for you yet, but I want to give you a head's up. The operation in Mexico and El Paso was an absolute home run. Was, until a loose end popped up. Best guess is that the cartel we took down in Mexico had some kind of CIA connection. We aren't sure, but that's the best guess we have right now."

"What? The C-I-fuckin'-*A*?" Dan was shocked.

"Yeah. What do you think?" Angelo leaned back in his chair, clearly interested in Dan's response.

Dan took a long pause and let out a deep breath. His mind was racing as he tried to assess the situation. His training taught him that the first step is usually to identify the exact problem. "Well, first I would say you need to try to find out if this is sanctioned or unsanctioned. If this is an agent getting rich by running a CIA op, telling his handlers one thing while telling his contacts something else, well that's one thing. If it is an op sanctioned by the CIA, well, then, you're fighting the whole fucking government, and that's different. Guess who wins?"

Angelo paused for a second, then said with a grin, "Hey, we shot the president once when he didn't fall in line. But you're right, I don't want a pissing contest with the whole government." Angelo's grin disappeared and was replace by his business face. "So, we might have to be targeting a CIA operative soon, and we now have him under surveillance. I'll let you know, but you might want to start looking at El Paso overnights again. If he's operating by himself, he's going to die by himself. He killed a friend of mine and tried to kill another. Motherfucker is going to go; it's just a matter of when and how."

Dan's brain had taken an exit ramp from the conversation at the comment about the president, but he decided that would be a conversation for a later time. He thought about what Angelo had said after and got his head back to the present subject. "I'm guessing if he is, in fact, CIA, he's going to need to disappear."

"Yeah, die. *And* disappear."

. . .

Sindee appeared in the doorway of the dressing room, and with the conversation handled, Angelo motioned her to the table. Dan opened the Blue Sky app on his phone. Without any other situation intruding on his life as an airline pilot, Dan would be flying his regular schedule. Rechecking his schedule on the app, he saw that it hadn't changed. His next report time was the next day at 2:10 P.M. at the DFW airport. Dan stood, said his goodbye to Angelo and, taking Sindee by the hand, headed toward the exit.

"I got our regular room, baby," he said with a smile.

"Oh, my captain, I love you. And now I'm gonna show you just how much!"

"I love you too, sweetheart."

Sindee had put on just enough clothing to walk across the parking lot without the risk of arrest. As the pair entered the hotel lobby, the man at the desk looked up at the pair, shook his head, and smiled widely. Dan smiled back. As the two of them stood in front of the elevator door, Dan heard the man tearing up a piece of paper. Dan whispered in her ear, "I got our room for free too, with your help. I'll tell you how later."

Sindee said, "With my help, you won't be able to tell me later. You won't even be able to speak." She looked back at the man behind the front desk, winked, and let him see her grabbing Dan's crotch.

50

Dan's trip was a simple two-day trip, and the overnight was in Tampa. He liked the Tampa hotel; it was downtown with a great selection of bars and restaurants close by. He had perfect weather, so he had plenty of time to take a nice long walk. He did some of his best thinking moving in athletic shoes. Dan was not much into social media, but Sharon was, and he had the thought during the walk to check her social media accounts. If she were having a girl week with an old friend—which he knew she wasn't—she would have selfies and pics by the dozens posted. On just an average day, she'd have at least a few posts on three different accounts. What Dan found was that she hadn't posted a thing since she left Texas.

Well, well, not even trying to cover her tracks, he thought, shaking his head.

The Tampa Riverwalk winds thru downtown right on the water-front, and Dan had covered much of it when he heard his phone make a noise that he didn't hear often. One of his social media accounts put up automatic, random reminders of posts from years prior. He never heard that sound because he didn't have the app open very often. Today was out of the ordinary since he had just checked Sharon's posts. What popped up was a post on his page from five years previous. It was a picture he had taken with Sharon on one of the rare overnights where she tagged along. She didn't go with him to places like Albuquerque or Des Moines, but the St. Thomas thirty-one-hour layover at a resort in the Virgin Islands sounded good to her. The two of them were smiling at the beach. He remembered that day; it was actually a pretty good day. *I got a blowjob that night on the balcony.*

Dan stopped walking and sat down on a bench facing the water. The smell of a nearby restaurant made him suddenly hungry, but the next thought in his mind was not about food, it was about Sharon. His brain wrestled with it like it had broken into his thoughts like an intruder. *Does she deserve to die?*

The thought hit him like a gut punch and then would not be dismissed. *People cheat all the time; marriages end. Should I really whack her? Would I be okay hitting someone else's wife just for that? The garbage I'm taking out is just that, human garbage. Sharon may be a shallow, superficial, worthless wife, and yeah, she is fucking around with what I though was a friend, but this? Of course I was pissed that night, I still am.*

Sitting on the bench, he wrestled further with his thoughts, shaking his head the entire time. Then, like everything else in his life, he formulated a plan. *She gets one chance to walk away. Just one.*

* * *

Back at the hotel room, Dan fished the other phone out of his overnight bag, dialing one of only two numbers on it.

Angelo picked up on the second ring. "Flyboy, what can I do for you?"

"Two things. I want to know if I can use your attorney to draw up some legal papers I need. I have his contact info; I just wanted your okay." Part of Dan's plan was to have divorce papers ready to sign the next time he saw Sharon.

"Sure thing, no problem. I'm sure you'll tell me all about it next time we meet."

Dan stepped carefully into the next request. "The other thing I need is related to the papers I want him to draw up. Believe it or not, what I would like is for you to delay that favor that you are planning on doing for me. I may be putting it on indefinite hold."

There was surprise and shock in Angelo's voice. "What? Are you serious? You mean the thing that we talked about the night we met?"

"Yeah, that thing." Dan heard the alarm in Angelo's voice. "Is it scheduled for today?"

"Let's just say I need to hang up this phone right now and make a call."

Click.

Oh my God, it was planned for today, whatever it was. Angelo sounded like he had to stop something immediately, like it's already in progress. Sharon gets back from Miami soon. If it is going down right now, I'd be notified when I stepped off the airplane in DFW. It would be just like Angelo to plan it all out that way.

. . .

Angelo picked up the phone that would get Nico the fastest. "Hey, I need you to call off today's op. I'm not read in on all the details as to why, but just call it off."

"Jesus, Angelo, her flight landed a half hour ago, my guy is already at the airport."

"Then you got a call to make!"

Click.

. . .

Sitting on Level Two of the Terminal A parking garage, DFW Airport, was a stolen pickup truck with a single occupant. The driver had boosted the truck not an hour before, and now he was sitting in the garage in a location where he could see the target vehicle. It was a BMW that he was there to rear end on its way out of the garage.

Don Barlow was Nico's go-to guy when it came to cars. Earlier in life, Don was a race car driver, but didn't do very well. He then moved on to stunt work in Hollywood. The money wasn't good in either profession, but the people he worked for now paid well. Don knew cars inside and out, working on them as well as driving. Today's task was to take the stolen pickup, hit the BMW from behind just hard enough to do some serious damage, but not enough that he couldn't drive away. If the truck was disabled, Plan B was to abandon it and catch the train away from the airport. It was stolen, so no matter what, it was a throw-away vehicle. If it were disabled, it would probably burn up, along with the driver of the BMW, in the post-crash fire.

When his company phone rang, he looked at the phone and noted it was Nico. Nico's calls were always answered. "Yeah, boss?"

"Got a total change of plan, and I need you to do it right fucking now. You gotta boost that BMW and get it to the chop shop."

Barlow had no idea why the plan would change like that, but Nico's orders were to be followed without question. "You got it, boss. I'm on it." Nico hung up before Don got the phone in his pocket.

Good thing I still got my tools.

. . .

The flight from Tampa to Dallas is a fairly long leg, and it gave Dan enough time to put the fine points on his plan. Before he left Tampa, he placed a phone call to Angelo's attorney, and they put him right through. Angelo must have said something to him because it sounded to Dan as if his call was expected, and the guy kept calling him sir. Dan had researched divorce enough to know about the Texas requirements, and why it was impossible to be divorced in ten minutes. But this attorney had work-arounds for every problem. Sharon didn't know it, but she was getting divorced tomorrow. That was door number one. She also didn't know it, but she didn't want to find out what was behind door number two.

To Dan, on the go-home leg of a trip, the radio call that switched his flight to the approach controller was music to his ears. It meant they were close to the home airport, and he was less than an hour from his truck.

"Blue Sky 1249, contact Regional approach on 125.77. They will have runway assignment and lower."

"Center, Blue Sky 1249. Regional approach on 125.77. Have a good day."

"Dan, I've been meaning to ask, what's with all the trip trading?"

"Call approach, let's get a runway and get the approach briefed, and then I'll tell ya."

Mike smiled. "Roger, boss."

"Regional approach, Blue Sky 1249. Checking in 1-5 thousand with information Echo."

"Blue Sky 1249, Regional approach. Expect runway 18-Left, information Foxtrot is current. Let me know when you have it."

"Approach, Blue Sky 1249 will get Foxtrot."

"You're slipping, Mike." Dan smiled. "Get Foxtrot and let's brief 18-Left. We can talk on the ground."

. . .

"So, we aren't friends anymore?" Dan knew Mike was just busting his balls. Their gate was occupied, so they had some time to talk before parking the airplane. It was a good way to bring up what they weren't able to talk about in the air.

"Fuck off, Mike. I'm the only friend you have. Aah, no, just trying to patch things up at home." Dan lied. He had to keep up appearances, and keep both avenues open until Sharon chose a door.

Just then, Ramp Control called to let them know their gate was now open.

"Roger Ramp, spot 122 to gate D-31."

. . .

Parking at the gate in Dallas, both men were thinking about the days off in front of them and the details they wanted to accomplish. Parking brake was set, engines shut down, and the Shutdown Checklist was completed. That marked the end of a successful flight.

"Mike, you get out of here. I'll hand off the airplane to the next crew. Enjoy your time off." Dan got paid as a captain, so he always told the first officers to take off as soon as they could at the end of the trip.

Captain Dan Hatfield, Blue Sky Airlines, stood in the doorway of the cockpit and thanked every passenger for flying with them that day. It was just as he had done on every flight he had ever flown as a captain. After the last passenger was off, he said his goodbyes to the flight attendants, and walked up the jet bridge, bags in tow.

Dan's other phone buzzed in his pocket, and he answered a call he was sure he was going to get just as soon as he landed. It was Angelo.

"Yes, sir?"

"I was hoping we could meet as soon as possible, work a few things out." Angelo's voice had a slight irritation that Dan could sense.

"I'm free right now. Your place?"

"That would be great."

Click.

. . .

Still in uniform, Dan pulled his F-150 around Angelo's house to the parking area in the back. Angelo was standing in the doorway as usual, but the look on his face was one of concern, and not the usual friendly greeting face. When Dan got out of the truck and approached the door, Angelo said, "Come on inside; let's go to the office."

Angelo didn't say another word as they walked through the kitchen, and down the long hallway to his office. Dan had the familiar feeling of being sent to see the principal. They sat, Angelo put folded hands on the desk in front of him, cocked his head and said, "Okay, what is going on?"

Dan breathed out a heavy sigh and started explaining. "Well, boss, it's this simple. I came to the conclusion that she might be a cheating whore, but I don't think that warrants death. But like I said, I only wanted to put it on hold. I'm going to give her one chance to sign the divorce papers your attorney is preparing. She doesn't, then she gets door number two, which was apparently scheduled to be opened today. By the way, she's called and texted me about twenty times in the last hour. I don't know what's up with her. Anything I should know before I see her?"

Angelo laughed. "Yeah, she's probably pretty pissed that she got to airport parking, and her car has been boosted. She probably wants a ride. Well, it is your call, and if you put the op back on later, I'll make it happen. But, I'm out about five grand in expenses because you aborted this mission, so I'm taking it out of what you have banked."

"I understand completely, Angelo. By my math, that means I'm at 170 grand right now, is that correct?"

Angelo nodded, with a smile. "That's what my math says too. You want that in nickels or quarters?"

Dan laughed at the joke, then brought up the next part of his plan. "Well, about that. I want to pay Sharon to fuck off. What's that old joke? You don't pay a hooker to stay, you pay her to leave? I was wondering how soon you could get a hundred of it in cash for me. If she doesn't take it, I will give it right back to you."

Angelo got up from his chair. "Stay right here." He left the office and disappeared into the house. About three minutes went by, and he reappeared with stacks of cash. Hundred dollar bills in bundles, ten thousand dollars each. Angelo laid the pile on the desk in front of him and counted out seventeen of them in front of Dan. "One-hundred-seventy grand. That should make us even."

Dan looked at the pile of cash with big eyes. It reminded him of scenes from Hollywood movies. "Holy shit, Angelo. I didn't need all of it. I hope you kept some pizza money for yourself."

Angelo chuckled. "Flyboy, I could buy a pizza joint with what I have here. You never know when you are going to need it. Like today."

"One other thing. Boss, I think I know you well enough to guess that you probably worked up some kind of briefing or intel file on Sharon. Do you have something like that?"

Angelo smiled a knowing smile. "I sure do. I'm assuming you would like it for show-and-tell during the divorce meeting tonight. It has everything you could want for that. I would suggest you go through it first and decide carefully what to show her. There may be some things in there you don't want her to see, but I'd like you to see them all. Dan, one of my rules in life is to play my cards one hand at a time, and never give someone the whole deck." Angelo retrieved a thumb drive from a small desk drawer, inserted it into the computer, and the folder was copied from his desktop in minutes. He handed it to Dan. "There you are: one 'work up,' as we call them."

"Thank you, Angelo. Truly, thank you."

. . .

Dan left Angelo's house with a paper sack full of paper notes. *That's gonna look very cool in the safe, sitting next to the Glock.* His next stop was the attorney's office to go over and pay for the divorce papers. Dan was ushered right into the attorney's office by the law firm receptionist. The attorney gave him careful instructions about how to proceed and exactly how to ensure a legal divorce before the end of the day. When the attorney gave him two folders with identical sets of paperwork, Dan didn't get a chance to ask why, as the attorney immediately offered an explanation as he handed the folders to Dan. "You might need a second set. First sets have a nasty habit of being torn up." Dan left the office and climbed into his truck.

Using the attorney's instructions as a guide, Dan practiced his delivery for what needed to be said in the upcoming meeting with Sharon. She continued to call and text. Now that Dan knew the reason, there was nothing on Earth that would be able to coerce him to answer that phone. *She's going to be talking to cops and finding a ride home. Hell, I may even beat her home.*

. . .

Sharon sat fuming in the back of a cab at the airport. After filing a police report with the DFW Airport Police, she spent almost an hour calling Dan, texting him, and calling other people to try to get a ride home. She finally gave up and flagged down a cab. Every few minutes she remembered another thing that was left in the BMW, and her anger spiked again. The officer told her something she knew already: she was probably never going to see that car again.

The caller ID on her phone showed that she was getting a call from Ed's attorney. She picked it up quickly. "Hello?"

"Sharon Hatfield? This is Kelly Tasker from Miami."

"Yes, Mr. Tasker, do you have some news?"

"Yes, I do. It's good news and bad news. The good news is that Miami-Dade has reviewed surveillance tapes from the bar and the hotel and were able to track down the woman from the bar. She admitted to drugging and having sex with Ed. With what she gave him, he probably doesn't remember it. She said it is something she likes to do to strangers, go figure that one out. I don't know. She is being held by the Miami-Dade police and will be arraigned tomorrow on a number of charges."

"So, Ed is getting out of jail? He's not going to be tried?" There was hope in her voice. The idea of Ed going to prison had been what she most feared.

"Mrs. Hatfield, not so fast. Ed showed up at the airport intending to operate an aircraft in an obviously compromised state. As far as the FAA is concerned, I'm told by their representative handling this, Ed should have known not to put on that uniform that day. Setting foot in the airport in uniform shows it was his intention to try to fly. They intend to seek permanent revocation of his pilot's licenses. With his financials, he will be fine without being a pilot. Last, Miami-Dade treats incidents like this as a person operating a motor vehicle while intoxicated. They are going to charge him, but obviously it will be taken far more seriously by the judge, as it wasn't a car. It was 172 passengers and a lot of jet fuel flying over our heads. We will negotiate by agreeing that Ed will not seek to fly ever again and try to get fines and probation. But you should be prepared, he could face a five-year sentence."

Looking out the windows of the cab, Sharon realized they were turning into her neighborhood. "Is that all you have, Mr. Tasker? I have to go." She was numb from the news.

"Yes, that is all I have for you right now. Call me if you need me or think of something."

51

Dan had arrived home long before Sharon. He expected fireworks at any moment as he went through his routine. But he had managed to get all the way to the part where he was in his office chair, in comfortable clothing, with a scotch rocks on the desk in front of him. Dan had had enough time to create a show-and-tell folder on his computer from the Sharon work-up when he saw a cab park in front of the house.

Here we go.

She stormed through the front door and looked genuinely shocked to see Dan sitting there behind his desk. "Why the fuck haven't you been answering your phone?"

"I think we have more important things to talk about, Sharon."

"You bet your ass we do! My car was stolen from the airport!"

Dan took a breath and made sure her anger did not work into him. He knew that he needed to be cool and in control of what was about to unfold. "Sit down. We need to talk, and you need to listen." Sharon opened her mouth to say something, but Dan held up a finger. "I am going to talk first, and then we will do some show-and-tell. In the folder in front of you are divorce papers. If we sign them, we are divorced today, right here, right now. I know all the reasons an attorney would say that's not possible. One of us has to contest the divorce in order for that to be true. You aren't going to contest. I am giving you half the 401k, and whatever you want from the house, but you need to get it out of the house in the next twenty-four hours. Anything left that I don't want, or reminds me of you, I will throw away. I'm also going to give you some cash so that we can separate immediately, and I do mean tonight. I was going to give you the car, but well, I guess that ship has sailed. Now, I know you'll have some questions, and I'm sure I know what the big ones are, so I'm going to answer them. I'm guessing the first question is, why? The answer is because you are fucking Ed and have been for a while."

Sharon's mouth and eyes opened wide, and then she said, "How did you know; how long have you known?"

Dan's jaw clenched with anger, and he took a moment to let it subside. *Gotta stay cool.*

Her face changed when she had a realization. "The flowers in the backyard."

"Yes, Sharon. The fucking flowers in the fucking back yard. I had an overnight cancel, so I buy you flowers, and head home to surprise you only to be surprised myself by watching my friend go down on you in the kitchen. You, wearing the French lingerie I bought for you, that you haven't even worn for me." More anger; another pause. "Oh, and how about that Miami trip, how nice is the Miami-Dade jail? Why don't we start show-and-tell with that?"

Dan clicked a few files and showed Sharon on his computer monitor the signed jail visitor log. Then he clicked a video file and played video of her visit with Ed. The audio was clear enough to hear Sharon sobbing through questions about how they were going to be together and "get rid of" Dan.

Sharon had the look of a trapped animal. "What is..? How? How did you get that? How could you even have that?"

"You've been followed since that first evening. I have friends, and trust me when I say, you do not want to meet them. I know everything. Everything. Ed? Jesus, Sharon. I guess you finally found someone with enough money to make you happy. Well, I'm going to give you what you want. Right. Fucking. Now. This is the deal; I will only offer it once, and you have two minutes after I make it to decide. And I will tell you right now, with God as my witness, if you turn it down, you will regret it." Dan let that hang in the air for a moment before he continued. Sharon was speechless, her ever-changing expression filled with apprehension, suspense, shock, and fear.

"You will sign these divorce papers in front of you, and you will contest nothing. The papers stipulate you get half the 401k, and so you will. They also stipulate you get your possessions from the house, and I'm giving you twenty-four hours to get everything out, and I mean everything." Dan reached down into the paper bag that she could not see and retrieved ten stacks of bills.

"What is that?" Sharon said in genuine shock.

"It is cash, and it is yours. Plain and simple, it is my way of making sure you can get completely out of my life as fast as possible. You have twenty-four hours, starting now. That is the deal. It is not subject to negotiation. Take it or be sorry."

Dan slid the cash across the desk in front of Sharon.

"How am I supposed to get my stuff out of here in twenty-four hours?"

Dan looked at the cash, and then at Sharon. "Hire a fucking mover."

"Where will I put it all?"

"Last I looked, Ed has a nice three-car garage."

"What am I going to do for a car?" Sharon seemed, to Dan, to be close to the end of her rope.

"I could have sworn the man you are fucking owns a car dealership. How convenient. Your two minutes are almost up." Dan opened the divorce paperwork folder and pulled out the papers. He took the last page, the signature page, and placed it in front of Sharon. Then he put a pen next to it.

. . .

Sharon thought she hit bottom when Ed was arrested. She thought she hit bottom again when she visited with him in Miami, and then once again when the attorney delivered the news of a possible prison sentence. She was shocked at how wrong she was. She didn't need any more time to make her decision. The bridge behind her was burned, and there was only one direction for her life now. Dan held all the cards. She didn't even care where he had gotten all that cash. It would, in fact, allow her to go where she wanted to right away. With a shaking hand, she took the pen, lined up the signature page, and signed on the line. She recalled practicing that signature when they were first engaged. Now she was putting it on divorce paperwork. She just closed her eyes and started to cry. *How did things get so bad?*

"I want you to watch this," Dan said as he took the pen from her hand. He picked up the signature page, turned it around, and signed it. "We are now officially divorced. I don't care where you sleep tonight, but this is no longer your home. Take the cash and your suitcase and get out. I'll see you and your movers tomorrow."

She wanted to say something, anything. She simply couldn't think of anything appropriate. It was an act of sheer willpower for her to stand; she felt drained. Looking at Dan, all she saw on his face was a casual calm and indifference. Taking the stacks of cash, she unzipped the suitcase just enough to shove them in, then she walked out the front door without looking at Dan again. Sharon waited fifteen minutes for the Uber to arrive. The light in the office went out after only about two minutes.

. . .

Dan went to the living room and turned on the TV. He felt as if a huge weight had been lifted from his chest, and he was able to breathe again.

He didn't know it, but Sharon was getting in a car about the same time he was refilling his scotch. He went to the office in the dark to see if she was still there, but she wasn't. He wasn't checking on her, he just wanted to know for certain that she was gone. He nodded, smiled, and walked back to the baseball game.

Dan picked up his phone to call Sindee, and before he could turn it on, it rang. *We must have some kind of psychic connection.* When he answered the phone, he greeted the woman he loved and filled her in on the entire situation.

After he had finished with the story, Sindee asked, "Are you okay, baby?"

"Yeah, yeah. I'm fine. It's what I wanted. I wanted my relationship with Sharon officially over, and I wanted her out of my life. That is what has happened. You know, there's going to be some attention on my life for a little while. I think we should keep up appearances. I don't want to give Sharon any reasons to do something stupid."

There were a few seconds of silence on the phone. "You're right about all that, my love. I miss you already, and I don't know how I'm going to be without you for, what, a few weeks?"

"Yeah, probably a few weeks at least. I love you, Sindee, I really do."

"I love you too, my captain."

.   .   .

After he hung up, Dan decided to take a walk around the house, in anticipation of tomorrow. Standing in the walk-in closet, Dan looked at the quarter of it dedicated to him, and then the three-quarters of it containing Sharon's collection. *Tens of thousands of dollars of clothes, shoes, and other shit she just had to have.*

Dan made one decision on the spot when he walked out of the closet, and into the bedroom. *That bed goes tonight.* The enormous, ornate, and nearly gaudy bed that Sharon decided they would buy the moment she laid eyes on it. It was no small task, and it was made larger by the way scotch slows a person down. In a half hour or so, the bed, mattress, sheets, and pillows were at the street.

I'll let Sindee pick the next bed. She won't pick it just because it looks good. She will pick a strong one that can take a beating.

He made his way back to the couch by way of the bar to discover that the game still had a few more innings. *This is gonna be my bed until I can meet Sindee at a furniture store.* He was just about to doze off when his cell phone rang, and the contact that popped up was Mike Chelsea.

"Hey, Dan, are you catching this Rangers game? It's a good ballgame. You should tune in if you're not." Mike was a bigger Rangers fan than Dan was.

"Yeah, I got it on now, scotch in hand, but I missed the beginning. I was busy disassembling my bed and piling all of it out at the street."

Of all the possible directions the conversation could have gone, this was not one Mike would have seen coming. "Uh wait, what?"

Dan told him the story, the parts of it he could tell anyway, with the punch line being that they are divorced and she's coming back tomorrow to move her stuff out.

"I think you should have some company for that, Dan. Toni and I will come over first thing tomorrow and drink some of your coffee. It's a good idea to have witnesses at times like this."

"I don't think Sharon is going to cause any problems, but I agree, good thinking. You and Toni haven't been over to *casa* Hatfield in a while. Thank you, Mike. I appreciate it." Dan felt the true friendship they had.

They said their goodbyes, and Dan turned to one last task before he hit the pillow, or rather, the couch cushion. Dan opened the alarm app on his phone and changed all the door codes.

52

When Mike and Toni knocked on the door at about 8:30 A.M., Dan had just gotten dressed after taking a shower. Dan didn't shave on his days off. He answered the door smelling good and looking rough. "I just put the coffee on. What have you got there?"

Toni was holding a brown bag in her hand, with the name of the bagel shop on the outside. "Mike said you guys have gotten bagels there before. Something about golfing, if I remember right?"

"Exactly right, that is my favorite bagel shop. Thank you," Dan said. He was about to usher the couple inside, when the sound of an approaching truck caused them all to turn. Dan was delighted to see it was a moving truck, and even more so when it stopped in front of the house. A white BMW parked behind the truck. Dan spotted the dealer tag on the front, and Sharon behind the wheel. *She moves fast. Good.*

One of the men who exited the truck cab was holding a clipboard with paperwork. Sharon was talking to him by the truck, and then they, joined by two other movers, walked up to the door. Dan was on the porch; Sharon wordlessly entered the house. Dan stopped the man with the clipboard. "I am the homeowner; she is just here to get her stuff. Move anything out that she wants but go through every room of the house with her. Do it one room at a time and take whatever she wants. My office, my clothes, the bar, that couch, and my TV are off limits. Be done by six o'clock tonight. Is that doable?"

"These guys could have the entire house in that truck by six." he said.

He then started flipping through the paperwork on his clipboard as if he were looking for something to show Dan.

"There's nothing on that clipboard for me. I didn't hire you, she did."

. . .

In an hour's time, the bedroom was done, and the movers were working on the rest of the house. When Sharon and the movers left a room, Dan went in and took anything that remained that he didn't want, and had a mover put it at the street. The pile in front of the house was sizeable and growing.

The process continued after lunch and into late afternoon. The flow out to the front yard slowed to a trickle. At least twenty people had stopped and were looking at the pile at the street, some even going through the stuff. Dan caught sight of Sharon numerous times; to him she seemed to be trying to maintain her cool, to give off the appearance that all of this was routine. Dan knew her better.

"There's that charity store in Southlake, they pick stuff up. Should I call them for the pile at the street?" Toni had a slight southern drawl that Dan had always found charming.

Dan said, "If you would, I would appreciate that, Toni. Great idea."

. . .

Angelo was just wrapping up a call when a different phone rang with a call he knew he wanted to take. "He's probably got ten people at his house right now, but try to call Dan tonight to see how he's holding up. I gotta take this other call, sweet cheeks." He disconnected the call with Sindee and answered the ringing phone.

"Talk to me." Angelo had been waiting for this briefing.

"Okay, boss, it's been a couple of days of snooping, and we now know quite a bit about them. They operate out of a single house, a big one. We can tell who is in charge, and the guy that goes everywhere with him seems to just be a field agent. There is a third guy who spent nearly every minute of the last three days inside the house. They got a fiber optic internet line, and an air conditioner that runs all fucking day. I'm guessing they have a dozen computers, servers, shit like that running in the house, making heat. We have no names, and the house is in the name of a dummy corporation with no other assets. They eat out at different places. There is a bar, a seedy dive of a place not far from the house, and that's the only place they went regularly. In at about five P.M., out at about nine P.M. all three days. Maybe they are meeting someone; maybe they have a good happy hour. I think the bar is where we grab them. How do you want to play it after that?"

"*Very*, very good work." It took Angelo a few minutes to lay out a detailed plan, one that he had clearly put a lot of thought into.

"I got it. Beautiful plan. *That* is why you are the boss, Mr. Genofi."

I know.

Click.

. . .

It was early evening, and true to their word, the movers were done before 6:00 P.M. Any time Dan had a pause in the action throughout the day, his thoughts went to Sindee. He was tantalizingly close to having her in his life full-time. Only Mike and Toni remained at the house.

"You sure you don't want us to stay?" Toni offered.

"Nah, but thanks, I do appreciate it. We'll do a sleepover some other time." They all smiled, happy to see that Dan had not lost his sense of humor.

When they had said their last goodbyes and left through the front door, Dan picked up his phone and secured the whole house with his alarm app. Then he fished his other phone from his pocket and dialed.

Sindee had concern in her voice. "Baby! How are you? You okay?"

"Oh, I'm fine, sweetheart, great actually. I finally have the house to myself. Had people over here all day moving Sharon's stuff out. Couple hours ago, a charity operation came by and picked up a pile from the front yard."

"Wow, well that is good, I guess. Now you can move on. I miss you terribly, in every way a woman can miss you. I know we have appearances to maintain, but we gotta figure something out. Angelo wanted me to call you too. He wants to make sure you are okay."

"I bet he does. Everyone can relax; this is a good thing for me. Tell Angelo I'm fine, and lover, I miss you too. I'm sure in all the same ways. I'll think it over. Hey, uh, you know, we could play on the phone right now if you'd like."

"I thought you'd never ask," she whispered.

. . .

Dan woke the next day, his second night on the surprisingly comfortable couch. All he had planned for this day was rearranging the house, and making a list of what he was going to need to make the place right. His plan was to put together a comprehensive list by room but wait until Sindee was in his life so they could shop together. It seemed like a nice way to move her in. Dan wanted to get on with this new phase of his life, excited to move on. Each day ahead would be one day closer to Sindee being a visible part of his life. Dan was retrieving a yellow note pad and a pen from his office when his other phone rang.

Sindee's voice brought Dan to attention. "Good morning, lover, how did you sleep?"

"Oh, baby, I slept well and think you are a big reason I slept so well. Thank you, my love."

"Anytime, flyboy, and I do mean anytime. When do you fly next?" Sindee asked.

"My next flight is a two-day trip starting tomorrow, and I'll be flying with my friend, Mike."

"That's great, flying with your friend again. Where do you overnight? Is it a nice hotel?" Sindee always asked that question, a very common question for those outside the industry. People who travel a lot develop a definition of a nice hotel quite different from the average traveler. For them it is about amenities, location, and the mattress; not how nice the lobby looks.

"Minneapolis. It's at the Master's Quarters Hotel, downtown. It's pretty swank. Long overnight too, so Mike and I will be able to do beer call."

"Beer call?" Sindee sounded puzzled.

"Yeah, it means meeting for a few beers. There's a whole new language I'm going to teach you: Pilot-ese."

Sindee had genuine interest in her voice. "Oh really? I want to learn, and I have a language I'm going to teach you, too. But we can talk about that later. I will call you tonight, but for now I got something I gotta do."

"Alright, I have some things on my to-do list, and then I gotta pack and iron a shirt, too. Talk to you later. I love you."

"Love you right back, my captain."

Sindee quickly dialed another number. "Hey, big guy. My captain will be flying tomorrow, and he overnights in Minneapolis."

. . .

Angelo, all business. "Talk to me."

"We have all the arrangements made, boss. Have my guys picked out, and they know their assignments. These guys are good, but so are the targets, so I'm being especially careful about the details. We can go any time. When are you thinking we are a go?"

"Let's surveil another day or two, make sure we aren't missing anything. I'm thinking we watch today, tomorrow, and one more day, then go the next. Double check everything, then check it again. Even the routes."

"You got it, boss."

Click.

53

The next morning, Dan walked up to the gate forty minutes before sign-in time, and Mike was already there, flirting with a gate agent.

Mike turned when he saw Dan approaching. "Hey, brother, how are you doing? Ready to aviate?"

"Yeah, Mike, I'm one hundred percent. Is the plane here?"

"Pilots just walked off; cleaners are in the cabin. Want to get in the cockpit early?"

Captain Hatfield and First Officer Chelsea signed in for their trips on the gate computer and headed down the long jetbridge. They set up the cockpit and their tablets, just as they had done for flights hundreds of times before.

Mike was a good friend and a good pilot. "Dan, how are you handling all the non-flying crap right now. You know, the house...?" He was trying to make sure Dan had his head in the cockpit.

"Absolutely fine. I appreciate you asking, but what happened was a good thing for me, and I am in a good place. Seriously. Now let's knock out this two-day." Dan was telling the truth; he was just doing it without the details.

The first day of the trip was a single flight from Dallas-Fort Worth to Minneapolis. A few hours later, they were strolling off the airplane, and the flight was textbook. Thirty minutes later, they were getting off a van in front of a very nice-looking and tasteful downtown hotel. Ten minutes after that, and Dan was finally doing what he'd been looking forward to, what he thought was going to be the highlight of his evening: The Removal of The Uniform.

The knock on the door was so light, he almost didn't hear it from the bedroom of the suite. When he reached the door, he made a check of the peep hole, and he could hardly believe what he was looking at. Dan tore open the door.

"Oh my God, what the fuck are you doing here? I'm so happy to see you, baby!"

Sindee ran into his arms for a strong hug and a stronger kiss. "It was Angelo's idea, and I loved it. My bag!"

The door had closed, leaving her bag in the hallway. Dan, in his underwear, retrieved it. It felt light. "Doesn't feel like there's much in there. What did you pack?"

"Oh, there isn't much in my bag, but what *is* in there, you are going to love." She took a moment to look around the suite, impressed. "It's been *days*, lover boy. I'm gonna fuck you all over this place."

Dan heard the text notifier on his phone: it was Mike. Sindee was on her knees in front of Dan when he texted back, "Skipping beer call, I got something I need to take care of in the room."

I'm glad he texted instead of calling. I wouldn't be able to speak right now.

. . .

The two lovers woke the next morning in a way that was routine for them. Dan first, then shortly thereafter Sindee, mostly because Dan started doing something Sindee couldn't—and didn't want to—sleep through.

After, Dan made coffee in the room. "This place is alright. There are choices of coffees and teas in the wood box on the table." Dan carried two cups back to the bedroom. He was greeted by the sight of a nearly naked Sindee in a shockingly sexual pose. He stopped in his tracks and admired her head to toe. Dan knew she loved that kind of attention.

"Damn, baby. You make it hard to even drink a cup of coffee!" He handed her the cup, and she didn't move a muscle.

"I can make it hard, anytime, anywhere." She took a sip and smiled. "Just like I like it. You are hired."

Dan sat next to her on the bed. She still hadn't moved. "Baby, I was thinking. This worked out very well. You could come with me on overnights any time we can work it out. A paid ticket for you, and then I have a hotel already arranged. We can still keep up any appearances we need to, but still see each other. At least until you and I can have a legit meeting, and I make you a visible part of my life. Interested?"

She turned in the bed and set a half-cup of coffee on the nightstand. "I'm going to my suitcase for a change of what I will call 'clothes.' Then I'm going to come back and show you just how *interested* I am."

. . .

"Before Start Checklist complete."

"Thanks, Mike."

Mike asked, "How are you doing today? You seem to be in good spirits."

"I had a great hotel day, got a good night of sleep, and woke to find out I still have one of the best jobs in the world. And when I go home after this trip, it will be my home."

"That is great to hear you say that, brother. I know in time you'll meet someone else who will make you happy. I have no doubt. You're kinda ugly, but the pilot thing and that mad cash you pull down sorta makes up for that!"

Dan liked the banter. "Mike, you're such a hound dog. Hell, I bet you wear your uniform to the grocery store on your days off to pick up women."

Mike smiled, "Of *course* I do!"

. . .

The flight back to DFW was routine. Both pilots packed up their pilot bags and left the cockpit—and the pilot life—for a few days. Dan was still walking up the jetbridge when his phone rang. Dragging his bags behind him, he kept walking as he looked at his phone. It was a Blue Sky number. "Hello?"

"Hey, Captain Hatfield, it's Kyle Davis the VP of flight again. I wanted to see if you had a chance to think over the offer of the chief pilot's office position."

"Yes, sir, I did. I was leaning toward no. Then with the recent divorce, well, I think it would be best to just stay on the line. I am honored you would think of me, but I am going to pass."

There was obvious disappointment in Davis's voice. "Okay, well, thanks for thinking about it. Stay safe and be well."

"Thanks, goodbye."

Dan got to the bus stop just as a bus pulled up. He boarded the employee parking bus and had just sat down when he felt the other phone buzzing in his pocket. It was Angelo.

"Boss?"

"Yeah, where are you now." Angelo sounded casual, nothing urgent.

"On my way home from the airport, but not in the truck yet. Want me to call you when I get in the truck?"

"Can you meet tomorrow, my place, regular time? I want to discuss a few things."

"Yeah, sure, boss. Regular time tomorrow. See you then."

Click.

Dan was in the truck a few minutes later, getting the air conditioning going full blast. He picked up his other phone.

Time to check in with the woman I love.

54

"You want a coffee or something?" It was clear that Angelo, when he wasn't working, loved to play host in his enormous house.

Dan thought for a second and decided to go with a day-off beverage. "Uh, you know, I think I'd like a beer. Got any?"

Angelo smiled. "Name one you think I won't have."

After a pause, Dan said, "Black and Tan."

Of course, the housekeeper walked in moments later with a cold Black and Tan, and a cold mug. Nothing could have removed the smiles from either man's face. "Remind me to never bet against you, ever, Angelo."

"I have a feeling you already knew that."

"True. Okay, so what's up, boss?"

Angelo got into business mode. "I wanted to brief you, in general, 'bout El Paso. Those guys are definitely spooks and definitely U.S. government. But my guys think, and I agree, it isn't sanctioned, at least not all of it. It's three guys working out of a house, tons of equipment inside, tech guy stuck in the house all day. If what they were doing was a completely legit op, they would have called for backup, they would be hitting back. But those two took a beating and are still sniffing around, just the two of them."

"What can you tell me about what you have planned."

Angelo nodded, impressed again. *He knows I already got a plan, and that I can't tell him all of it.*

"Well, it's pretty simple really. We are grabbing those two guys and the car too. Then a crew breaks into the house, takes that tech guy and anything of value or that might be incriminating. Whatever we find. Then all of it goes away, poof, never to be seen again. I think that will tie it completely off, with no future issues after that. I will probably have someone set up a camera to see who shows up at the house afterward, but I'm guessing no one will... for a long time."

He could see that Dan was processing it all, looking for problems and finding none. Dan nodded. "Sounds good, boss. Are you gonna need me for any of this? Should I be looking at my *schedule?*"

"Nah, I may have some things in a month or so, but business is pretty quiet everywhere else. I'd like to keep you far from this El Paso thing, actually. Nico and the locals will handle this. They have a good crew down there. I believe your end of that operation is already tied off, and in a day or so, it will *all* be right. Hey, flyboy, did you enjoy your overnight in Minneapolis?"

A smile rapidly spread over Dan's face. "Angelo, sir, thank you so very much for that. Yes, I enjoyed so much of the overnight I got very little sleep. We are going to do that again, until the time comes when we can meet legitimately, and she can openly be my girlfriend. Hey, um, I wanted to run this by you before I make a move. I would like for Sindee to quit the club and maybe work on some kind of business that would free her to be able to travel with me. Are there any problems with that?"

"No, Dan, in fact, I love the idea of getting her out of there. Don't get me wrong, you know she was my favorite, and she is what she is, but I always felt like that place was beneath her. I *love* the idea of you getting her out of there. I have a few ideas. Let me put something together, and also I will smooth things over with the club owner. I'll get back to you on this."

"If that's it, boss, I'm gonna take my leave. I'd like to tell Sindee in person, and if I leave now, I'll catch her before she goes to the club."

"Go get her, Dan. I'm very happy for the both of you."

. . .

Dan found the right contact and dialed. "Hello, Vincent, it's Captain Hatfield. I was wondering if the meeting room could be made available for dinner?"

"If you could hold briefly, I will check that for you." Vincent texted Angelo and got the okay. "Yes, Captain, it is available, and Mr. Genofi wanted me to let you know that he will be buying dinner tonight for you and your guest."

The man does not miss a thing! "Thank you, Vincent, we will be there in about an hour."

The GPS told Dan he'd be at Sindee's apartment in five minutes. He picked up the other phone and placed a call.

"Baby doll, I have a surprise. I need you to just trust me. Dress for a nice dinner and meet me downstairs as soon as you can. I'll be there in four minutes."

He could hear in Sindee's voice that she was puzzled. "Sure, baby, I can do that. I just got done getting ready for work. I know just the dress. But I'm supposed to work tonight."

"I have that taken care of. See you in four—nope, now it's three minutes."

. . .

The pair strolled into Vincent's with Sindee holding Dan's arm. "Hello, Vincent, and thank you for this."

"But of course, for such a splendid couple! Ms. Simpson, Captain Hatfield, right this way."

Vincent led the pair into the meeting room. They were seated at the table, but this time it was Dan sitting in the seat normally occupied by Angelo. Vincent had seated him there, and the sign of respect was not lost on Dan. An excited Dan was already speaking when Vincent was closing the large, mahogany doors.

"Baby, I've been thinking. I want you to hear me out before you tell me what you think. I make a very good living, I have savings, investments, and no longer have someone spending it recklessly. I would like you to quit the club and work with me on some legitimate business. Something that doesn't tie you down so you can travel with me anytime. I ran this by Angelo, and he thinks it's a great idea. He said he would smooth it over at the club with the owner, and that he had a business idea he's going to get back to me about. In the meantime, I will cover anything at all that you need or need to pay. What do you think?"

Sindee just sat there for a moment, thinking, processing. Dan guessed that she was wondering if it was real. Dan knew they loved each other, and that it felt like they were about to make a drastic change in direction of their lives. Dan hoped she had the courage to join him.

Sindee pulled in a deep breath, and staring into Dan's eyes, said, "Yes. Dan. Yes. Yes. This is what you want?"

"Absolutely. I love you, and I know there will be a time when we can live and be together. It's not yet, but maybe this will help get us there."

"What is Angelo's idea?" she asked.

"I don't know, he didn't tell me. I don't think he likes to discuss things until he has a complete plan. But you know it will be good; it's coming from Angelo. So, you don't even need to go to work tonight. Let's start right now."

"Thank you, Dan, so very much. I love the idea, and I love you too." Sindee paused and looked all around the room. "Hey, uh, how secure is this room, really."

"Completely. No cameras or microphones, you can't even get the internet in here. No one comes in this room unless we signal them."

"Oh, really?" That smile told Dan what was about to happen next. He knew better than to try to stop her.

55

Dan found it very difficult to drop Sindee off at her apartment. He was no longer sure he could wait the proper amount of time to be dating after divorcing his wife. But if Sharon decided to do something stupid, to call undue attention to Dan, Sindee would be out of the picture even longer. Door number two would be very difficult now. Dan knew Angelo liked his people to maintain a low profile. *Last thing in this world I want to become is a liability to Angelo.*

On the drive to the apartment, Sindee had confessed to Dan a fear she had. She truly enjoyed the attention she got at the club, and the way she turned them on. She also truly enjoyed being openly sexual, and that had been her life for quite a while.

"You are by far the best lover I have ever had in my life. But what if it isn't enough. What if the change in lifestyle is too much? What if I find that I need more release of that energy than I am able to get in my new life? You are gone a lot, and I can't fly with you on every trip."

Her words hit Dan like a punch, but they immediately inspired an idea. "What if we set up a high-quality camera in a spare bedroom, turn it into a playroom, and you set up a web fan account? You can make money, work only when you want to, it's safe, make your own schedule, and you will be performing for more people than you ever could at the club."

She loved the idea and thought it was perfect. Then they arrived at the apartment and did something they hadn't done much. Dan reclined his seat all the way, Sindee climbed on top of him, she curled up in his arms, and they lay there for a long while. Neither of them wanted that moment to end, and when they were finally saying goodbye, it was their most difficult yet.

. . .

Back at Dan's house, he entered his code on the keypad, and walked into an empty house, dreaming about when he'd be greeted by someone who was actually glad he'd arrived: Sindee running up to him, barefoot and barely dressed, throwing her arms around him. *Soon, but not soon enough.*

. . .

Surveillance noted that the spooks parked behind the bar in a parking lot with a wall around it. They backed into a parking space against a wall every time. All good ideas tactically. Angelo's entire plan was to start by flattening a tire on the car.

When the two men walked out of the bar and looked at the car, they could see the flat left front tire, even in the darkness. Agent One was in charge and took the lead. "Fuuuck! Get me the lug wrench. I'll start working on the lug nuts while you get the spare out of the trunk."

Agent Two, the subordinate, had clearly changed more tires than his superior. "The tools are under the spare. I'll pull it all out."

Agent One pulled the key fob out of his pocket and popped the trunk. Agent Two went to the trunk and started unloading. The two were at the back of the car when the tow truck pulled up. "You guys need some help with that or a tow? I'll change it for you for twenty bucks." He sounded friendly and professional.

Neither agent was interested in changing a tire, so the offer was music to their ears. They didn't see the two other men crouching down in the cab of the lifted tow truck. They also didn't see the two stun guns in the hand of the driver as he exited the cab.

When both agents hit the ground, each having been stunned multiple times by the driver, the other men moved quickly. While the two men from the truck loaded the agents and tools into the trunk, the driver got behind the tow truck wheel and started hooking up the car. By the time the tire was thrown in the back seat, the car was being lifted by the front end and ready to move. One of the men opened the driver's side door, reached under the dash, feeling for a device plugged into the car's computer interface plug. He found the wires quickly and ripped hard, removing the small black location tracker from its hiding place. He held it up for the tow truck driver to see and slammed the car door shut. The tow driver operated the lift controls; the car was ready to haul away less than two minutes after he first spoke to the targets. Backing into the parking space had made the tow crew's job so much easier.

The moment they started moving with car in tow, one of the men picked up a cell phone and dialed. "We got them, heading to the meeting point."

Click.

On the other side of town, on the other side of that phone call, a passenger in a box truck said to the driver, "We're a go."

The driver started the truck moving while the passenger opened a pass-through window to the back and let the two men inside the back of the truck hear the same message. They all knew they were only a few minutes from the target house. The driver was carefully executing the plan, turning away from the house at the driveway, then backing the truck up to the garage door.

On the forward security camera feed, the man inside the house saw the truck park. He assumed it was some kind of delivery for their op house. The delivery and the time of night were not at all unusual. The man, Agent Three, went to the garage and opened the overhead door to receive whatever it was. In this case, it was three suppressed pistol rounds to the chest. He fell to the floor with a shocked look on his face.

"So much easier than the front door entry plan." The man would be the first thing they loaded into the truck. All four men spent the next hour going from room to room in the house, removing all electronics, files, paperwork, and anything that looked like work product from the agents. They found a safe, conveniently open, with more paperwork, folders, hard drives, guns, and stacks of cash. They took it all.

The box truck had way more room than they needed, but the pile in the back was still sizeable. Certain they were looking at a task completed, they climbed back in the truck and pulled away. The garage door was left up. Hopefully, some teenagers would find the place and trash it further. The driver started down the street while his cab passenger dialed his phone. "We got it all. Heading to the meeting point."

Click.

The drive to Metal World was maybe ten minutes. Ralph Toccino had been alerted that there was a special being delivered that night, but he wasn't tipped off as to just how special it was. When the tow truck with the special arrived, Ralph was waiting, and asked if he should warm up The Beast.

"Nah, we have a little while before the rest of the special arrives. I want to take the time to fill you in on something I think will be of interest to you. Listen. The boss identified the three people who were responsible for what happened to your father. My condolences, again, on your loss. Your father was a great man. Two of those people are in the trunk of that car."

Ralph's eyes got wide, then he slowly turned his head to look. "Are they dead?"

"No, but they will be in a little while. The third one is meeting us here.

Those two in the trunk are who's truly responsible for your father and, if you like, they can die the same way. Would you like to crush that car?"

Turning his head all the way to face the car, Ralph spit at it. "Fuck yeah." Hearing the box truck pulling in, Ralph turned to the sound of the noise. "That them?"

"Yeah, that's them."

Anger in his voice, Ralph hissed, "I'll warm up The Beast."

It was Nico talking to Ralph. As much as Nico wanted to do the honors to the two assholes who gave him a beating, he knew Ralph deserved the job way more than he did. By the time Agent Three was loaded into the back seat of the car, The Beast was all ready to go to work. Nico nodded, and Ralph stepped over to the car, leaned down to the trunk and shouted, "Now you fucks get to die like my father did. This is for you, Papa!"

Shouting and pounding on the trunk began in earnest at Ralph's promise, and it continued all the way until the press came down and The Beast was fed. Ralph knew he'd be hosing out The Beast again tonight, but he didn't care. He woke missing Papa that morning, but he'd go to bed knowing he avenged his father.

Nico looked at his cell phone. The time was 10:47 P.M. *With a little luck, we'll be in Northlake by breakfast time.* He was taking two of the men with him to drive in shifts. Angelo had changed the plan; the opportunity was just too big and was worth the risk. IT guy had been warned to clear his calendar for the next two months. He'd be sifting through a literal truckload of intel.

56

"New Castle 9, Pegasus 7. Be advised I'm seeing movement on the pilot's beacon. Not much, but probably two hundred feet."

"Roger, Pegasus 7, keep us advised."

Dan lined up the hand grenades on the hood of the truck. He was going to use the front wheel and engine as cover when hot shrapnel started tearing through the air. He pulled two pins, then threw the first two grenades into the tent opening as fast as he could. Then rapidly repeated that action with the third and fourth. Oddly to him, he heard four loud pops when he threw the grenades. That's how the Russian grenades work and, even though the sound was unfamiliar to Dan, it was a very familiar sound to the waking Iraqis. There was shouting before the first two detonations. That shouting descended to low moaning after the second two.

The voice on the radio was as loud as it was fast. *"New Castle 9, Hacksaw 1. I'm seeing small flashes, could be detonations or small arms, dead ahead, and also making out vehicles of some kind. Suggest you loiter back and let us deal with it."*

"Hacksaw 1, New Castle 9 is loitering in present position. Go hunting but remember there's a friendly out there."

"Hacksaw 1, roger."

"Pegasus 7, New Castle 9. How copy all of that last?"

The sound of the helicopters was closer now, and even with Dan's ears ringing a bit, he still heard them. That's also when he heard the shouting from the other man on watch. He was running back toward the tent from the other side of the compound. Dan didn't understand the language, but it was clear that the man was in a full-blown panic. Dan leveled the AK-47, flipped off the safety and unloaded half a magazine at the man when he got close. The Iraqi soldier fell to the ground in a lifeless shape.

"New Castle 9, Hacksaw 1. Seeing more what appears to be small arms fire. Where the fuck does Pegasus put the pilot beacon right now? The vehicles are looking like a mobile SAM position, over."

"Hacksaw 1, Pegasus 7. Radar is picking up some ground clutter in the same location as the beacon. He could be in the location of those vehicles. Wait, wait one, all standby. All mission aircraft be advised, pilot beacon is moving again, this time toward New Castle 9, away from the vehicles."

His job done, Dan began running as fast as he could toward the rotor noise and away from the vehicles. Major Hatfield correctly guessed that they were about to light up the site with high-order explosive munitions, and he did not want to be there when they did.

"Hacksaw 1, Pegasus 7. I show you about to pass over the pilot beacon location. Can you get a visual?"

"Pegasus, Hacksaw, I see a person in night vision. Appears to be wearing Air Force jumpsuit, going to make positive ID, standby."

The Apache pilot turned on his forward landing lights and flooded Major Dan Hatfield, USAF, with brilliant white light.

"Pegasus, Hacksaw 1, pilot positively identified. Guide in New Castle. Request permission to eliminate enemy vehicle position."

"Hacksaw flight, Pegasus, you are weapons free. Give 'em hell."

As fast as it had gotten there and lit Dan up, the Apache turned off his light, and took off toward the SAM position. Dan watched the fireworks show that was destroying the Iraqi position, knowing the next helicopter would be picking him up, returning him to his fellow aviators, his unit, and his life. He heard the approaching heavy helicopter and crouched down in anticipation of the landing. A few airmen jumped off and guided Dan to the helicopter door. Explosions were still going off not far away when the door was closed, and New Castle 9 headed back to base.

"Pegasus 7, New Castle 9, rescue complete. RTB. Great job, Pegasus. Thanks, Hacksaw flight."

There was a medic on board, who was relieved to find out he was unnecessary. Dan had been shot down, had evaded capture, neutralized a SAM site, eliminated the anti-aircraft weapons that could have killed his rescuers, and guided assets to a SAM position for prosecution and elimination. Not bad for a single night.

Dawn was breaking when New Castle 9 touched down in the hospital triage area of Prince Sultan Air Base. They brought out a gurney as standard procedure, but Dan waived it off. He walked into the building where a doctor would spend less than a half hour declaring Dan entirely fit. There were Colonels and a few Generals who were interested in the disposition of the downed F-16 pilot. A Lt. Colonel was telling Dan he wanted a debrief on all events as soon as possible. Dan was still very jazzed up by the experience, but also was a human who had been through combat and hadn't slept for a full twenty-four hours. Adrenaline only goes so far. His priorities now were that bottle of Dewars he'd been saving and a quiet place to drink it.

Everything else could wait. That was on his mind when he heard the shout of one of the embedded reporters that seemed to be everywhere on the base.

"Hey, Major. Major! I have some great shots of you coming off the helicopter. I'm hearing some real hero shit happened last night."

"Find me later, get me a copy of the pictures, and I'll give you the whole story."

57

"So, it would appear that the thing we discussed is all tied off and history. In fact, all of the ops are that way." Dan could clearly hear the tone of satisfaction in Angelo's voice.

"That's good to hear. Thanks for the update, Boss."

"Hey, we should get together soon, talk through the details of your future enterprises."

"Future enterprises?" Dan was puzzled about what Angelo had planned.

"Yeah, remember I said I had an idea for you two? I have put a plan in place. We need to talk over the details. And also, she told me about your idea for an online thing. IT guy is going to be busy as hell for prob'ly the next two months, but that would be an easy thing for him to handle. So, if you want to make that happen, I'll have him set it up."

Angelo's offer was generous, and Dan was happy to hear it. The computer and internet stuff was outside his realm of capabilities. "I really appreciate all that, I really do. How's tomorrow, same time, same place?"

"Sounds good, see you then."

Click.

There was an odd feeling that Dan recognized having had before. It was the feeling of *surviving* a series of events and coming out without a scratch yet changed forever. He turned his office chair to face the wall of pictures and awards in his office, better known as the "I Love Me" wall. In the center was a picture of him from the Gulf War, stepping off a Pave

Low helicopter in early morning hours. Staring at the picture, nodding his head, he thought, *Yeah, I have almost that same feeling right now. But this time is different.*

The framed article from Stars and Stripes, hanging right next to the picture, detailed his heroism the night he was shot down, and it was also the price he paid to get those photographs. Back then, Dan was just happy to have a new lease on life, to have any life at all. This time, Dan had Sindee in his future and huge income potential. There were already stacks of cash in his safe from the last few weeks, and whatever business deals Angelo had in mind.

Wait a minute, wait a minute. Dan stood and walked up to the picture on his wall. Removing it from the wall, he turned it around to look at the back. *May 23, 2003* was written on the picture. "Holy shit!" Dan took out his cell phone to confirm that which he already knew. The date on his phone was May 23, 2023

What the fuck does that *mean?* He sat back down, picture in hand, staring at the date as if some meaning would pop out of the words any second. Dan just kept shaking his head at something that he thought was too specific to be coincidence. Angelo had told him at their first real meeting, "I don't believe in coincidences. I believe there are forces in this world we simply don't understand completely, but that doesn't make them not real."

I wonder what Angelo will say about this. Well, it was Dewars in the early morning back then, so Dewars sounds pretty good right now too. I'm going to drink to getting out without a scratch.

He stood and started for the bar when he heard a soft knock at his front door. Dan opened the door to the sight of Sindee standing on his front stoop in broad daylight, a huge sexy smile plastered across her face. It took him a few seconds to take in the whole picture. She was wearing scrubs, head to toe, and white sneakers. In her right hand was a bucket full of cleaning supplies. He looked over her shoulder and saw a small white crossover parked in front of the house with a large magnetic sign that said *Maid for You*. He chuckled and shook his head. *Angelo*.

"Hello, Mr. Hatfield? I'm Sindee, and I'm today's Maid for You!"

Dan smiled wide. "Of course you are, and yes, I'm Mr. Hatfield. Very nice to meet you."

He stepped aside, letting Sindee bounce into his house. He closed the door and pulled out his other phone. Placing it on speaker, he dialed.

"Talk to me." Dan could hear the smile in Angelo's voice.

Dan, still shaking his head, said, "I like your idea. Maid for You?"

"Yeah, that was her idea, but I like it. We'll talk details tomorrow, but for now you have your introduction, a business, and a great cover for her spending all day at your place."

Sindee wrapped her arms around Dan and kissed his neck. She called out to Angelo. "Thank you so much for all that."

"Oh, sweetheart, you're welcome."

Click.

Dan looked down at the name tag high on Sindee's left breast, then took her in his arms. "'Cindy' is it? Where would you like to start?"

A knowing smile spread across her face, one that Dan felt in his chest. "I was thinking the master bedroom shower."

"Perfect."